TAKING AFTER

Also by Tina McElroy Ansa

BABY OF THE FAMILY

UGLY WAYS

THE HAND I FAN WITH

YOU KNOW BETTER

TINA McELROY ANSA

TAKING AFTER MUDEAR

A NOVEL

DownSouth Press

Library of Congress Control Number: 2007907228
Ansa, Tina McElroy
Taking After Mudear/Tina McElroy Ansa.
ISBN 2001012345

Cover Designed by Varnette P. Honeywood
Cover Execution by Audra George
Art by Varnette P. Honeywood
Printed in the United States of America
First edition
10 9 8 7 6 5 4 3 2 1

For Jonée,

whose love sustains me

ACKNOWLEDGMENTS

When a writer finishes her first book, she feels she has experienced all the "firsts" she is going to have.

For me, however, a blessed child, this has not been the case. With this novel, I have been reborn and allowed to experience a whole passel of "firsts," all blessings.

Taking After Mudear is indeed a sequel; however, it is also very much an original. It is the first novel published by my new press, DownSouth Press. It is the first of my babies that I have shepherded through from conception through gestation and on to birth, acting as publisher, author, and cheerleader.

And to have accomplished this feat, I have a whole lot of acknowledgments to make and a great many thanks to dispense.

The spirit of God has so settled on each word of this novel, that I know whatever your beliefs, each of you readers will feel it, too. I thank God.

The spirit of camaraderie and sisterhood had such a hand in creating and nurturing this novel. My friend and editor Blanche Richardson continues to support, improve and respect my words and stories in such a way that she honors not only me but all the ancestors whose stories we live by. I thank Blanche.

Just look at the beautiful and meaningful image on the cover of this book and all my novels. My goodness, Mudear is that black flower on the cover. What, I ask you, would Tina McElroy Ansa's novels be without Varnette P. Honeywood and her artistry, spirit and deep, deep understanding of our culture and people? I thank Varnette.

A new friend who has moved into my life and work as an old spirit is Catherine Meeks. She shares my love of literature, family and being a grown woman and has supported me and DownSouth Press in real and meaningful ways. I thank Catherine.

The spirit of family supports me in ways that continue, after all these years, to surprise and delight me. My family by blood, the McElroys, have my unending thanks for treating me, still, like the baby of the family. As does my family by love, headed by the stalwart love and generosity of my St. Simons Island sister, Consuela Floyd, who continues to believe in us. I thank Consuela.

My new family at Indigo Publishing in my hometown of Macon, Georgia, is a blessing and a continuing source of support and surprise. They have taken me and DownSouth Press under their wings and stepped up to help over and over. I thank Henry Beers and Indigo Publishing.

The spirit of friendship and support is typified in my circle of Good Lil' School Girls. What would I do without them? From publicity to my websites to marketing to promotion to speaking and book tours to the Sea Island Writers Retreats, they are there for me. I thank them all, especially Bernadette A. Davis, Kara Walker, and Shelia Worthy.

My readers deserve a special thanks for loving me, my novels, and my characters. This novel exists in part because my readers kept saying, "Now, what you need to do is write a book where Annie Ruth has that baby and Mudear comes back to interfere with everything." My dear readers, this is for you. I thank my readers.

The spirit of one of my most important mentors, the writer Bill Diehl, has encompassed me throughout the founding of DownSouth Press, the writing of *Taking After Mudear,* and my entire career. Bill, who passed in the last year, is with me always. I thank Bill.

Finally, the spirit of my twenty-year companion, Zora the cat, is evident in one special character in this novel. Zora passed just as I was completing *Taking After Mudear.* And though Jonée and I were distraught over this real loss to our lives, our household, and our hearts, the spirit of Zora continues to hover over us and encourage me to do what I do: write my stories and encourage and support others as they do the same. Thank you, Zora.

TAKING AFTER

CHAPTER 1

"Didn't ya'll hear me?" Annie Ruth asked as she lumbered into her big sister's sun room in one of their mother, Mudear's, silk pastel vintage nightgowns with the water from her broken uterus still streaming down her legs into her copper-colored, leather Easy Spirit walking shoes.

Her water had broken with a gush as she stood at the bathroom sink flossing her teeth before bed, making a big odd-shaped puddle at her feet on the Italian tile floor.

"Didn't ya'll hear me?" she again asked her sisters who sat staring, stunned silent at the sight of her. "I called for ya'll to come get me."

"Sisters," she said when neither of them still reacted. She looked down at her dripping gown, then back at them. "It's time."

That's all Annie Ruth had said—quite calmly, too, considering that she had just experienced the first signs of the birth of her first baby.

Moments before, the sudden burst of water had surprised her

so that she could not seem to get the buttons on the intercom by the bathroom door to function correctly so she could call for help from Betty and Emily, her two sisters, downstairs.

After yelling for them to "come get me" the way she had since she was three years old, she had made the laborious trek down the wide formal staircase of her big sister Betty's house by herself and walked splay-legged into the solarium, leaving small wet tracks all the way on the shiny hardwood floors.

All three Lovejoy sisters stood stock still for a moment: Annie Ruth in her soaking wet peignoir, Betty still dressed in the jewel blue shantung silk outfit she had worn out to dinner with her young man— her very young man—and Emily barefoot and comfortable in what her sisters called "a playsuit," a red halter top and matching shorts.

They looked at each other, frozen for an instant in a time—one final time—when they would be the only Lovejoy girls on earth. They lingered there in the sunroom a moment, appearing petrified in the amber light thrown off by the Tiffany floor lamp in the corner. Then, as if suddenly released from a paralyzing drug, Emily and Betty sprang into action. Emily slipped on her soft, scarlet, leather moccasins and grabbed the keys to Betty's car, a brand-new Lexus, roomier and more reliable than Emily's old clunker, which was sitting outside in the garage needing some mechanic's attention before she could safely put it back on the road.

Betty dropped the tangle of extra-soft, lime green baby yarn that she was determined to knit into a fluffy crib blanket before the child was school age, onto the foot of the pink and green striped chaise lounge where she was sitting, leapt to her feet and rushed past Annie Ruth to blow out the lavender-and-lemon-scented candles burning downstairs in the opulent house and grab the packed overnight bag that had been waiting at the foot of the big curved stairway in the hall for the past week.

Emily hurried outside without throwing any kind of wrap over her playsuit, exposing her bare shoulders, back, thighs, and the bottoms of her butt cheeks to the cool, late spring, night air. She jumped in Betty's Lexus, turned the key in the ignition, gunned the motor, and pulled the car up to the side of the house. Betty and Emily hadn't told Annie Ruth, but for weeks, whenever Annie Ruth was napping, they had been practicing for this time, making dry runs of their dash to the small Georgia town's Medical Center.

"Turn here," Betty had ordered.

"No, we should go this way," Emily had countered, making a huge U-turn in the middle of Forest Avenue to avoid driving past the Pleasant Hill Cemetery and their mother's grave site. They had bickered and strategized and mapped out and then re-mapped until they had finally settled on the most efficient route to the hospital.

"Would ya'll come on?" Emily yelled out of the open car window as she gripped the steering wheel like a vise, in the process nearly piercing the black leather wheel cover with her long scarlet nails. As she sat there rocking in the driver's seat, she went over and over in her head the quickest route to the Mulberry Medical Center that she and Betty had settled on.

"If they don't bring their asses on, I'm gon' lose my mind out here," she said aloud through gritted teeth to the empty car as she continued to rock slowly to and fro in the driver's seat. "I swear I am."

Just then, Betty ran to the car with Annie Ruth's purple T. Anthony overnight bag, threw it in the back seat of the big, silver Lexus and jumped in the front next to Emily. Then, she looked around bewildered. "Where's Annie Ruth?"

"I thought you were going to bring her out," Emily said, panic seeping into her already rising voice.

"I thought she was with *you*," Betty shouted wildly as she threw open the car door and leapt out.

She ran back through the solarium at the rear of the house, passed the kitchen, raced through the formal dining room, rattling the French crystal and bone china in the cabinets with each stride she took, and came to a dead stop out in the front hall. She braked so suddenly, the soles of her high-heeled sandals made a "screeeech" sound on the Georgia hardwood floors. Standing there like stone carved from the quarry outside of town, Betty tried to speak, but all she could do was open and close her mouth a few times and gasp.

Right there in front of her was Annie Ruth, as big as the colonial-style house she was standing in, squinting into the large gilded mirror in the entry hall, her feet planted wide apart for stability, the insides of her spread legs still dripping birth water onto Betty's imported Red Flower rug, as she leaned in as close as her big belly would allow, trying to apply Copper Nut Brown eye shadow that she had taken from her giant black zippered M.A.C. makeup bag on the antique table in front of her.

Betty continued to gawk in silent amazement for a few seconds. Then, she found her voice.

"Lil' Sis? Girl? Have you completely lost your mind?"

Betty didn't mean to, but she shouted it at her preening baby sister. Annie Ruth, startled by Betty's shriek, tossed the mirrored compact she was holding high above her head. It sailed through the air, fell, bounced once on the thick pile of the rug, then, landed on the hardwood floor with a loud "crack."

"Oh, Betty," Annie Ruth whined as she stared at the broken compact mirror on the floor, "look what you made me do! We don't need no seven years' bad luck tonight!"

"Leave that damn mirror and that makeup alone, Annie Ruth, and bring your pregnant ass on! We having a baby!" Betty ordered.

"Oh, I just want to brighten up my eyes a bit," Annie protested breezily as Betty strode across the long Persian runner toward her with a determined look on her face. Betty wanted to grab her baby sister by her long, curly, newly-thick, henna-tinted hair and drag her out the front door by the scruff of her neck the way she had a couple of times when the girls were teenagers and Betty had to get them all home from a party before Poppa discovered they had slipped out of their bedroom windows. But this time, she didn't have to.

Just as Betty reached for her, Annie Ruth experienced something she had only read about in books and seen in films: her first real contraction. It hit her so hard in the pit of her stomach, it made her knees buckle as if she were a disjointed, brown-skinned, pregnant Barbie doll.

She let out one sharp cry of anguish and reached toward the delicate antique table for support.

"God 'a mighty knows!" she gasped—half-exclamation, half-prayer—and froze for a moment with her eyes screwed shut, her mouth hanging open in an incredulous little "o." Grabbing her stomach with one hand and thrusting her other arm across the surface of the scallop-edged table, she swept all the tubes and cases and sable brushes to the floor and turned to seek her sister's help.

"Betty, come get me," she implored for the second time that night with her eyes still closed in pain.

Betty was right there this time for her baby sister, and, taking her arm tenderly right above the elbow in the fireman's position, she lifted Annie Ruth to her feet and slowly led her out of the formal entrance at the front of the house, forgetting to close the big pine double doors behind them.

Outside, Emily was still sitting and rocking behind the wheel of the car with the motor running, looking for all the world like a wild wolf, gnawing on her bottom lip and bouncing her left breast rhythmically in her right hand the way she did when she was deep in thought or plain nervous.

Emily felt so torn about the impending birth of her sister's baby that she feared she just might leap out of her own body and run in two different directions at the same time, up and down the deserted street like crazy Miss Cliona from Yamacraw.

Every morning since moving back to Mulberry from her apartment in Atlanta and sharing her big sister Betty's house with Annie Ruth, Emily had promised herself that that would be the day she finally, definitely, completely put behind her the anger and resentment that came and went like the tide. Each day, as she wiped the sleep from the corners of her eyes, as she brushed her teeth, as she chose her cutest clean outfit to put on, she swore under her breath, "I won't be mad at Annie Ruth today."

Then, she would leave her sun-lit room, all positive and showered and moisturized and made up, her chin tilted up, "looking to the stars" the way her Mudear had taught all her girls to do when they had gone out of their house to face Mulberry and all the talk about their strange family. But as soon as she would meet Annie Ruth at the top of the winding staircase looking all healthy and pretty and fecund as a sprouting, green field of corn, smelling of Carol's Daughter ginger bath oil, her pregnant stomach taking up way too much room in the wide hallway, Emily would feel her control begin to seep away, and she would start to lose it completely. She'd be right back on the porch of her dead mother's house out in Sherwood Forest six months earlier in the chill of an autumn evening hearing the news that Annie Ruth had broken her sisterly vow, had let herself get pregnant and was going to be a mother herself. Emily would have to turn abruptly and go back into her bedroom and pump herself up all over again.

Now, more than half a year later, on this cool middle Georgia spring night, as she sat in the driver's seat of Betty's car gently gunning the motor and waiting for her sisters to emerge from the house so she could get on with what couldn't be stopped, she prayed for the strength to pump herself up one more time for the birthing ordeal that lay ahead and she wasn't for a minute thinking of her pregnant baby sister's ordeal.

As Betty came out of the house supporting Annie Ruth, she could see Emily clearly in the glow of one of the floodlights that were scattered in the trees around her property. Betty couldn't stand a dark house, inside or out. She knew what it felt like to sit up after dark in a house without lights, without heat, without the hum of the refrigerator or the static from the radio, the electricity turned off. She had promised herself at age eleven that if she had anything to do with it, it would never happen again. So, lights inside and outside her home were on timers that clicked on automatically at dusk, and continued to burn until she turned them off.

Winter, spring, summer, and fall, but especially in winter.

After years of dreading the approach of the fall with its foreshadowing of shorter days and early dusks, she had consulted her doctor and discovered she had more than the winter blues and a fear of the dark. Betty suffered from SAD, Seasonal Affective Disorder. She had gladly taken her doctor's suggestion and installed a few lamps throughout her house that emitted artificial broad spectrum light. The light over the sink in her bathroom that she clicked on before she brushed and flossed her teeth, took her shower, washed and moisturized her face, and applied her makeup ("Lovejoy women don't go out the house without no makeup," their mother had instructed them, although she herself hadn't worn so much as lipstick in decades), had her humming to herself by the time she drove to her beauty shop over in East Mulberry in the winter pre-dawn darkness.

However, some parts of the spacious front and back yard didn't need the floodlights she had installed. In the dead of the last winter shortly after Mudear's death, Betty had hired a yardman to begin putting in a myriad of plants and bulbs that produced white blossoms—tea olives, crepe myrtle, rose bushes, camellias, dogwoods, crocuses, tulips all around the edge of her house and down the long curving driveway that could be easily seen in the dark. Week after week, more and more of the monotonous verdant grass that for years had covered the entire huge yard front and back was being eaten up with brilliantly flowering shrubs and plants. And the oak and mulberry trees that had stood at the perimeter of the yard for decades were joined by flowering trees like peach and plum and pear that had the nerve to bear fruit.

By the first week of that spring, the grounds around the massive house were beginning to look like something on the cover of *Southern Living*. Now, three months later, when Annie Ruth's water broke, the whole property could have passed for a small town botanical garden, from tall, spiky, native middle Georgia grasses to colorful bedding plants to bushy budding local peach trees. And although no one quite wanted to acknowledge it, all of Betty's plants and trees seemed to have a mind of their own, blooming all out of season and proportion to their size.

Winter-blooming tea olives flowered in May right next to spring-blossoming gardenias. Camellias that usually came into their own in winter were bearing big heavy cabbage-sized flowers in Betty's new yard in April.

Betty, who had sworn all her life, along with her sisters, that she would never suffer a plant to grow in any yard of hers, now had a garden that, at the end of a forgiving Georgia spring was as fertile and fruitful as her pregnant baby sister and was actually beginning to rival her mother's legendary sumptuous garden out in Sherwood Forest. And although she had skipped planting vegetables in her yard, she did have a thriving herb garden already thick with parsley and basil and rosemary and thyme and all varieties of chives planted next to her kitchen door. Furthermore, Betty, a neophyte in horticulture and floriculture, refused to question it or fathom how amazing it all truly was.

"I can't believe you turning into a gardener!" Annie Ruth had exclaimed as she struggled to get her expanding body out of the car in March when she had returned to her tiny, middle Georgia hometown from her Southern California home to stay with Betty for the final trimester of her pregnancy. Annie Ruth said the word "gardener" like it was some nasty morsel of rotten food in her mouth that she had sucked out of her teeth and had to spit out.

Betty had smiled as sheepishly as if someone had discovered the hidden cache of sexy Polaroids she and her twenty-year-old lover, Cinque, had taken and stuffed under the king-sized mattress in her bedroom.

"Yeah, who'da thunk it? Like Mudear used to say, 'Keep living,' huh?" she replied playfully as she had helped Emily haul Annie Ruth's pile of luggage into the house and up the stairs to the room she had prepared for her, trying nervously to make light of a sea change in her life.

Annie Ruth, trailing into the house behind her sisters, didn't press Betty any further about the garden. She just exchanged a rare conspiratorial glance with Emily that said, "Now, what the hell is this all about?" A little later that night before Emily headed to her own bedroom down the hall to change into more comfortable clothes, Annie Ruth grabbed her and pulled her into the bathroom while Betty was downstairs making them all a pot of blueberry tea.

"Quick, Em-Em, before Betty comes back. Tell me what in the world she's doing growing a garden in her own yard? Right outside of where she sleeps?" Annie Ruth demanded quietly, using her childhood nickname for her middle sister, as she peeped around the door to the bathroom that she had left slightly ajar to keep an eye on the curved oak staircase. "The only thing she ain't growing out there is corn!"

"Well," Emily began as she sat on the side of the big, marble Jacuzzi tub and pretended to examine the fronds of the lacy fern Betty had cut and brought into the bathroom in a tall crystal vase with white pebbles in the bottom. But she was finding it nearly impossible not to watch Annie Ruth struggle to pull down her panties, sit on the toilet and sigh in relief as she peed. She was so fascinated by Annie Ruth's new, round, ripe-looking belly and her big, full breasts, it was difficult for her to concentrate on a succinct explanation.

"Stop staring at me and talk, girl," Annie Ruth admonished her jokingly. "I ain't no porn site called 'Knocked Up Women on the Toilet.'"

Emily, caught in the act, chuckled at her hungry curiosity, shook her head sharply to clear it and started to explain in a rush, glad to have her baby sister around to share the strange turn of events.

"Well, for starters, these fern leaves here are not made out of plastic," she began in a hushed voice. Then, pausing for effect she added, "They're real."

Annie Ruth's stream of urine stopped sharply and she let out a little gasp. "Uh."

"Yeah," Emily said, nodding her head knowingly.

After a moment of silence as they both stared at the fern, Annie Ruth gathered her wits and continued peeing. Emily breathed deeply and went on.

"Annie Ruth, girl, last fall, right after you left Mulberry after Mudear's funeral, Betty started checking out gardening sites on the computer. I came into her office downstairs one day in November and caught her. She tried to log off real quick, but I saw the flowers and the plants."

"Get out!" Annie Ruth said as she slowly rolled off white toilet tissue and reached around and under her belly to wipe herself.

"Yeah. And then next thing you know, she's hired herself a gardener! Not just a lawn service to mow the grass and clip the trees and hedges like she's always had. But a real gardener with a helper and tools and a truck and an old broke-down hat and everything!"

"You lie!" Annie Ruth was astonished.

"If I'm lyin', I'm flyin', and I'm too fat to fly," Emily said, trying to make light of the few extra pounds she had gained in the past couple of years. But even as she smugly scanned her baby sister's newly rounded figure, she couldn't shake the self-conscious feeling about her own voluptuous body.

"Shh, here comes Betty," Emily whispered as she stepped out of the bathroom. "Don't say anything. I haven't said a word about it to her."

"What?" Annie Ruth asked as she scurried out as best she could behind her sister, as she dried her hands. "You just gonna' act like that garden's not out there growing around us like Mudear come back from the grave?"

They both ran softly and jumped onto the high 1880s four-poster bed in Annie Ruth's new room just as Betty reached the landing, carefully carrying a silver tray with a full, silver tea service on it.

"Yes!" Emily whispered firmly and put her index finger to her lips as Betty came in.

The Lovejoy women, even in their thirties and forties, were like most sisters. Each of them knew that when she was absent the other two were talking about her because when one of the others was out of the room, that's what she did.

As she entered the bedroom with the tea service, Betty called out laughingly as they each had since they were teenagers, "Stop talking 'bout me, here I come!"

But this night with Annie Ruth's water broke and her baby on the way, Betty knew that this was no time for collusion and division. This night, the Lovejoy girls needed to pull together!

"Oh, God!" Betty muttered to herself as she saw the look of confusion cross Emily's face when they came out of the front door instead of the back. If she can't handle a change in exit routes, Betty thought, how are we gonna ever get through this baby's birth?

"You alright, Em-Em?" Betty asked as she helped ease Annie Ruth into the back seat where she immediately stretched out with her head resting on her overnight bag, holding her stomach and her back and moaning in pain.

Emily didn't say anything. She merely nodded a couple of times, quickly, sharply, but she was thinking, I wonder how many times Annie Ruth been stretched out in the back seat of some car. Yet, when her baby sister let out another primal scream, like something out of the Old Testament, Emily bit her lip in true sympathy, and she felt like shit for her petty judgment.

Betty had no idea what Emily was thinking, but seeing the look on her face made Betty want to suggest that perhaps she, herself, should be behind the wheel of her Lexus instead of Emily. However, Betty immediately thought better of saying anything. If she didn't know anything else on earth, Betty knew her sisters, and she feared Emily might see the suggestion as a criticism and go off on her.

All I need now is to have another Lovejoy in crisis mode, Betty thought as she sucked her teeth at the memory of Annie Ruth, with her big, old, pregnant self, trying to put on makeup to "brighten her eyes a bit."

But as soon as Emily turned the car around and pulled out of the driveway into the deserted street, Betty saw a veil of calm descend upon her like a mantle of benediction.

For once, Betty was grateful that her tiny hometown seemed to shut down after midnight. There wasn't another car on the street. With one eye trained on Annie Ruth in the back seat, Betty watched Emily focus all her attention on the empty road ahead as she headed cautiously but speedily for Mulberry Medical Center precisely as they had practiced.

Betty leaned over the seat and took Annie Ruth's hand.

"How ya'll doing back there, Lil' Sis?" she asked, trying to keep the weighty atmosphere in the car light. But the look on her baby sister's face, so changed, so different from any Betty had ever seen there stole any levity she had to offer the situation and made her gasp.

If it hadn't been at night and if they all had not been totally engrossed in the imminent birth of their first baby, one of the girls probably would have noticed how spring had arrived, not only in Betty's yard, but all over Middle Georgia.

The peach trees that the city had planted throughout various neighborhoods expressly for the upcoming Peach Blossom Festival were all in their glory. Even rosebushes growing in the yards of deserted houses along the route of the new highway that cut through town were blooming.

But inside Betty's car, it was beginning to feel as still and grave as winter. Emily, who hadn't said a word since they pulled out of Betty's driveway, suddenly spoke up.

"When I was pregnant that time with Ron's baby before I got rid of it, the way we all promised we would if we ever got pregnant," Emily began, "I got mad and told him it might not even be his, when I knew it was. He didn't really believe me, but it hurt him just the same.

Betty, grateful for once for her middle sister's knack for inappropriate comments, quickly joined in the siblings' ritual game as they made their way on to the hospital.

"Once, when I met Cinque at his mother's house for the afternoon— the only time I ever went to his parents' house, I swear—and we were alone there, we fucked on his mother's new leather sofa."

For a moment, both sisters were silent, waiting for their baby sister to outdo them as she always did. But Annie Ruth let out another wordless primitive scream in reply, and Betty felt Emily press down on the accelerator and barrel through a yellow traffic light so suddenly the momentum threw them all back against their seats.

When the three women pulled up to the emergency entrance of the Mulberry Medical Center, both Emily and Betty jumped out and ran inside to the admittance desk, leaving Annie Ruth alone in the back seat writhing in pain.

When they returned in seconds dragging two attendants and a gurney, she looked at them and implored, "Will ya'll please stop leaving my black ass?!"

"Sorry, Lil' Sis," Betty apologized as she reached into the back seat to help her out. "We'll never leave you again. We swear."

"Good," Annie Ruth replied with a grunt and continued, unaware that she was finishing up the Lovejoy sisters' ritual game they had begun in the car. "'Cause all I got is you two. You know, I don't know who this baby's daddy is."

From there, things moved so swiftly, they barely had time to get Annie Ruth inside the hospital and up to her room. Her labor contractions started coming so close together that by the time they had her feet up in the stirrups at the end of her birthing bed, she was still wearing her Mudear's peach-colored nightgown.

So it looked as if the newest Lovejoy girl—like a princess in the local Peach Blossom Festival coronation—was about to come into the world down a corridor draped in curtains of gauzy fruit-colored silk. It was a grand entrance that suited her dead grandmother, Esther "Mudear" Lovejoy, just fine.

CHAPTER 2

I don't know why these young girls make such a big deal about having a baby.

I might be dead as a doornail, but I still remember that having a child wasn't no big thing.

Nowadays, they got to have Lazarus classes.

They got to go to these expensive especialty stores that only sell maternity clothes that look like only a streetwalker would wear. Stretch jersey dresses all low-cut and tight across their big old stomachs and big old butts so everybody can see they pregnant.

They got to take certain vitamins. Heaven forbid they don't take they folick acid and iron and such.

They got to do these exercises and wear these special clothes when they doin' 'em.

They got to lay on these special mats while they stretchin' and strainin'.

And they got to have this certain kind of music playing.

Then, after all a' that, they end up screaming and caterwauling like something in the barn yard when the real work begins.

Me, I ain't never had no bad time having no baby. All three of my girls popped out just like that. One. Two. Three. And I didn't have all that fancy stuff they got—clothes and exercise and music and kowtowing— before, during, or after neither.

But then again, I ain't never had no problems with <u>my</u> body.

When I was a girl, I didn't never even have no bad menstrual pains. Never did have a day of cramps. When my middle girl Emily got her period, you woulda' thought she was the first woman to bleed. She'd have to stay home from school and lay in bed and hold a hot water bag to her stomach and to her lower back for a couple of days. Of course, she couldn't do nothing around the house for those days. Emily always was a fanatical fool. But back then I think she was just being lazy.

Lazy like them girls now—and women, too—who have the nerve to not only have cramps during their periods, but also claim they having cramps and bloating and irritability before their times of the month. Even got a name for it. Pre-menstrual symptoms. Hell, if they come up with some post-menstrual symptoms, they'll have the whole month covered and won't have to do nothing but sit around and complain all the time!

Uh! Triflin' women.

Look at Annie Ruth there in that fancy hospital delivery room with everything made to be all comfortable and gentle. The walls painted a special soothing color. Soft music playing on a channel on the television. Hell, my own old bedroom out in Sherwood Forest wasn't that special, and I had made me a pretty sweet nest out there in that little cracker box house Ernest called himself being proud of.

You should'a seen the hospital ward I was in back when I had my girls! Shoot! I only had what they gave you in the colored section of the county hospital and that was old used stuff from the white section. I wanted to go to that St. Luke's Hospital, the one for coloreds, run by coloreds. Good place. Probably the best hospital in all of Mulberry County, colored or white. But, of course, back then, Ernest couldn't afford no private hospital for me on his little kaolin mine salary.

Good God, Daughter! Stop all that attention-getting fuss and just birth that baby!

I don't know where my girls get all that hysterical melodramatic stuff from.

Wait a minute! Is that my good peach gown that girl got on? Uhhh. You mean to tell me she found one of my only <u>real</u> silk bed gowns to go and birth a baby in?

That heifer!

CHAPTER 3

"Where is my epidural? Will somebody please give me my damn epidural?" Crying and cursing, her contorted face free of everything but sweat, Annie Ruth had finally for once in her life abandoned any concern with eye shadow and mascara and bronzer and perfectly, seemingly casually-coiffed hair, and looking pretty. She knew she looked like hell and didn't care one little bit. Her Mudear's sheer peach nightgown clung to her sweaty body, her long hennaed curls were matted to her tiny skull, and she wasn't even wearing any translucent Lancome copper lip gloss. All she wanted was for the pain to stop and for someone to hand her her baby.

After the flurry of confusion at the Medical Center emergency entrance, the sisters had to go through the frantic parade into the hospital room where the delivery would take place with folks craning around corners and over bed pans to get a good look at the Lovejoy girls having a baby. Annie Ruth had been at less than four centimeters when her sisters checked her into the hospital. For the next five hours, she advanced about a centimeter every hour. Then, things had come to a painful halt, and all the Lamaze training went right out the window.

On one side of the birthing bed, her big sister Betty held her right hand. On the other side, her middle sister Emily clutched her left one. They both grimaced in pain as their baby sister crushed the bones, skin, and sinew of their hands and dug her frosted peach nails into their flesh so hard it brought tears to their eyes.

Now, Annie Ruth wasn't the only one crying. All three Lovejoy girls—looking like models of the same woman from different ages in various shades of brown skin in varying stages of smoothness with high cheek bones and dark arched eyebrows—were weeping in pain, huffing and puffling in unison as they had been instructed in birthing classes.

But when Annie Ruth, exhausted and overwhelmed, stopped even trying to execute deep breaths and began whimpering pathetically, Betty could take it no longer. She spun around, turned on the attending physician, and screamed at her, "Dr. Hamlin, give my baby sister the fucking epidural!"

When the poor woman didn't move quickly enough, Betty took a menacing step toward her. The doctor, beginning truly to fear for her own safety, backed off and tried to explain that Annie Ruth was too far into the delivery to administer safely the kind of anesthetic she wanted.

"Miss Lovejoy," the physician spoke calmly, sensibly, as if she were sure this intelligent well-known local businesswoman would understand if she spoke to her of facts. "Betty, she's already dilated eight centimeters. I don't like to give an epidural after eight centimeters.

Many women who prepare for natural childbirth change their minds when the pains start. But I'm afraid your sister waited too..."

But right then, Betty felt her baby sister give her hand a feeble squeeze as another stabbing pain wracked her round, sweaty body. Then, to Betty's horror, Annie Ruth went into a dance of jactation. She watched her sister's bloated body toss to and fro, twitching on the delivery bed for a few seconds like a woman possessed by a demon. Without hesitation, Betty grabbed the doctor in her chest, gathered a fistful of her turquoise scrubs with her one free hand, pulled her to within inches of her own face and hissed, "My sister is in agony! Give it to her! Now!"

Like magic, one of the nurses produced a long hypodermic needle and looked to Dr. Hamlin for instructions.

The doctor, a tall, curvaceous, pecan-tan-skinned woman who wore her short sun-streaked hair in bouncy braids, just nodded curtly to the nurse. But when the nurse approached Annie Ruth with the hypodermic, the mother-to-be caught sight of something in the direction of the nurse's shoes and pulled her hands away from Emily's and Betty's and began thrashing about again, looking around the delivery room feverishly. At first, Betty supposed that Annie Ruth had seen the long needle and become frightened. But when she leaned forward to take Annie Ruth's hand again and comfort her, Annie Ruth screamed right in Betty's face, "Oh, God, what they doing letting cats in this hospital?!"

"Oh, shit!" Betty said under her breath.

Emily bit her bottom lip, raised one arched eyebrow and muttered, "Uh-oh."

She and Betty exchanged knowing looks. But Annie Ruth's exclamation freaked out the doctor and attendants, who then immediately began forgetting their duties and started searching around their feet for a feline intruder.

"No, no, Annie Ruth, you know there're no cats in here," Betty tried to assure her sister. Then, in a quieter voice, she added as she gently pressed her palm to Annie Ruth's sweaty forehead as if the laying on of hands could help exorcise her demons. "Come on, sugar, get a grip. You just seeing things again."

She tried to project as much composure and sanity as she could muster, but the whole time, she was thinking, Those damn cats again! She didn't think Annie Ruth had had an hallucination for months now. The last time that she knew of Annie Ruth seeing cats was on the plane trip to Mulberry that Annie Ruth had taken from California to attend their mother's funeral. And that had been the previous fall, nearly seven months earlier. Betty had hoped against hope that her sister had buried those delusions in the grave along with their Mudear's body. But the look on Annie Ruth's face and the sincere terror in her voice in the hospital room squashed those hopes.

"Shh, Lil' Sis, you know it's only in your mind," Betty tried to assure her sister.

But Annie Ruth would not be comforted.

"No, Betty, it's not like on the plane and at the awards banquet and at the television station on air that time. This time, it's for real," she insisted loudly.

Betty noticed that the doctor and attendants had all taken a couple of steps back from the bed and were looking at each other oddly out of the sides of their faces.

"Where, Annie Ruth? Where? Where you see 'em?" Emily asked suddenly, nervously looking around on the floor and under the birthing table.

"Dammit, Emily!" Betty shouted at her skittish sister. "Don't you start," she commanded her.

Emily ignored Betty and kept looking around her feet and over her shoulder in the hot dimly lit room for a sign of the hallucinatory felines.

"Betty! I swear! There's something in here! For real!" Annie Ruth whispered fervently to her big sister. "I see it... and feel it! Don't you?"

"Yeah, Betty," Emily chimed in. "I think I feel it, too."

"Emily!" Betty chided sharply.

"Ladies," the doctor said finally with authority, remembering that this delivery room was her arena. She felt her control slipping away and was determined to reclaim it. "We're trying to have a baby here. Let's focus on that."

Annie Ruth reared up on the table and rested on her elbows. With her knees in the air and her elbows all akimbo, she was a study in jarring angles.

Using all her remaining strength, she took a deep slow breath and screamed at the doctor, "What the fuck do you think I'm trying to do?"

The physician, new to Mulberry, but trained to deal with the stressful situation of delivery, didn't say anything in her defense, but thought, cats in the hospital? Shoot, what folks in this town say is true. These Lovejoy women are crazy!

Betty had never been at a delivery before. And she was trying to keep it together for Annie Ruth's sake, but to her, things didn't seem to be going well in there at all.

Even after the cat scare had settled down and all the attendants seemed to be going back methodically about their business, her baby sister continued to thrash about and scream, wailing like something out of the woods, piercing, primitive screams that clawed through Betty's body like sharp pointed fingernails on a chalkboard. And although the leader of the Lamaze classes had shown them all the instructional films and had walked the mothers-to-be and their labor coaches through the delivery innumerable times, to Betty, none of this birth seemed to be going according to anything she remembered seeing.

Then, without warning, in the midst of the cat scare, Annie Ruth's bowels suddenly seemed to explode and grayish green waste came spewing out of her butt, covering the draped linens and most of the doctor's scrubs.

Seeing the sisters' shocked faces, Dr. Hamlin assured them, "Oh, that's very common. It's nothing to worry about."

But Betty and Emily were plenty worried.

When the doctor grabbed a scalpel from the metal tray at her elbow and performed an episiotomy to widen the vulval opening, the blood that flowed from the small incision seemed redder and more abundant than Betty expected. Annie Ruth's cries seemed more savage and wrenching. And despite the air conditioning, the room seemed hotter than high noon outside in the unusual early spring heat that had descended on the middle Georgia town during the days of the last week. All three sisters were soaked in sweat, their hair glued to their heads, their clothes and scrubs stuck to their bodies.

In each of their minds, they could clearly hear their Mudear's voice intoning, "Lovejoy women don't sweat under their arms."

"There's the head," Dr. Hamlin said finally, trying to sound calm and encouraging in the sea of chaos that swirled around the three Lovejoy sisters and seemed to be engulfing the room.

"You hear that, Annie Ruth? We're almost there," Betty said cheerily, trying to buck her up. "Hang in there, girl! We're almost at the end. You're doing *good. Real good.*"

Annie Ruth screamed in pain again, but this time, the suffering that accompanied the baby's crowning head appeared to clear the mother's head and bring her back to the situation at hand.

Conversely, Annie Ruth's cry seemed to send Emily straight to Nutsville. She had looked up into the mirror over the foot of the bed just in time to see what looked like a specter emerging from her sister's vagina. A tiny head draped with a white membrane that the baby seemed to be struggling to free herself of appeared in the reflection.

Emily took a half step back from the bed and spoke in a half-whisper to her equally startled sister. "Oh, Betty, it looks like a ghost!"

The sight of the child's strange birth mantle had alarmed both Emily and Betty, but the milky mantilla of skin only seemed to amuse the doctor.

"Well, what do you know," Dr. Hamlin said to herself with a chuckle as she struggled to deliver the baby without disturbing the birth caul. "I haven't had a child born with a veil all year. See, ladies, there's nothing to worry about. This is my lucky child. See, she's coming here with a caul," the doctor said proudly as she returned to the task at hand.

Betty had never before seen a child born at all, with or without the birth veil that she had only read about in novels and slave narratives, short stories and memoirs.

But the entire process, which had gone on for more than five hours, was beginning to take its toll on her as much as on Annie Ruth. She could feel her knees growing rubbery beneath her sweat-soaked silk slacks and her hands, always a little sore from years of holding hot combs and curlers, ached when Annie Ruth squeezed them with each birthing pang. Betty looked over at Emily for spiritual support but was dismayed to see her sister's dark brown skin begin to drain of color from her forehead under her shiny black fringe of bangs to her arched eyebrows right down past her full red lips to her long exposed throat. Then, just as her face completely blanched, her eyes started to roll back in her head at the sight of Annie Ruth's blood and placenta and feces spread all over the doctor's cotton scrubs.

Betty knew Emily. Now that Emily was no longer focused on catching sight of cats running around the delivery room, she was on the brink of reeling across Annie Ruth's tight extended stomach. Betty could tell.

"Don't you faint on me, Emily," Betty commanded sternly.

"Don't you dare faint now. I need you here. Annie Ruth needs you here. Come on back now, girl. Now, come on back."

Dr. Hamlin looked up at Betty and thought, My, she's handling her sister's sinking spell well. But the doctor had no way of knowing that Betty had repeated those words—"Alright, Emily, come on back now. Come on back, girl,"—countless times throughout their lives as Emily teetered and danced, pirouetted and pranced on the precipice between sanity and insanity, between clear-headedness and out-of-her-head.

At the sound of her big sister's strict, authoritarian voice, Emily blinked a couple of times, shook her head sharply, tossing the ends of her thick straight black hair around her face, took a deep breath and slowly nodded.

"I'm here. I'm okay. I'm alright," she said with all the confidence she could muster. When she saw Betty's eyes crinkle up at the corners in a smile, she rallied, smiled back bravely, and firmly grasped Annie Ruth's clammy hand.

"Come on, Annie Ruth, you heard the doctor. Give us one more push. Just one more."

Betty knew what it took for Emily to say those words of encouragement. Suddenly, Betty was no longer fearful; she was proud of both her sisters.

Smiling beneath her sagging surgical mask, Betty joined Emily's cheer-leading chants. "Yeah, Lil' Sis, come on. You can do it. You 'bout to be a mama. One more big push. Come on, make me an auntie." She spoke softly, rhythmically, soothingly, as she gently brushed her sister's long brown ringlets from her face. She sounded as she had on many nights decades before when she had to settle them all down and put herself and her younger sisters to bed while their mother wandered blissfully outside in her garden.

Annie Ruth looked up plaintively into her big sister's face and whispered, "Help me!" But even Annie Ruth knew no one could help her now. And she had come too far to turn back.

The baby was coming. And even her sisters couldn't save her from what she had to do herself.

"We can't do this for you, Annie Ruth. You the only one who can birth this baby. Come on, girl!"

Annie Ruth's eyes rolled back in her head and Betty feared her little sister just might faint. Instead, Annie Ruth seemed suddenly to be gripped by mystical hands on her broad Lovejoy shoulders and steadied on the birthing bed. She shook herself one time as if to free herself of the invisible grasp, pushed herself up on her elbows with surprising strength and bore down one more good time.

That was all it took. The baby's head and shoulders pushed through her mother's birth canal, and the whole body slipped slickly into the physician's waiting hands.

Betty couldn't watch anymore. She kept glancing away, then looking, then glancing away again. Emily, however, couldn't take her gaze off of Annie Ruth's crotch and the infant who was struggling to get out of the veil of colorless membrane enshrouding her.

This don't look nothing like it did on film, Emily thought as she leaned forward, despite herself, for a better view.

As soon as Dr. Hamlin gently lifted the veil off the baby's face, Annie Ruth's daughter let out a loud, lusty cry that brought fresh tears to all the Lovejoy women's eyes.

Dr. Hamlin seemed determined to keep the velum of skin hanging around the baby's head and tiny shoulders intact as she maneuvered around the bed and side tables and lights and, with the baby in her hands, headed for the corner of the room and the long surface that looked like a metal changing table.

Annie Ruth fell back onto the birthing bed, still panting and blowing a bit dizzy from the extra oxygen, with her eyes closed. Her sisters had forgotten her for the moment in their eagerness to get a good look at their new niece.

The first thing Betty thought as she laid eyes on her niece kicking and squirming in the doctor's hands was the Nikki Giovanni poem that ended, "Oh, what a pretty little baby."

The first thing Emily thought when she caught sight of the baby's head full of jet black, tightly coiled hair, she leaned over and shared with Betty. "Well, at least that settles that," she whispered. "With all that thick nappy-looking hair, the daddy sho' ain't no white man."

Annie Ruth, however, had other matters on her mind. With a surprising spurt of strength, she reached up and pulled Emily and Betty down to within inches of her face. They had laughter and words of celebration and pride on the tips of their tongues for their baby sister. But she didn't want to hear any of that. She interrupted them.

"Six weeks 'til I can have sex again, my ass," she said in a deliberate breathy whisper, "Sisters, I may never fuck again."

Then, she fell back exhausted on the white sheets of the delivery bed as the doctor returned from the corner table and placed Annie Ruth's baby girl on her stomach, then stood back with a satisfied smile.

Annie Ruth seemed to regain some strength at the sight of her child, and a bit of her old spirit returned as she gazed lovingly on her baby girl.

"Daughter," she said softly, "you have worn your mama out."

Then, she sighed, closed her eyes and went limp because she couldn't buck up one more second.

CHAPTER 4

Well, what d'ya know? Like the old song they used to sing when I was young say, "Annie had a baby!"

And listen to her, talking about private things like relations with men in front of a room full a' strangers. Shoot, if Annie Ruth know like I know she ought not 'a be thinking about ever "fucking again." Seeing as that's how she got messed up and broke a leg like this in the first place.

Yeah, "Played so well, Daughter, but slipped and fell." Hee hee.

But Lord ham mercy, messed up or not, I got to say, that is a pretty child that Annie Ruth just brought into this here world. Prettier than any of my girls were when they was born. Betty, Emily, and Annie Ruth was all right funny-looking little things when they was first born. Umm, but look at her. My first grandchild! Um. Um. Um.

I know I'm her grandmama, and as old Miss Carrie used to say, every mother think her little, black crow is a tall, sleek swan. I never could stand them women who went on and on 'bout their children and their grandchildren. But I got to say it again. She is a pretty thing.

And she got the nerve to be born with a caul over her face! Just like her grandmama! I knew that child was gonna' take after her Mudear. I just knew it! That oughta' tell 'em something right there. A child born with a caul ain't no everyday ordinary thing. In fact, it's extra-ordinary!

Don't tell me I didn't mark that child! Don't tell me I didn't mark her as my own. I knew it!

Ever since I been dead, there's been some things I just know that I didn't have a inkling of before. Even though the old folks always used to say that a child like me born with a caul—we always called it a veil, but it's the same thing—over her face had powers to see ghosts and spirits and to look into the future and such, I don't think I never could do any of that. Shoot, if I had, I wouldn'tna' married old Ernest Lovejoy. Wouldn'tna had no children. Wouldn'tna had this grandchild.

Frankly, I don't think I look nearly old enough to be somebody's grandmother. Even in death I don't look that old. 'Course, nowadays, grandmamas are grandmamas at thirty-five or even younger.

I ain't thirty no more, or forty, or fifty for that matter. But I figured I still looked pretty well. Then, I got a good look at myself in a still fish pond in Betty's yard the other day – or it could 'a been the other month, I ain't got no sense a' time now – and it like to scared me to death... Well, you know what I mean.

I thought, God, is that what people look like when they dead?!

I wasn't never what you call a pretty woman, not in no regular everyday ordinary kinda' way like Betty and Emily and Annie Ruth. But you know, I always thought there was something 'bout my looks... Even that old dog I was married to seemed to think so at one time. I know I look better than them old hags that used to call themselves my friends at one time. I know I done aged better 'n them. I saw one a' em, Agnes, the other day. One of her boys I guess was driving her down the street past Betty's house toward the colored Catholic church, and I swear her face look like fried tripe. I know even dead I look better 'n her.

Anyhow, when I caught a look at myself in that still water, I couldn't hardly believe it was me. You see, it looked like me, but then again, it didn't look like me. It scared me more than a little bit 'cause it made me feel almost like I was losing my mind. I mean, that kinda' thing is something I'd expect Emily, with her crazy self, to be thinking, "I look like myself, but then again, I don't look like me."

But still it was the truth. I didn't remember my head being so little and pea-shaped. And I could have sworn that I was taller than I looked. I guess mostly it was that God-awful outfit I've been wearing for months now. I ask again, why would those girls go ahead and bury me in this ugly navy blue dress? No matter how much I seem to be able to do now that I'm dead, I can't for the life of me seem to change clothes. I always did look lovely in pastels. And with spring here, I'd give just about anything to have on a nice light pinkish color instead of this dead-looking navy.

By rights, I ought to have been laid out in that pretty peach-colored peignoir that Annie Ruth just ruined for life by giving birth in it and covering it in blood and mucus and, Lord help me, shit. Couldn't they find that girl no hospital gown?

Not that I'm one to be complaining. I never was a complainer. Me, I'll take it any way I can get it.

Anyhow, no matter how old I feel or look, I am a grandmother. There she is—the proof laying right up there on her mama's stomach. Even if she wasn't laying up there next to Annie Ruth, you could tell she was my grandchild by how different and how much better she looks from all those other ugly, crying babies up there in that hospital.

And she got a head full a' thick strong colored folks' hair on her head. It's all soft and curly now, but you know it's gon' turn.

I shouldn't even say nothing 'bout her hair. I'm so sick a' colored folks and hair I don't know what to do. Even before the baby is cleaned up good, colored folks always gotta ask, "What kinda' hair the baby got?" Even before they asked if the baby was alright and healthy and had all its fingers and toes.

"Is she got good hair?" the baby's people always want to know. If don't nobody in their whole family, on either side, got any straight hair, they still ask, "What kinda hair the baby got?" Foolish folks! They ought to be asking what's in her head not what's on it.

But I can tell just by looking at my grandbaby that she got something going on in her head, too! Brightest-looking child in that whole big hospital they call a Medical Center.

But, shoot, then again, look at the daddy's nappy hair. What else she gon' have?

Oh, they claim they don't know who the daddy is. They don't even talk about it. Even Annie Ruth got the nerve to say she don't know. Personally, I think she lying. But whether she is lying or not, I know the truth. I know who the real daddy is.

And I tell you something else. My grandchild is the onliest one in that whole hospital who was born with a caul over her face. I bet you that much! We used to call 'em "veils," but everybody with any sense all over the world know it's the same thing as a caul.

I was born with one, but they didn't never do too much talking about it in my house when I was little. But it ain't gon' be that way with my grandchild. Oh, yeah, she gon' know who she is. And it ain't gon' take no change like it did for me when I was a grown woman for it to happen.

I'm working on that thing rat now! Ha!

CHAPTER 5

Betty's cropped, jewel blue, shantung silk pants and matching camisole and even the short swing jacket she hadn't had time to take off before slipping on the hospital scrubs were still damp with the sweat of the effort of childbirth. Her entire body felt clammy. The soles of her feet ached as did her back, legs and fingers. Even her butt was sore from straining and pushing in sympathy with Annie Ruth. And her neck was one big knot from sitting up in the leatherette lounge chair provided in the room for sleep-over visitors.

It felt as if she had not only been her sister's labor coach, but as if she, too, had just experienced labor and given birth herself. Yet, strangely enough, she also felt full and complete. After seeing life, her own flesh and blood, come into the world through her sister's open legs, Betty knew anything else she ever experienced without that tiny new creature, her niece, would always seem right this side of empty and barren.

But even buoyed by the memory of new life, Betty was so weary and drained she could not begin to think about leaving Mulberry Medical Center, finding one of the two or three cabs that ran after dark and heading back to the top of Pleasant Hill and her big house by herself. She had remained with Annie Ruth in her room watching an old Tina Turner concert on the television and staring at the tiny newborn miracle that lay in the bassinet next to Annie Ruth's bed until she saw the sun peek over the cotton candy, pink blossoms of the crepe myrtle trees planted outside the wide hospital window.

When a nurse came in to take the baby to the nursery and whispered, "Doctor's orders. So, Ms. Lovejoy can get some rest," Betty realized that she, too, could have used some of that rest. On top of everything else, she hadn't had a cigarette in more than two weeks, and at that moment, she would have killed for a glass of wine or a shot of tequila next to a burning Kool Light. She had been cutting back on her smoking for months. And although she was determined not to take one puff around her new little niece, she didn't have that same resolve about drinking.

Betty flopped into the first comfortable chair she saw in the lobby of the hospital next to a lanky, dark man who looked like an old Chuck Berry and was dressed like a young Elvis.

At least I stayed around longer than Emily, she thought and ran her hands through her thick cropped hair. It, too, was damp but had not lost the swing that she had taught the best cutters in her shops to add to make black permed hair, even short hair, bounce like Oprah's. A couple of hours after the birth, her sister Emily had brushed her dry lips across Annie Ruth's damp forehead as the new mother dozed in her private room, picked up her red leather purse, the keys to the Lexus, and headed for the door. Then, she turned suddenly, went back to retrieve a white plastic bag with MULBERRY MEDICAL CENTER printed on it, then slipped out of the room with only a blown kiss toward the baby's bassinet and a "call me" gesture and a walking fingers motion toward Betty. Betty understood that in "sisterspeak," the sign language meant "phone me when you're ready to leave."

So, she knew that Emily was merely a phone call away, but her leaving pissed Betty off just the same.

As soon as Emily had left the room, Betty had a good mind to follow her out into the hall and read her big round ass from one end of the hospital to the other for not sticking around with her baby sister after she had just given birth to her first child. But she didn't have the heart to try to chastise Emily. Shoot, she thought as she watched her sister's retreat, at least she stuck it out through the birth.

Betty could sense the confusion and regret written all across her sister's broad bare brown back like long angry welts as she left the room. Actually, she was amazed that Emily had gone through with their sisterly promise to be with Annie Ruth through it all. "More than I thought she'd be able to stomach," Betty had said softly to herself as she tried to find a comfortable position in the hospital room chair.

Emily had spent much of the previous few months trying to pretend that she wasn't so angry with her baby sister that she could hardly be in the same room with her, especially after Annie Ruth had started showing and glowing with good health, hormones, and pre-natal vitamins.

Since they were little, all sleeping together in one room praying that Mudear couldn't hear their thoughts, since the day they first felt their mother pull away from them into her own private, selfish world, since the evening they realized Mudear wasn't even going to rouse herself to cook dinner for them, the sisters had made pacts with each other that were as binding as the religious vows of innocent, virginal novitiates.

Over the years, the promises made to each other in youth, meant to cement and support them, had twined around them like some living vine that tripped them at every turn.

When Betty was ten, Emily eight, and Annie Ruth five, they had stood in the family's backyard among their mother's flowers and vegetables and swore that they would be friends for life and never need outsiders, who thought they were as strange as their reclusive mother. Two years later, after an afternoon of weeding and watering in the hot Georgia sun, they had stood on the very same spot and vowed never to work like slaves in a garden when they were adults and out of their Mudear's clutches.

"I ain't never gonna' even grow a weed!" Betty had sworn as she wiped dirt and sweat from her brow outside the old house in East Mulberry.

And seven years later, as teenagers sitting cross-legged on the floor in the safety of the cove between their single beds in the Sherwood Forest house, they shyly joined hands and made the one pledge that had grown to hinder them the most.

In hushed tones, they had pledged never to have children.

"I'll never be a mama," they had each vowed. "That way we'll never be like Mudear."

Their mother had insisted that they call her that, "Mudear," but the self-involved, self-focused, selfish, little brown-skinned woman was as far from a dear mother as anybody could have gotten. Mudear didn't think the sun rose until she got up and since she didn't rise 'til late afternoon, as far as she was concerned, the day didn't start until dusk. Then, she lounged around idly all the afternoon and evening in the pretty pastel nightgowns and robes and negligees that her daughters went downtown on Mulberry's green and cream public buses to purchase for her at Davison's Department Store. She just seemed to be waiting for night. It was only way after dark when she felt her natural gifts really shone and she truly came into her own.

Mudear had many gifts. Even her worst enemies—women in town who had been her friends and confidantes at one time only to find themselves tossed aside in Mudear's self-sustained march to freedom— had to admit that.

"Esther Lovejoy may be a strange old heifer," they said in hushed tones as they sat up in one of Esther Lovejoy's eldest daughter's two beauty shops—an old-fashioned one in East Mulberry and a new state-of-the-art one out at the Mulberry Mall—waiting to get their hair done, "but she sho' did raise some smart girls."

Mudear, however, didn't care anything about what people thought about her talents. In fact, not caring was on the Top 10 List of her proudest achievements. The gift she was truly proudest of, that caused her the most hubris, was her night vision, because it allowed her to indulge her one real passion: tending her garden after dark when the heat of Middle Georgia summers became more bearable. And that's just what she did. Night after night after night, dressed in a pastel nightgown or bathrobe, like some petite specter, she floated around the prodigious garden that took up the entire back yard and the vacant lot behind that yard, hoeing and weeding, watering and fertilizing, planting and transplanting. Then, as the sun began to lighten up the sky, she'd crawl back into her big four-poster bed—sometimes without even washing her hands and feet—like some small-town Southern vampire precisely as her husband Ernest was rising to head to his job out at the kaolin mines on the outskirts of Mulberry to help pay for her singular lifestyle.

Content and tired, she slept the sleep of the innocent all through the day, then rose later in the afternoon to bathe, eat, watch T.V. and lounge around again until dark. The way her days shaped up, she didn't see any reason to get dressed. So, she didn't. Instead, she wore nightgowns, not pajamas, and robes in light airy shades of cotton candy and cornflower and lilac and lime that she swore flattered her medium brown complexion and that she preferred to the dated street clothes that hung unworn from year to year in her bedroom closet next to her husband's starched and pressed khaki work clothes.

Mudear was lucky enough to have three daughters, so one day, the fiendishly clever woman had simply decided to stop performing any household duties. One by one, Mudear had dropped the domestic chores: the cleaning and the cooking and the washing and the shopping. And the girls — still barely little things — picked them up. For a while, it seemed that every day brought another task that Mudear eschewed — combing her daughters' hair, bathing them, making sure they brushed their teeth, fixing their school lunches, replying to notes from their teachers, ironing, sweeping the kitchen floor. And every day, Betty or one of the other girls made sure the task was done.

And as they put their hands to the oars and took on the tasks at hand, they felt themselves placed in a leaky rowboat and set adrift like three little abandoned sailors.

For that's what they were: abandoned.

Oh, Mudear didn't abandon them all in the traditional sense. She didn't just pack up one day and walk away from the family household. All through their childhood and into their teen years, as they mopped the kitchen floor or paid the bills or ironed their school clothes for the next day, Annie Ruth always pointed out, "Oh, she was too slick for that."

Although none of them ever dared to say it aloud, even with Mudear out of earshot and not caring even if she had overheard their conversation, each girl had at one time or another thought, I wish she would just leave. Even Emily had thought it once or twice, though she clung to the fantasy of Mudear changing back suddenly to a halfway caring mother in the exact way she had seemed suddenly to transform into the distant, self-focused woman she was 'til the day she died.

The one time Emily had dared to speak her secret desire — "I wish she would just leave," — she had immediately clamped her hands over her mouth so forcefully that she had bruised her thick full lips.

And even when Mudear wasn't anywhere nearby, all three girls could hear their mother cackle in their heads and say, "Wish in one hand. Shit in the other and see what you got." It was as close as she ever came to what she called motherly advice.

Mudear had not only discarded physical household work in her march toward her personal freedom. She also abandoned any nurturing role. And just as she had expected, again her girls took up the slack. As the eldest, most of those caring duties naturally fell to Betty. They were a heavy load. But she didn't mind. Betty, wise like old folks' children, saw more clearly than her sisters that all they had in the world was each other.

It was Betty who showed her sisters how to strategically place a sanitary napkin in their panties, and later how to insert a Tampax gently. It was Betty who assured Emily that the acne that ravaged her teenaged face would soon clear up. It was Betty who combed her sisters' hair and made sure they did their homework. It was Betty who taught them how to iron a blouse, to shave under their arms, to tie their shoes, to take a douche, to pin curl their hair.

For more than three decades, Mudear seemed not to notice who did what as long as she didn't have to do it. Oh, once in a while, when they were teenagers, Mudear would look up from a photo-filled magazine or her favorite television program and instruct Betty, "Pick up that rug, don't sweep around it. Daughter, don't be so trifling." Or to one of the younger girls, "Oh, let Betty do that. Let her pick up that box. She big-boned, she can handle it."

But that was about as far as she became involved in household duties.

One Saturday afternoon, when the girls were in the kitchen raking their mother over the coals as they washed breakfast dishes and wiped off the table and swept the floor and began preparing the next meal for the evening, Annie Ruth, the baby, not even a teenager yet observed dryly, "Mudear, she got it made."

From down the hall in the house's largest bedroom, they heard their mother add, "Made in the shade."

Mudear reveled in her self-made situation. The girls, who felt they had to carry so much shame—shame for having to care for themselves, for having a mother who was unlike any they knew of, for never being sure of others' opinions of them—in hushed voices, called their mother shameless.

Mudear lived by the philosophy that "when I done et, my whole family done et." Betty had actually heard her mother say that early on one night to her father when he had come home from work hungry and tired to a cold dark kitchen and three unfed little girls.

"When I done et, my whole family done et," Mudear had stated flatly, then turned over in her nice warm bed and gone back to sleep.

Mudear left the cooking to her eldest daughter who couldn't bear to see her baby sisters go hungry, waiting for a meal from their mother that never materialized. It was what kept the household running for decades. It was what Betty figured her mother expected of her. All the things that Mudear refused to do.

Every one of the girls did that, just what Mudear expected of them. Betty cooked delicious meals and ran the household. Emily washed dishes and clothes and paid the bills. Annie Ruth did the dusting, studied hard in school and made sure the teachers never insisted on a parent-teacher conference.

Throughout the girls' childhoods, adolescence, and young adulthoods, and up until the day she was taken to the Mulberry Medical Center and died, Mudear didn't leave the sanctuary of her comfortable home—first, the small wooden one in East Mulberry, then, the more spacious brick one out in the Sherwood Forest development—except to tend to her lush garden after darkness of night fell. Instead, she lay around her home dressed in pretty nightgowns and sent her girls out into the world of Mulberry alone to buy the groceries, to pay the bills, to shop for their own clothes, to attend school, and to fend for themselves and each other.

Even Emily's psychiatrist, Dr. Axelton in Atlanta, who had heard a story or two in her time, had difficulty accepting the life that Emily uncovered for her session after session in explaining Mudear.

"And you and your sisters were how old when your mother stopped performing any household duties?" Dr. Axelton had asked, fixing her patient with a steely gaze of her faded blue eyes.

"We were little," Emily had informed her, relieved for once to be able to share the enigma that was Mudear with someone other than her sisters. It was for the sheer release that her forty-five minutes with Dr. Axelton every week for nearly a year afforded her that Emily put up with the grilling her state government insurance clerk dished out regularly. "Betty was ten, I was eight, and Annie Ruth was almost five."

The psychiatrist was trained to mask her own feelings as she took notes on the clip board resting in her lap. Yet once or twice, Emily saw the older woman's grey head shake imperceptibly in sympathy and disbelief.

"Oh, but Mudear did wash out her dirty drawers every night," Emily added quickly.

"And she didn't once leave the house other than for the back yard for how many years?" Dr. Axelton had asked as she made notes on her clip board.

"Um, let me think, oh, about twenty-five, thirty years."

"Never?" Dr. Axelton asked.

Emily had been tempted to reply, "Lady, what part of 'never' don't you understand?" But instead she merely softly but emphatically repeated, "Never."

No matter how many patients Dr. Axelton had treated, no matter how many hair-raising stories she had heard, Emily knew that the analyst had no true understanding of what her Mudear was truly like. Even though the town of Mulberry never seemed to tire of talking about her, few people, other that her daughters and husband, truly knew the crags, crannies, and valleys of Mudear.

Decades after Mudear had drilled the three girls on the tone and proper inflection of the endearment—"No, sugar, say 'Mu-dear'—even with Mudear nearly a year in the grave, the woman's voice could still ring in her family's ears like a cursed echo that would not stop resounding.

It was a voice that continued to drain her daughters and husband of any routine pleasure. Betty could attest to that. Hearing her mother's voice in her head criticizing the clothes she wore—"Ain't you too old to be wearing a skirt that short?"—the way she ran her two beauty shops—"Daughter, did you see on the television 'bout this here woman who lost every single penny she had when she went and extended herself too far and opened up two stores?"—the men she dated, such as they were—"That lil' boyfriend a' yours got any curly hairs downstairs yet?"—had always sapped her of any joy and energy she felt, even though she succeeded at times in closing her ears to the carping.

This morning—the morning of the birth of her brand new niece, when she should have been filled with joy and vigor—Betty was even more exhausted than usual. She could just feel a bad Mudear mood creeping up on her like a ravenous, stalking, salivating animal in the dark. For the past several months, she had been fighting that feeling almost every week. Usually the fight felt good, as if she were changing, getting stronger, and making progress against a relentless yet invisible enemy. This day, however, it merely felt sad.

"Don't let nobody steal your joy," Mudear had instructed her girls all their lives. She said it with deep feeling, verging on tenderness, as if she weren't the grand-theft joy felon in the house.

"I refuse to let Mudear steal my joy this day," Betty avowed when she heard her mother's words of wisdom again ringing in her ears. And she bound out of the chair in the hospital lobby with renewed, determined energy.

Forgetting the cigarette she was craving, Betty bypassed the double doors leading out of the medical center, headed straight for the bank of elevators in the hall and got onto the first one that opened.

"Forget you, Mudear. I know where my joy lies," she said as she punched the elevator button for the nursery floor so hard with her thumb that she thought she heard her knuckle crack.

CHAPTER 6

Humph! She may try, but she and her sisters ain't never gon' forget <u>me</u>. And she ain't got no right to be talking 'bout me, me of all people, stealing their joy.

Stealing their joy? Shoot, them girls just ain't got a clue, do they? They don't know nothing 'bout getting they joy stole.

But then them girls never did know all I did for them.

And they never even asked either. As far as they was concerned, I was always like I was. I was always the strong one who ran my own household. They just took it for granted that that's the way it was, but they had no idea how long I had to think and plan and work that thing before I became a woman in my own shoes.

And I got to admit, there was a bit a' luck involved for all the pieces to come together the way they did when the girls was still little things.

If I hadn'na' saved a little piece a' money from those few pennies Ernest had been giving me since we first got married. If Ernest hadn'a spent all his money on tryna' be the "big man" 'round town. If the girls hadn'a all come down with the whooping cough at the same time. If it hadn'a been wintertime. If they hadn'a turned off our heat. If I hadn'a stepped in and caught the bus downtown to pay that gas bill when Ernest didn't have an extra penny to his name. But them girls don't know or seem to care all that happened to me.

Self, self, self. That's all they care 'bout. God, them girls is selfish. They got some ugly ways!

But that's a'right, lil' heifers. That's allright. Just keep living, daughters. You'll all gon' learn a thing or two before it's over.

CHAPTER 7

Betty knew in her spirit that the baby girl lying in the hospital nursery with "Lovejoy" printed on her tiny I.D. bracelet was the main source of her joy that night and would be for every day and night she lived. With Emily moping around the last few months reminding her every time Annie Ruth left the room, she couldn't ignore the fact that the tiny child was also proof of the vow the sisters had made and Annie Ruth had broken.

"But, Betty, we promised!" Emily had whined for months until her big sister told her if she didn't shut the fuck up about broken promises that never should have been made and honored in the first place, she was going to raid her secret marijuana stash and set fire to it in the big brick barbecue pit in the backyard of her house.

"I swear to God, Emily. I swear. I swear I'll do it. I swear. I'll do it," she told her earnestly as she closed her eyes and slowly shook her head for emphasis. "If you don't stop talking about Annie Ruth breaking promises, I'll burn that dope. I swear I will."

As far as Betty was concerned, their vow of childlessness was a covenant she was glad to see shattered.

In the last year, Betty thought as she leaned wearily against the wall outside the hospital nursery, there had been any number of family pillars she had seen fall, crash, and burn on the fires of Mudear's funeral pyre. The previous fall, when Mudear had died, things had begun to change so phenomenally and rapidly, it all made Betty a bit light in the head. The mere thought of the last few months made her bring her fingertips up to her temple and run them through her damp hair.

The gesture, one that she had been doing most of her adult life, made her smile despite her exhaustion. It reminded her suddenly of Cinque, her friend—she refused to call him her "boyfriend" because he was, in fact, at age twenty still so close actually to being a boy—and the habit he had when they were alone together of casually running his fingers through her short hair and gently scratching her scalp with his short bitten-down nails until her whole head, then her entire body, tingled. If her arms, like the rest of her body, had not been so bone weary there at the hospital, she would have stretched her hands up to her own skull and scratched all around in her hair herself just for the memory of the pleasure it gave her. Recalling the joy that the birth of her sister's child had given her only heightened the unpleasant knowledge that, other than Cinque, there was precious little pleasure in her life. Not from her thriving beauty businesses, not from her bulging closets, not from her hefty bank accounts, not from her unlined face and firm butt. And it had been that way for quite some time.

Oh, she tried to tie it to her mother's death the autumn before, but she knew that that emptiness had been there long before Mudear had passed. Her mother's death had merely thrown the void and the valleys of her life into sharp relief for her. It had done that for all the Lovejoy girls.

Even though they were far from "girls," folks in Mulberry still called them that. "Girls."

Betty, who had lived in Mulberry her whole life and knew precisely how small towns functioned, prayed that she and her sisters would not end up like the Sellars sisters. Those three grey-haired "girls" were all well into their eighties, living in the same house together and were still referred to as the "Sellars Girls" by everyone in town.

She had nothing to base it on and she didn't dare utter the longing, but she still held out a shred of hope for the Lovejoy sisters that they would indeed one day find love and joy in one-on-one relationships.

"Hell," she'd say to herself many times as she closed up her beauty shop in East Mulberry and headed for her car to go close up the second shop out at the mall, "who knows? Maybe Cinque will even mature and grow up enough for us to commit to each other before I get too old to really enjoy a long-term relationship with him."

The spring that Annie Ruth had her baby, Betty was twenty-three years older than her nearly twenty-year-old lover. Emily was just turning forty and freaking out about it. And even her sisters had a hard time remembering how old Annie Ruth actually was. She had been lying about her age for so long, since she had left college, in fact, that to determine her true age, Betty and Emily always had to pinpoint their own ages, then count back six or three years respectively.

Although she couldn't define it, Betty felt that Mudear had something to do with the fixation all of the girls seemed to have with age. Annie Ruth swore she just couldn't keep track of the dates and that in her business of TV news—much like in films and television entertainment—it didn't pay for a woman ever to get too old. Emily, on the other hand, proclaimed her age at every opportunity, then quoted her mother that she had "earned every one of these years." Betty fell somewhere in between her two sisters' philosophies on aging: Approaching her mid-forties, she felt near her prime even as she sensed her prime slipping away.

As much as they tried to be free women in the world, the Lovejoy girls knew they were far from liberated. All three women had spent most of their adult lives trying to outrun Mudear and her long, tight grasp. Betty attempted to put business success, her evening glass of wine, and her social standing between her and her mother. Emily thought the hundred miles or so between Mulberry and her home in Atlanta would do the trick. And Annie Ruth tried numbing herself with a string of men and public adulation to forget the kind of mother she had.

None of it worked.

No matter how achieving or crazy or professional or well-dressed or sexually adventurous they were, they were at heart still the Lovejoy girls, Mudear's daughters, the offspring of the strangest, craziest woman in Mulberry, Georgia.

There seemed to be no avoiding it. The town of Mulberry itself seemed to be in cahoots with its citizens to prove to the Lovejoy girls precisely how strange and particular their family and lives had been.

The week after they had buried Mudear, Betty suddenly had more traffic and business through her popular beauty shops, Lovejoy 1 and Lovejoy 2, than any time in her whole career. And that was saying something. Women and some nosy men, too, crossed the shops' thresholds who had never darkened her doorstep before. Some professed merely to wanting "a trim." Others laid out the $35 for a shampoo and blowout. And some even thought the privilege of seeing one of the Lovejoy girls close up in her professional environment was worth the full fee of $65 for a perm.

"Look to the stars! Look to the stars!" Betty had had to keep repeating to herself for days after her mother's funeral as she walked through both her jammed-packed beauty salons with all eyes trained on her.

Fortunately, Betty's employees, usually as nosy as the new customers, remained loyal. They couldn't stand the way the townspeople ogled their generous and considerate employer, and tried to pick them for more information on Esther Lovejoy's death, setting up, and burial. So, the beauty shop staff continued to do heads and shut down the sly inquiries every chance they got.

"Me, I wouldn't be turning my hair over to some strange beautician just to get a little scrap of gossip to chew on with my old dried-up girlfriends," the chief shampoo girl at Lovejoy's 2 said loudly as she poured out a pink gel and roughly scratched suds up in a new customer's hair. The woman in the shampoo chair, too busy looking around the shop for a glimpse of Betty, didn't even hear her shampoo girl's comment.

"Yeah," the colorist at the next sink chimed in. "I'd be afraid the good Lord would make all my hair fall out for being so un-Christian-like."

When a chorus of "um-huhs" and "amen to that" rose up all over the shop, three women waiting in the comfortable reception area grabbed up their purses and marched out the door. Then, the woman in the shampoo chair, finally realizing that the chatter was aimed at her, and with the words cutting too close to the bone, suddenly whipped off the shop's signature short red and purple plaid wrap she was wearing, threw it on the chair and stormed out behind her friends with soapy water dripping down her face and back.

Just about everybody in the tiny town seemed to want to get a peek at the Lovejoy girls, who—stressed out, pregnant, and determined to take advantage of their last chance to tell Mudear just what they thought of her—had had the nerve to get into a fight down at Parkinson's Funeral Home right over their dead mother's body, roll around the parquet floor in their expensive black frocks and high-heeled shoes and finally tip their mother's corpse over right out of her silk-lined casket like a toasted Pop-Tart. Oh, most folks in Mulberry just had to get a good look at them after that.

And even in a small town, where Esther Lovejoy reveled in telling her girls that "pretty women were a dime dozen," the Lovejoy girls were something to behold, especially when they were all together. Each of them—a mite taller, heavier, curvier than her younger sister—was a slightly different shade of smooth, pleasing brown.

Annie Ruth had a little undertone of burnished copper to her skin that she punctuated with her curly, hennaed hair. Emily had a bit of deep red in her coloring. And Betty had the pure lustrous dark skin that street artists in the '60s immortalized on velvet canvases of black women with huge round afros and even bigger round butts.

While growing up, they had been right cute, little stair-stepped girls in matching dresses and brightly colored hair ribbons that Betty, just a child herself, purchased in the notions section of Dannenberg's department store and kept starched and ironed for them all. In their teens, each one blossomed into an individual, with certainty about what was her most flattering style. From the age of twelve, Emily seemed to know intuitively that she looked good in red. Annie Ruth wore nothing but gold hoop earrings, large and small, from the moment she had her ears pierced at age thirteen. And Betty never bothered with growing her hair below the nape of her long, elegant neck.

And they just got better with age. Even their Mudear had to admit that they were the kinds of brown-skinned women who grew better looking with each passing year. As young women, whenever they complained that folks in town seemed to stare at them whenever they ventured out of the house, Mudear merely stretched her little body out further on her cushy chaise lounge and instructed them to shout at the rubber-neckers, "Ain't ya'll never seen a bunch of good-looking, brown-skinned colored women before?"

"Good-looking, brown-skinned colored women" indeed, each of

the girls had thought at one time or another.

Mudear may have said the words, but she didn't give the compliment. All her girls knew that she would never even think of giving any one of her daughters praise that didn't bubble and churn with a subtle hidden acid.

Emily took no pleasure in the elegant slender hands that Mudear had told her couldn't accomplish anything but washing dishes. Annie Ruth couldn't pass another woman on Rodeo Drive without comparing her looks to the stranger's. Mudear's words, "Pretty women sho' nuff a dime a dozen out in Hollywood, California, daughter," made her check, then double-check her makeup four or five times a day. And even as she lay snuggled beside her tall, muscular young lover, Betty still felt like a big old raw-boned, big-boned, heavy-duty country gal.

Thanks to Mudear, they couldn't be completely secure or sure of anything. Shoot, none of them, even a pregnant Annie Ruth, could even wear a pair of white slacks without worrying about coming on her period.

Mudear had made sure of that with her off-hand pronouncements and casual curses spoken over their lives from her throne of a La-Z-Boy or propped up on her comfy king-sized bed. All their lives, all Mudear had had to do was mutter to herself, "Trifling women! Nothing's worse than a trifling can't-do-nothing woman," and her girls would start examining themselves and each other for signs that she might be talking about them.

With that dead woman's voice still ringing in Betty's head, the small brown woman who had insisted that her daughters address her with the endearing name she called her own mother, seemed as alive to her eldest daughter as she had a full year before when she was still lounging around out at the house in Sherwood Forest yelling orders down the hall to her husband or her "girls." Betty had spent so much time in Mudear's house, she didn't even have to walk into that nearly vacant three-bedroom ranch-style structure in the Mulberry suburb to envision a still-living Mudear stretched out on her favorite lounger in the family room, dressed as always in some pretty flowing pastel nightgown and robe, popping pieces of spicy red cinnamon candy into her cruelly luscious mouth and clicking through the cable channels on her wide-screen television with the universal remote in her hand.

For the two decades that she had lived on her own, Betty had traveled across the bridge spanning the Ocawatchee River five or six times a week and driven out Orange Highway to Sherwood Forest to Mudear's house. Sometimes, she took meals she had cooked or picked up to go on the way. Other times, she strapped on an apron there and prepared a meal to be served at once and two or three additional ones to refrigerate or freeze for later. While the food simmered, she took the opportunity to wash a load of clothes and sweep up the neat house.

Folks who knew her schedule and what it took to run two thriving beauty shops as well as her own household and fulfill all her professional duties could not figure out how Betty managed even to visit her mother and father's house so regularly, let alone help run it. But that was because they had no idea how Betty and the girls had grown up.

Keeping half a dozen bubble balls in the air while making the outside world think that everything was okey-dokey was something at which Betty excelled. She had done it most of her life. However, like all the Lovejoy sisters, whether they were in their parents' house in Georgia or three thousand miles away in California, Betty felt as if she were in shackles all the while she performed that sleight of hand.

Betty had hoped and prayed, along with Annie Ruth and Emily, that their mother's death would have broken those fetters. And in some ways, it had. Since the autumn, Betty had driven out to the house in Sherwood Forest less than once a week. She knew she should have gone there more often to see how her father was faring alone. But besides the harsh memories the ranch-style house evoked, Betty found it difficult to watch her father seem to fade away right before her eyes. Over the years, the girls had watched Mudear overshadow him and his personality with her own powerful one, leaving him a cipher in his own home. But since her death, he had practically become a phantom.

"Who would have thought Papa would have wasted away without Mudear around?" Emily had pondered one evening earlier that spring as she watched Annie Ruth try and fail, then try and fail again to hoist her heavy round frame from the brightly flowered overstuffed easy chair and ottoman Betty had bought for her weeks into her pregnancy when she complained of slightly swollen ankles.

"Well, like Mudear used to say, 'If Mother Nature don't get you, Father Time will,'" Betty said from the classic chaise lounge she had had the local craftsman down the street from her house in Pleasant Hill re-upholster in a pink and green stripe satin material.

"If it had been me," Annie Ruth offered with a grunt as she finally succeeded in standing, "I would have been dancing a little jig to be unshackled from that woman."

"Well, I don't see you dancing no 'jigs,'" Emily said as Annie Ruth kind of waddled over to the white-stained, antique, pie-crust table by the window and picked out a piece of marzipan shaped and colored like a tiny peach from a crystal dish.

Annie Ruth polished off the piece of confection, smacked her lips and reached for another.

"Well," she said smugly after swallowing the candy, "I'll accommodate you just as soon as I'm in jigging shape again. As Mudear herself used to say, 'I'd get up out a' my wheelchair to dance on that one's grave.'"

"Sisters?" Betty asked soberly. "Have you noticed how often we've been referring to and quoting Mudear lately? We're even beginning to sound like her. If I hear one of us say 'Well...' one more time." She let her voice trail off.

From her tone of voice, they could tell Betty had been thinking about this for a while. So, they paused and gave it some serious thought, too.

For decades, nearly their entire lives, talking about Mudear was what they did. It was simply part of life for them. The three of them had discussed their totally self-focused mother anytime they found themselves in the same room together. As children, they prepared meals, mopped the bathroom floor and talked of their reclusive mother; they tried on clothes by themselves at Davison's department store downtown in Mulberry and talked of whether she ever tired of wearing nightgowns all the time; they finished homework and huddled on the floor between their narrow beds at night and bemoaned the fact that every one of their little friends who couldn't come in and use the bathroom in the Lovejoy house or run and scream in the yard while Mudear was still abed thought they were as   strange and crazy as the woman who birthed them. In fact, the whole town did. And instead of feeling sympathy for the girls who were held prisoner by their mother's whims, the townspeople seemed to assume they had inherited Mudear's idiosyncrasies and shunned them.

As adults, the girls had chatted on the phone every day about the Mudear of their past who seemed simply to cease household or motherly duties overnight, about the Mudear of their teens who sent them out of the house to pay the bills and deal with teachers and figure out on their own how to write a check or shave under their arms for the first time.

It was as if Mudear were the deity of their lives and they the acolytes who kept the ceremonial temple fires burning with their resentful fascination.

Many times over the years, Mudear had overheard her daughters' ceaseless complaining patter about her. Mudear didn't care. She had been like that her entire life. As a child, her favorite expression was, "So?

I don't care." She seemed to believe that she was innately notable, worthy of being the regular topic of conversation. Even when her girls were little and she was still perfecting her suddenly reclusive life, she showed no concern when the stories of how peculiar she was somehow filtered back to her.

"She laying up there drunk all day in that house," town folks gossiped.

"I heard she burned herself with hot fish grease, and now she just covered with hideous scabs and scars," some people said.

"I bet'cha Ernest beating her ass up in that house and won't let her come out."

That last one merely made Mudear laugh.

"Don't nobody make me do nothing now," she told her last friend in the entire world when Mamie let that one tidbit slip out one day over the phone. Then, before long, Mudear didn't hear anything folks were saying about her because she ceased to talk with her friend Mamie or anyone else except her three daughters and her husband Ernest.

And still her girls talked endlessly about her.

But for weeks after Mudear's death and their graveside vow to change the crazy spiral of their lives, they had all made a conscious effort not to keep Esther Lovejoy and her memory alive by continuing the constant three-way conversation about her. And they had stuck to it. For a while.

Then, it seemed that slowly after only a couple of weeks, Mudear had slivered back into their thoughts and conversation, like a garter snake at a garden party.

At the very idea that they were somehow unconsciously keeping their dead mother alive and kicking, Annie Ruth stood over the candy dish and shivered dramatically as if a cat had walked over her grave. Then, she let her entire cute round body continue to shimmy and shake for a moment or two longer than necessary.

"Oooo, I think you're right," she said when she had finished jiggling. "We are talking 'bout that woman almost as much as we used to. Next thing you know, we gon' be quoting one of her favorite out-of-context, misapplied Scriptures like 'I know how to abound and how to abase.' All this talking about her again. Sisters, what the hell does it mean?"

Emily spoke right up, nodding her head assuredly as she spoke, as if she had been waiting for an opportunity to share her insights. "I think it just means we've had time to re-consider Mudear and her life since she died and come to the conclusion that she had her good points we might want to remember."

Betty ceased her knitting and Annie Ruth dropped her fifth piece of marzipan back into the crystal dish.

Emily kept right on talking.

"You know, some of the things we could really use, like telling us to wash our panties out every night and always moisturize our faces even if all we had was Vaseline and to drop our keys and stoop down to check if our stuff was smelling out in public. You know, some of her good points."

Annie Ruth and Betty looked at each other for a second, then both turned and stared at their middle sister for half a beat, and turned back to each other for another long moment. Finally, they both burst into hysterical laughter.

"No, sugar," Betty said when she was finally able to catch her breath. "That ain't it." And she continued to shake her head and chuckle softly.

Emily's feelings were hurt. "I don't know why I even bother to offer my opinion on anything around here. Ya'll don't never listen to me."

"Not when you talking crazy talk, girl!" Annie Ruth abruptly stopped her laughter and shouted at her. "'Good points?' Mudear?! Shit!"

"Well," Emily sniffed, "it may sound crazy to ya'll, but if you ask me, it's possible that we miss our mother. I think Poppa actually misses being in Mudear's shackles."

Then, all together, the girls—even Emily—shuddered a bit, shook their heads, sucked their teeth, and murmured sadly, "Um um um." They didn't plan to, but for the rest of that evening, they sat silently in Betty's solarium lost in their own thoughts about their mother.

All the girls seemed much more pensive now that Mudear was dead. At first, they didn't notice it among themselves, but just about everybody around them for any real amount of time recognized the change. Where before they had been all "ya-ya-ya-ya-ya," yapping at each other and at life, now, they were muted, more thoughtful, more focused on some private interior voice.

Oh, now, they still cared about what was on the outside, how they looked and what they wore, how flattering the colors and hairstyles and fashions they wore were, but somehow after Mudear's death, they were changed. In the late spring of that year, even the girls themselves started looking at each other differently.

Did Emily always have that tiny mole on her left shoulder like Mudear, Betty wondered one day as she spied the beauty mark on her sister's bare back for the first time.

Is Betty moving more slowly and deliberately lately? Emily noticed one day a couple of months after she returned to Mulberry.

"When did your laugh get so deep and hearty, Annie Ruth?" Emily had asked. "You sounded exactly like Mudear just then."

They tried to shake it off.

Underneath, however, there was the echo of the voice, their mother's voice, that still spoke into their lives.

"Hold your head up! What you got to be 'shamed of?"

"Look to the stars!"

"I don't care how many pairs of silk panties you got, wash out them drawers every night instead of throwing 'em in the dirty clothes hamper!"

"Get out ' that bed and go on to that good job you got! You ain't sick,

crampy, or crazy enough to call in sick!"

"A man'll lead you a dog's life!"

None of the girls said it. But they all knew it. Mudear was as much with them half a year after her death as she had ever been.

Even as Betty stood in the hospital corridor outside the nursery and gazed on Annie Ruth's new baby girl, she felt something almost like a cool presence at her back, looking over her shoulder. She turned around quickly to find only an empty space behind her. Then, she spun around again when she sensed that same entity still lurking behind her. Betty tried to ignore the feeling. She chuckled nervously at her skittishness and blew her new little niece a kiss through the wide glass window the way Emily always did whenever she saw a red bird, in hopes that the old wives' tale was true and she would see her lover that day. Betty blew the kiss but felt more like throwing salt over her shoulder in the devil's face to ward off evil spirits.

Then, impulsively, she pulled her trim cell phone out of her purse. And even though she knew she was probably throwing off pacemakers and other sensitive instruments all over the hospital, she hit number three on the speed dial menu and rang up Cinque.

"Heck, Annie Ruth may not be interested in getting laid any time soon," she said as she stepped onto the empty elevator and heard her lover Cinque answer on the first ring. "But what I really need right now is a good, quick, unconditional fuck!"

CHAPTER 8

U h uh uh. *Betty done got so coarse since she been sleeping with that young boy. I ain't never heard her use no language like that before.*

I bet she been sitting up watching them filthy rap music videos on television tryn'a stay all young and everything and fit in with that youngster. Oh, well, it's her funeral if she want to talk like that. I guess she grown.

But as far as I'm concerned, none a' them girls will ever be grown enough to make fun a' me. Talkin' 'bout "Mudear's shackles."

"Mudear's shackles?"

That's what they said. But they ain't serious. Them girls a' mine ain't finally discovering how their Mudear suffered before she took control a' her life. Them girls just tryna' be funny at my expense. Uh, with them ugly ways about 'em, they sho' don't take after me.

They can make light a' me if they want to. They just don't know. I know all about shackles. Back in the days when Ernest was calling himself courting me, we went to a movie one Saturday night downtown at the Burghart Theatre. I don't remember what movie it was, but there was this black man in it—that's the only kind a' picture they showed at the Burghart back then. If the movie didn't have a black man, woman or child somewhere in it, they wouldn't run it or the folks in the audience would start a riot! Anyway, if my memory serves me correct—and I do have a excellent memory—in this movie, the white folks would shackle this man to his bed at night and every time they showed that man shackled to that bed, every one of the folks in that movie house, and it was packed, it being Saturday night and all, every one just moaned and said, "Umm, umm, umm!"

That's how I felt when Ernest was walking around all over me, calling hisself ruling his roost like some barnyard fowl. I felt like that poor, poor, pathetic man chained to his bed at night.

'Course, like most things, it didn't start out like that. Me and my little spirit all shackled and everything by Ernest.

At first, it seemed like Ernest had to have me. Like he really liked what he saw. He even had the nerve to tell me one time when he was tryna get in my drawers that he liked my free spirit, that I wasn't like no other girl he had ever met. Which, a' course, _was_ the truth. He said that I was like them fireworks and sparklers folks light up on the Fourth day of July.

Oh, all that sweet talk and that little honeymoon period didn't hardly last no time. As soon as he got me, soon as we got married, it was like he was mad all the time for what I was. Don't ask me why. Don't ask me to explain it. It was just some more a' that crazy man shit as far as I could see.

If I knew how to do something better 'n him, he got mad. If I won at a game of Tonk, he got mad. If I cooked good pork chops for dinner, he got mad. If I seemed to be enjoying myself in bed—with him, mind you—he got mad.

I thought for sure after they put me in that pine box, well, it wa'n't no pine box, it was all fancy and shiny bronze and everything. You know them girls didn't want nobody saying they put they mama away in some cheap casket. I figured that once I was put away in that box, dressed in this ugly unflattering navy blue dress—I still can't for the life of me understand why them girls would think of burying me in navy blue when they know how good I look in pastels. Don't anybody look good in navy blue. Anyways, when they dropped me in that hole in the ground out at Pleasant Hill Cemetery, I just knew that that would be all she wrote, the pencil broke. Oh, I knew I had been floating around right well all the time they was gettin' ready for the funeral and everything. I thought as long as my body was laying up there in Parkinson's Funeral Home, I had free rein all over Mulberry. Checking in on this one and watching that one of my girls. But I figured that was only up until my burial.

After that, I thought I would be stretched out there in the cemetery for all eternity and be mad about missing out on everything with nothing to do but lay there without even a television set to keep me company.

But that ain't how it worked out at all. I guess I had to die for my luck to change. 'Cause since they planted me in the cold, cold ground, I been busier than I ever was when I was 'live.

And it's a good thing, too, considering how them girls a' mine been acting since my passing: Annie Ruth flouncing her big pregnant ass all over the country like she ain't even shame, Betty dating that boy who ain't hardly old enough to have any hairs and Emily losing her good government job and everything.

Oh, them girls made a big deal right after I died—carrying on out in public, driving like bats out 'a hell all around Mulberry, putting on that shameless display down at Parkinson's Funeral Home the night before my burial, getting into a actual hand fight, falling all over each other and "accidentally" knocking my casket over and flipping me out on that funeral home's beautiful parquet floor for the whole town to see. Oh, yeah, they cried and scrapped and hugged sitting on that floor around my cold dead body, carrying on something awful for anybody who happened to be in that funeral home building to hear. Talking 'bout how they were gonna' bury me and all my stuff—got the nerve to be saying I got issues! Talking all sincere in those little high trembly voices about putting me in the past and forgetting 'bout me and moving on.

<u>They</u> the ones with issues.

But ha! The joke's on them 'cause I ain't gone nowhere!

Shoot, they may be my daughters, but they can kiss what I twist and I don't mean my ankle and I don't mean my wrist.

You know, being dead, it can be so boring. Sooooo boring, even at night, which is <u>my time</u> a' the day, it's still boring. Boring. Boring.

Shoot, if I didn't have my girls to look after, I don't know what I'd do with myself.

Oh, yeah, I've found out that if I stay connected to them, my girls keep me plenty busy. Especially with Annie Ruth and all her mess. When I was a girl they called a girl who got herself pregnant out of wedlock someone who had "broke a leg." But now it ain't hardly as bad as "breaking a fingernail." But then, when you can claim that you been with so many men that you don't even know for sure who the daddy is. Well, now, that's a different ballgame, ain't it?

And Emily, bless her crazy heart, she as loony as ever.

You talk about a fanatical fool. The other girls be trying to ignore it, but Emily'll still go to Nutsville on 'em in a minute.

Change, my ass! They still the same. 'Cept for Annie Ruth having a baby, they the same as they was when I breathed my last breath at the Mulberry Hospital. I refuse to call it the "Mulberry Medical Center." I don't care how many new signs they put up.

And even though that old piece a' husband of mine been going steadily downhill ever since I breathed my last breath, he ain't really changed either. Not where it truly counts.

I know 'cause I checked in on old Ernest out at the house in Sherwood Forest a couple of times. Oh, at first, I spent a good deal of time out there in my garden. My garden has always been my most favorite place in the whole world to be. But I hardly ever thought about going *in* the house and seeing what that old man was up to. Mostly 'cause I know he ain't up to nothing much. Just like when I was there. If it hadn'a been for me all those years to keep him on his toes, ain't no telling how much he would'a gone to the dogs.

Hee-hee. Just 'bout the way he doing now.

Lord, I ain't never seen nobody go downhill so fast in all my life. You know Ernest always was a strappin' kinda' man. You know, a laborer. Lord knows he ain't never been no bookish smart kinda' man. Even after I about took over that household way back when the girls was young and made it my own, Ernest made sure he stayed in some kinda good physical shape working out there at the kaolin mines. But now, in the few months since I been dead, he just 'bout wasted away.

Heh! He better watch it 'lest he find himself laying up next to me out at Pleasant Hill Cemetery.

But I ain't all that surprised that he in the position he in now. My mudear used to say, "Don't nothing go over the devil's back that don't come back and buckle up under his belly."

So, far as I'm concerned, Ernest getting just what he deserve, and he can sit out there in that house in Sherwood Forest and rot for all I care.

But my girls, now that's something different. Whether they know it *or not, I got plans for them.*

    If they think they thinking a lot about me now. Ha!
    Just they wait. I got som'um for their asses!

CHAPTER 9

Betty may have thought that her middle sister merely couldn't stand another moment in that close hospital room with her, Annie Ruth, her new baby, the nurses, and a cleaning woman mopping under and around the bed where her baby sister had just given birth. She may have suspected that Emily simply wanted to get out of there and light up a joint to settle her nerves. And she certainly knew that the half-hearted smile that Emily had spackled on her face like another coat of Revlon long-lasting, scarlet lipstick hid a well of jealousy and pain and resentment.

But Betty didn't know the half of it.

What Betty thought about her sister was true enough. After the long and arduous birth, Emily did feel as if she were about to jump out of her own skin. But Emily also left her sisters in the hospital room because she had an assignment to complete. And the words of the assignment—*"Get that veil in the earth! Get that veil in the earth!"*— kept playing like a scratched record snagged in a groove by an Old School nightclub D.J., repeating in her head as she moved through the antiseptic halls of the Medical Center pulling her tight red shorts down out of the crack of her butt when the nurses elbowed each other and raised their eyebrows in her direction as she passed them.

As she walked toward the bank of elevators, she tried to lift her chin off her chest and "look to the stars." But that recording now playing over and over in her head made it difficult for her to follow any instructions but the ones she was hearing now.

Then, as she stood in the empty hospital elevator, her eyes pressed shut, her head tilted back so far she could feel the blunt tips of her freshly cut hair-do brushing against her bare shoulder blades, breathing deeply just to calm her nerves, she clearly heard her mother's voice saying, *"Daughter, stop standing there like a fool! Go on and take care a' that business for me!"*

Her eyes flew open, and she quickly pressed the elevator button for the ground floor of the hospital.

Now, Emily had heard voices before. At one point in her life after her abortion and her husband Ron had left her, she heard them almost all the time—when she rose at dawn from a restless sleep, as she listlessly dressed for the day, while she drove her clunker of a car toward downtown Atlanta to work, as she sat across the desk from some researcher looking to her for guidance through the cavernous state archives. At different times, they were the voices of childhood classmates, of old lovers, of her unborn child.

They were always voices of reproach and confusion and fear and derision.

She had never told anyone about them, not even Dr. Axelton, for fear that some day the men in the white jackets would show up on her apartment doorstep in southwest Atlanta and cart her off to Milledgeville, the site of the state's old public insane asylum.

She knew that hearing voices was one of the last steps in the descent into true madness. Her mother may have spent nearly her entire adult life inside the confines of her home and still been able to come and go at will in her garden at night. And her sister Annie Ruth may have been seeing cats out of the corners of her eyes for years now and still been allowed to function as a well-dressed, high-powered TV personality. But Emily knew that she would never be given that kind of leeway. No one could know about the voices in her head and still hire her as some big city television news anchor the way they had with Annie Ruth. Emily was no baby of the family, allowed to fail and fall and get pregnant and act crazy and see cats and such and still remain comfortably ensconced in polite society.

Shoot, Emily had been summarily fired from her low-level state government job when all she had done was lose her patience with a clerk in the government insurance department. That's all she had done, merely lose her temper a bit. Somebody should have told her the clerk was the latest conquest sleeping with the head of the archivist division instead of just another skinny young white woman in white pumps and a cheap, pink, polyester suit.

So, she knew better than to broadcast any new manifestations of her own personal craziness. Just as she had told no one of the earlier voices which eventually subsided, slowly dwindling like an echo in a cave, she had no plans to tell anyone about the voice of her dead mother in her head the night of her niece's birth. As a matter of fact, she had been hearing her mother's voice speak to her a good bit lately. And still she told no one of the voices in her head. However, that restraint didn't mean she could ignore the voices' commands.

"Go on, Emily, do what I say!" she heard as she pulled Betty's car out of the covered parking garage next to the hospital. She had no idea where she should be going, so she turned the car west and headed for what felt comfortable and familiar: the Spring Street bridge.

No matter how hard Emily tried to keep whatever car she was driving headed straight across the bridge spanning the muddy river that ran down from the mountains of north Georgia through the middle of the state and on to the middle of her hometown, she always seemed to end up on the banks of the Ocawatchee. Even though the river waters were usually a shade of her favorite reddish color, she never could understand why in the world that river had such a pull on her. It spoke life to her, but it also summoned death.

Emily was a teenager more than twenty years earlier when she first considered drowning herself by jumping from the Spring Street bridge into the river's muddy waters.

Thereafter, whenever anyone suggested that she should learn to swim like her "water baby" sisters, she objected. And when some boyfriend tried to teach her by splashing her into the deep end of a friend's pool, she fought him off like a Trojan and never spoke to him again. She figured she couldn't chance knowing how to stay afloat. She never knew when the optimum opportunity to drown herself would arise. For years, it seemed that the water levels were either too low or the area was too crowded for her to take a successful plunge. But whenever all conditions seemed just right for a suicide attempt, she wanted to be fully ready by being totally unprepared for survival.

As she drove, she lowered both front windows of the Lexus and allowed the cross ventilation of the breeze to blow across her face and body. After the ordeal at the hospital, she felt she needed a good clearing out, like with a strong laxative of Epsom salts and warm water. The sight of her tiny niece slipping out of her sister and then lying so sweetly on Annie Ruth's breast just about broke her heart.

All she could think about was the child she had not allowed herself to have. The last words her ex-husband Ron had spoken to her years before had been the accusation that he would never forgive her for "flushing his baby down the toilet." Whenever she sat alone and lonely down by the river and watched the deep swirling muddy waters of the Ocawatchee, she knew that she could never forgive herself, either.

Emily was now perpetually lonely. Always had been. Whether she was sleeping in the same bedroom with her two sisters, her mother and father down the hall, or standing all alone in the middle of her one-bedroom garden apartment in Southwest Atlanta, she felt enveloped in a bubble of solitude. At least, Betty got her old stand-by male friend Stan and her little do-right boyfriend Cinque, she thought. And now, Annie Ruth got her own baby girl. Emily had no one. For her, it all felt so hopeless. She knew better than anyone that if it weren't for her sisters, she would truly be a little abandoned girl, a little lost world, a motherless child.

Her sisters never knew about Emily's plans for suicide by drowning, but Betty worried about her hanging around the river banks all the same. And then she got Annie Ruth to worrying, too.

For years, Annie Ruth would make a special phone call to Emily at least once a week to say, "You know, Mulberry's no L.A., but you still have to be careful out there in those streets, Em-Em."

"Em-Em, no matter how much the city try to clean up down by the river, that place still attracts derelicts and the hopeless," Betty, on the other end of the three-way conference call, cautioned her time and again. "And now that all that Cleer Flo' shit is happening down there, Sugar, it's just not safe."

Emily would merely smile and say, "Um," with a shrug in her voice and go right on ignoring Betty's and Annie Ruth's warnings. Down by the river was one of the few spots on earth where she did feel safe. And all "that Cleer Flo' shit," as Betty so glibly called it, was proof to Emily that all those years of being attracted to the waters of the Ocawatchee River had been for some larger cosmic reason, greater than all the

Lovejoy girls' fears put together.

"There's just something special 'bout those waters," she would tell her exasperated sisters in attempting some kind of explanation for the river's supernatural attraction for her. So, Emily wasn't a bit surprised when the phenomenon that the Mulberry town folks called "Cleer Flo'" began to exert itself.

A couple of years before Mudear's death, for no discernible reason, the waters of the Ocawatchee River—perennially red ochre and thick with the clay, mud, and dirt of the middle Georgia land that it flowed through—suddenly turned clear and clean as a north Georgia mountain stream.

Then, all varieties of fish began appearing in the crystal clear waters, fish that had never frequented the waters of the Ocawatchee before. Trout and bream and freshwater catfish joined the regular dark fat mullet on the hooks of surprised and delighted anglers. One or two days a month, there was even a jubilee-type harvest of the new freshwater fish washing up on the banks of the river, flipping and flopping as lucky folks strolled by and picked them up like farm workers harvesting peppers and squash and tomatoes.

Folks who would never even spit in the murky waters of the river before now happily brought their children and grandchildren down to the Ocawatchee to swim and splash at the waters' edge.

And although the local health department posted warnings against it, some brave souls in and around Mulberry even took to sipping the clear water from mason jars they kept in their refrigerators because they believed the stories that the water had curative powers. This would go on for a few days or weeks, then, just as suddenly as it appeared, Cleer Flo' would pass and the Ocawatchee would return to its formerly muddy state. And as suddenly, the river's acolytes and worshippers would disappear until the next magical-like occurrence.

Emily, however, was no fair-weather Cleer Flo' friend of the

Ocawatchee. She loved the river, muddy or clear.

So, when she got to the bridge, instead of heading on out Spring Street to the Sherwood Forest subdivision—"I think that's where I'm headed," she muttered to herself—she seemed to turn automatically down the little muddy dirt road, hardly wider than a path, that led to the river banks.

It hadn't rained in Mulberry for days, but Emily knew that somehow it would be muddy down by the river.

If Betty knew I had her new Lexus down here by the river driving through all this muddy red clay, she'd have a fit, Emily thought as she pulled the car up and parked on a small rise she remembered from her last visit. Then, she realized that evidence of her trip to the river would be all over the tires and bottom of the car.

"Well, damn!" she said as she got out and examined the sides of the car. Muddy red splashes dotted the car from the front to the rear. "If I don't wash that mud off her car before she sees it, I'm gon' be busted for real!"

The mud on the car really irritated her because one of her newest resolutions was to be more focused and responsible. Right after their mother's funeral the year before, all three sisters had met back at Betty's house, just as the sun had set, kicked off their shoes, sat down ceremonially in a circle on the Georgia pine floor of her beautiful, elegant, living room and, still dressed in their exquisite black wool and crepe suits, they promised each other that things were going to change. And they meant it.

Like all other families in their situation, they had been touched, altered by the death of their matriarch. And Mudear wasn't merely any matriarch. Everything about her life and death pointed that out.

"We gon' laugh about that funeral home thing one day," Annie Ruth had assured her sisters the year before as they had sat in Betty's living room after Mudear's grave-side services. Emily had gone along with the group, aping what they did and said with such seeming confidence. She had held her hands out to her sisters in the circle. She had intoned the promise and nodded her head solemnly as each of them voiced her own commitment to change, to transforming her life in ways that disentangled it from their dead mother's tentacles.

But even after the tail end of an autumn and a full winter and most of a spring had passed, they could not bring themselves to laugh when they spoke of their dead mother's funeral and the days leading up to it.

Even Emily, who declared loud and often, "ain't no shame in my game," whenever she had to go to her prosperous big sister one more time for a loan to tide her over 'til the next payday or when she needed money for an unexpected car emergency or a must-have pair of red, high-heeled, Marc Jacob mules, found herself unable to bear the humiliation of their public display at Parkinson's Funeral Home the day before their mother's funeral.

If she still couldn't laugh about it, she yearned to be changed by it. As her sisters had pledged their commitment to change the course of their lives, Emily had sat cross-legged on the living room rug racking her brain for some step to take.

"I swear I'm going to stop accepting less than I'm worth from men," Betty had said with her eyes closed.

Annie Ruth had smiled in spite of herself as she wondered to which one of Betty's men she was referring: Betty's new attentive twenty-year-old lover Cinque or her old neglectful fifty-year-old boyfriend Stan.

"I swear I'm going to do right by this baby," Annie Ruth had said as she gazed down at her stomach. "I swear on my mother's grave, on Mudear's fresh grave, I'm not gonna be like her."

Emily didn't know where to start. She knew her life was ripe for transformation in so many arenas. So, she lowered her eyes, squeezed her sisters' fingers and said, "Me, I'm gon' change."

"We all gon' change," they had promised each other.

But as she sat by the slow-moving Ocawatchee River, still spent from the delivery room drama she had just gone through, Emily couldn't for the life of her think of one thing she had accomplished in the previous seven months to turn her life around. Of course, she had had that incident on her job, walked out of the archives building and moved back to Mulberry. But even she knew that coming back there had not changed anything. In fact, it had only brought her closer to the way things had always been for her: the family's middle child, the one everyone thought would be the first to go truly crazy, the only married Lovejoy girl, though the union was doomed from the start. And her return to Mulberry had also brought her back inexorably nearer the scene of her mother's crime: the spiritual abandonment of her and her family. The realization that she was right back where she had started—the unmarried, childless, jobless, unexceptional, confused, rudderless middle child—was almost more than she could bear. Standing by the Ocawatchee River, she felt close to bursting into the tears that had seemed to be sitting right behind her eyes all night as she watched her baby sister do what she had never done: bring life into the world.

She tried to recall what Dr. Axelton had told her to do when she felt a crying jag coming on, but she was too exhausted from the emotionally draining hours in Annie Ruth's birthing room to remember much of anything. So, she simply gave into the feeling and, leaning back against the side of Betty's car, wept.

With big, fat tears tumbling over her cheekbones and rolling down her face, she suddenly remembered the joint in the pink tampon holder in her purse she had rolled the night before from the stash she kept in an Altoid's tin under her bed at Betty's. With that thought, she immediately felt better. She dried her tears with the backs of her hands and, as she pulled the pot from her purse, sighed as if she had just been rescued from the thick murky waters of the Ocawatchee when she hadn't been in the mood for suicide.

She had to fight a bit of anger rising in her throat at her therapist, Dr. Axelton, for having more than once suggested, gently, very gently that perhaps she was medicating herself with the pot she smoked.

She had wanted to retort, "Well, hell, yeah, I'm self-medicating! You won't give me anything to make my life better but these anti-depressant pills that fuck with my sex drive and barely lift the darkness around the edges! Now that I don't even want to screw all that much, how am I supposed to fill that deep hole of despair in the middle of my soul if I don't smoke?"

As she lit up and took that first deep drag and held the smoke a while in her lungs, she could feel herself and the stress of the night lift, seeming to dissipate along with the smoke that floated from her lips and out into the damp night air. The light, disconnected feeling was as close to comfort and joy as she figured she was going to get to that night.

Months earlier when she had first moved into Betty's house, Emily had thought she would have at least gotten some joy and satisfaction out of seeing Annie Ruth's pregnant body swell up and lose its cute little shape. For years, Emily herself had been having to fight like a warrior to keep her curvaceous figure from slipping over the edge of voluptuousness into plain chubbiness. In the end, however, Emily found no solace in her baby sister's fecundity. It was too rich, too beautiful, too ripe, to feed Emily's idea of retribution.

As week after week of her pregnancy passed, Annie Ruth didn't get fat. Oh, she got bigger, but she also grew more luscious, more delectable, more beautiful, more appealing, more tender. Her copper-brown skin glowed like burnished gold. Her face rounded softly at the jaw line. Her dark brown eyes glowed with the gentle radiance of contentment. Even her eyelashes seemed to grow thicker and longer, more lush, more flirtatious.

When the Lovejoy sisters went out to dinner or when they went shopping out at the Mulberry Mall or when they traveled to Atlanta for an arts fair or to catch a performance of India.Arie, people—perfect strangers—stopped Annie Ruth to tell her just how beautiful she was. Plump food vendors insisted that she taste their lemon cream cheese pound cakes and take samples home with her for midnight snacks. Smiling shopkeepers draped brightly colored scarves around her shoulders and demanded that she walk back and forth in front of their stalls for the sheer delight of seeing their wares so beautifully displayed.

Seamstresses and textile artists laid tiny pink and blue baby shirts and booties on her bulging belly and wouldn't take money for the items. Instead, they would make Annie Ruth vow to return with the baby dressed in the soft snuggly clothes as soon as the infant was big enough to travel.

"Pretty as you are, that's gon' have to be a pretty baby you carrying," they told her as they made over her as if she were a furbelowed little first-grader at Easter services.

As beautiful as Annie Ruth was obviously becoming in her growing ripeness, all the girls knew that their mother, if she were still alive, would have sniffed at the compliments her baby daughter elicited.

Mudear had told them their whole lives in that flat, matter-of-fact tone she used on them when imparting wisdom, "Pretty women a dime a dozen, daughters." The peculiar older woman always chose the exact time in which her girls had felt their prettiest and most vulnerable: Betty's first prom night, the day Spelmanite Annie Ruth called from the Atlanta campus to say she had been chosen to run for campus queen at neighboring all-male Morehouse College, the afternoon Emily noticed that her sensitive skin was clearing up.

Mudear was like that. She had a knack for picking the exact moment when she could best deflate her daughters' egos and joy with one swift comment. The woman's philosophy concerning her daughters' egos was the opposite of the approach she took with her husband Ernest and, in fact, with all men.

With her daughters, it was: hit 'em while they high. With men, she believed, and drummed into her girls' heads: hit 'em when they low. Both approaches called for such an astute subtlety, a shrewdness so particular, so sophisticated, so worldly that it was difficult to believe it came from a high school-educated small town woman who hadn't ventured out into the world past her front or backyard for the last thirty years of her life.

And the little ordinary-looking woman could perform this deflating feat without breaking a sweat, without disturbing one fluffy curled hair on her tiny peanut-shaped head.

BAM! She would knock Betty nearly to her knees with a comment on the likelihood of her eldest daughter growing old all alone surrounded by a gang of mangy cats she had taken into her home. WHAP! She'd give Emily a back-handed compliment on how pretty her useless hands were. SMACK! Wasn't it a good thing that no one at the television station in California knew about the nervous breakdown Annie Ruth suffered at her last on-air job in D.C.?

Even as Emily feared her over-reaching jealousy was a nascent sign of inheriting Mudear's ugly behavior, she secretly kept waiting for Annie Ruth to show ugly signs of pregnancy: the bloated face and hands, the swollen ankles and feet, the varicose veins, the darkened patches of skin on her chin, upper lip, and chest, the dark circles under her eyes from lack of sleep, the crankiness, the hemorrhoids at least.

But there was none of that with Annie Ruth. Even her thin brown hair— Mudear had called it "that t'in t'in cat hair"—usually so sparse and scanty without the aid of falls and extensions and wigs and pieces that Betty created and applied precisely for her, became thick and luxurious and full of bouncy life with the natural infusion of hormones and the prenatal vitamins she took. It trailed around her oval-shaped face, grazed her high-cheekbones and brushed against the gentle valleys below her shoulders and above her clavicles like something in a Clairol hair commercial.

On the girls' weekly forays into the world to keep the little mother-to-be entertained and happy, Emily would walk beside her tall, big sister and her round, baby sister, her face steeled for the compliments the world insisted on showering upon Annie Ruth. Emily never headed out without first plastering on her public face. Her "public face." That was another tip from her psychiatrist, Dr. Axelton.

The fragile-looking, older white woman had sat across from Emily during one of her first appointments and stared into her face for at least a full half-minute. Then, she had leaned toward her new patient and said, "Emily, we're going to have to work on a few faces for you."

"Faces?"

"Yes," Dr. Axelton had said firmly. "Right now, your teeth are clenched. Your jaws are tight. Your nostrils are flaring. Your eyes are wild, darting all over the room. Until we have some time to work on some of the issues you're confronting and get some medication in you at levels that will alleviate your present anxiety, believe me, that's not the face you want to present to the world."

Dr. Axelton spoke so gently, in her soft, white, Southern woman's voice, the only kind of accent that could pronounce the word "camellia" with the true inflection, that Emily wasn't even offended at the words of this white woman who was then only a stranger to her. The analyst's knowing gentleness was one of the things Emily loved about her. It was why she had still driven to Atlanta once a week to see her, long after her job's insurance had run out and Emily had to get the money from Betty to pay the doctor's fees.

"Well, Dr. Axelton," she said, addressing the Ocawatchee River as she stubbed out the half-smoked joint on the cement underpass and dropped it back in the tampon holder in her purse, "I don't know 'bout your stuff, but my 'medication' still works."

She carelessly plopped down on the riverbank, lay back on the grassy embankment, and let out a long, expansive stream of air. For the first time since Annie Ruth had waddled into the solarium with her announcement of imminent birth, Emily felt some measure of mellowness. She could feel the tension drain out of her body as clearly as she could feel the cool grass against her bare back. She was so relaxed and grateful for the feeling that she didn't even care that the dew-damp rust clay and green turf she was lying on was probably staining the seat of her short jersey pants.

Shoot, it's worth it, she thought with a sigh as she closed her eyes, stretched her bare brown arms above her head, and took another deep breath of the damp night air. The Ocawatchee River smelled the way she had remembered it smelling all her life—fishy and fertile and fecund.

"Humph, like a pregnant woman," Emily said aloud with a little chuckle.

Suddenly, she remembered the plastic bag she had left on the front seat of Betty's Lexus and sat straight up.

For a second or two, she couldn't for the life of her recall what was in the bag or why she had brought it with her. Then, as if someone were whispering instructions to her, she saw the thin colorless membrane lying in the bag and realized she needed to get moving and do something with it. She didn't know or couldn't remember exactly what she was to do but felt the urgency nonetheless.

She got right up and brushed debris off the seat of her red shorts and her bare back. Then, for a second or two, she looked around the dark riverbank like a lost animal.

For a moment, she wondered if she was supposed to go to the car, take the plastic bag from the seat, return to the river and throw the contents as far as she could into the muddy waters of the Ocawatchee.

"*No!*" was the whispered command she heard. "*Get that veil in the dirt!*"

"Nooo, that's not right," she said out loud as she stood on the riverbank with her hands on her sweetly rounded hips, her head tilted to the right, and gnawed on her bottom lip in concentration.

"*Yes, it is right, you fanatical fool! Put it back in the earth!*" Mudear's voice came through so loudly to her this time that she could almost hear it resound over the river's waters.

"Hummph," Emily said suddenly, a look of comprehension crossing her face as she got a fleeting image of her mother's garden in her head. "It's just like Mudear to try to blow my high. Well, at least now I know where I should go."

Without stopping to question her movements or the voice's instructions or the fact that she was hearing her dead mother's voice, she brushed a hand across her round bottom again to insure she wasn't going to soil Betty's pristine gray upholstery with red dirt and grass stains, got in the car, turned it around on the narrow shoal and headed out toward her parents' house in Sherwood Forest.

"Well, Dr. Axelton, there goes the buzz from my medication," she muttered to herself as she shook her head a couple of times and turned onto Orange Highway.

CHAPTER **10**

W hat I'mo' have to do? Ask Jesus Christ Himself to get down off the cross and go down by the Ocawatchee River and tell that girl what to do with my grandchild's birth veil?

Those girls used to be a whole lot easier to work with when I was 'live than they are now. Especially Emily. But then I guess that's what I get for trying to work with the only one of my girls who is a certified pure-T fanatical fool.

Folks talk about watching television is a waste of time, but that ain't the truth at all. Shoot, I learned all kinds a' things on the TV, got a lot'a good information that way. On one of them talking shows in the late afternoon, I saw this expert person talk about how you can tell whether a person is crazy or not just by the looks of them. *And I sho do believe that. Humph, I used to look at television all the time, but since I've had my girls to entertain me, I ain't missed it one bit.*

So, like I was saying, this woman on television said that people who show a lots a' whites of their eyes when they look at you are likely to be skittish-something. No skitso-something. Anyway, what she meant was crazy one way, then, crazy another. And that's just like Emily: crazy one way, then crazy another. And damn if she ain't got a lots a' whites showin' in her eyes. too.

Look at her. All that effort and she just now heading out to the house. If I wasn't already dead, she would'a been the death of me by now!

CHAPTER 11

E rnest hardly slept at all anymore. It was well past midnight, but he was still up and fully dressed when he heard the car pull in next to his brown Ford Tempo in the carport at the side of the house.

Since Mudear's death, he had spent most of his days keeping up the house and the front yard as if he feared she might show up suddenly for a surprise inspection. He cut the grass whether it needed it or not. He smoothed down already-made beds in the room he had shared with his wife but called "her room" and in his daughters' old rooms that no one had slept in for months. He wiped sparkling clean kitchen counters and washed and re-washed coffee cups and saucers from which he drank his morning and evening instant Sanka. And he tried his best to get up enough dirty and soiled clothes to make up a decent load for the avocado green washing machine that sat with its matching dryer nearly forsaken and forlorn in the tiny utility room off the carport.

When Mudear had died the previous fall, he still had a year to go until retirement at his job as a manager out at the kaolin mines on the outskirts of Mulberry. But after her death somehow, he couldn't seem to force himself to continue to rise at dawn, drink his first cup of Sanka and get out of the house each weekday morning in time to punch a clock. For more than three decades, he had spurred himself on with the thought that he was taking care of his family, which mostly meant Mudear after the girls grew up. That he was paying the bills the way a real man did. Now, he couldn't for the life of him come up with a real reason to keep on working to bring home a regular paycheck anymore.

He had told himself a man needed to work, especially a man whose wife had spent money the way Esther did, as though she had a job herself. She didn't. Mudear never worked outside the house and the yard a day in her life. And after her girls were old enough to attend school, she didn't work inside the house either. After one long-ago cold winter night in their old house in East Mulberry with the sound of the girls' coughs rattling their little frames in the frigid air, Mudear had changed.

Changed so deeply that many nights back then Ernest expected to hear the convulsing of that shift throughout the wooden structure of his own house. And when Mudear had changed, the whole household had changed. In fact, Ernest had thought many times, Hell, the whole damn world had changed.

After that, his home, which had been his castle, his domain, his fiefdom, was no longer a refuge, an asylum. It had shrunk to more of a torture chamber. The change had seemed to happen suddenly, like a tsunami overwhelming him and his orderly life. To him, it had felt abrupt, but it had actually been a steady and measured shift. One day,

Mudear was up early, before first light, fully dressed with a starched apron tied at her waist, cooking his full country breakfast of grits and cheese and eggs and link sausages and toast, with his lunch of three ham sandwiches, an apple and a big chunk of homemade lemon pound cake sitting in a brown paper sack on the hall table awaiting his departure. The next, there was only a pot of oatmeal bubbling on the stove like hot lava and two baloney sandwiches and a Moon Pie in a greasy used paper bag on the kitchen table. The next day, there wasn't even the oatmeal. And by the fourth day, even the sack lunch had vanished.

If it hadn't been for his oldest girl, Betty, who was no more than ten years old herself at the time, getting up to try and cook her father and sisters something before school, Ernest felt like he would have starved in those first days of his wife's—Mudear's—change.

That was what they all called it at first, "Mudear's change." In hushed tones and embarrassed incredulous whispers, the girls and Poppa would say the words, "After Mudear's change...." "Since Mudear's change...." "'Cause 'a Mudear's change...." Then, over the years, they shortened it to "the change." And finally, they would just say "change," and everyone in the household knew what was meant.

It wasn't menopause, not that "change of life." Rather, it was a life's change, a seismic shifting that transformed the shape of life for the entire family forever.

When his wife changed, everyone had to change. Even he himself had changed. Instead of marching into her bedroom to demand his breakfast and his full bagged lunch, he had found himself standing outside the flimsy bedroom door feeling unsteady, unsure, almost afraid to enter a room in his own house. A new feeling for him. Ernest had always prided himself on being the head of his household. That was what he had bragged about among his cronies.

"Shoot," he'd say over a Pabst Blue Ribbon beer downtown at

The Place, his favorite hangout, "I'm the man in my house. I go home when I feel good and damn ready to go home."

After those few cold days decades before, he couldn't bring himself ever to brag again. Mudear saw to that.

How could one little woman having the money only one time to pay one gas and one electric bill when I was flat broke change so much in the lives of an entire family, he would ask himself over and over through the thirty years that followed.

He never had an answer.

Then, finally after Mudear died in the fall, the question was moot, and the point of his entire life seemed pointless. So, even though he knew he would forfeit a good portion of his pension by retiring early, he just couldn't see any good reason to continue. He walked into his supervisor's office the week after Mudear died and, without any hesitation or warning, handed over his retirement papers.

For the rest of the autumn and through the winter, he had filled his days with busy work. Even into the spring, which brought no hope with it at all, he continued to while away most of his nights wandering from room to room of the suburban brick house, dressed as he always did in crisply starched and ironed khaki work pants and a long-sleeved white or khaki shirt. Then, he'd go to the outside faucet at the edge of the short cement driveway to turn on the soaker hoses for his wife's garden that filled the backyard and beyond. When he wasn't rambling around the house, he sat stonily on the edge of the seat of his big brown armchair and stared into the flickering images on the big screen TV that his wife had so treasured.

Many nights since the fall day that Mudear had entered the Mulberry Medical Center with a bad cough and not come out alive, Ernest had been tempted to go out in the back yard and roam around in the lush garden his wife had created and tended with a mother's love. It wasn't that he longed to be near his dead wife and her spirit. He had

had enough of that while she lived. No, now with time and leisure on his hands in the house all by himself, he found himself drawn to the sheer beauty of the yard.

The verdant space not only covered the majority of the house's backyard, but also extended on to cover the field behind the garden. Poppa had saved up for more than a year to afford the extra lot for his wife's passion.

She didn't appreciate it. Although she often and loudly vowed that she did not take a Vanilla Wafer for granted, what she really took for granted was everything: a sweet cracker, a Saltine cracker, her self-focused schedule, the gifts her daughters showered on her, a clean house, a cooked meal, cable television, unrestricted leisure, a warm bed in winter, an air-conditioned home in summer, seemingly unlimited resources. Everything. She took everything for granted.

"You think I'm impressed with that little piece 'a land you scrimped and saved to buy?" she'd throw in his face after a hard day's work at the mines when he had the nerve to mention their home to her. "Shoot, I don't care nothing 'bout nothing that can disappear tomorrow. You know me, I know how to abound and how to abase."

Then, Mudear would pause as she adjusted whatever pastel bed jacket she was featuring that evening and add, "Ernest, you taught me that, don't care 'bout nothing that don't care 'bout you."

She didn't give him no credit. But Poppa knew she loved that yard.

After her death, Poppa was so tempted to try to savor what it was that had given his wife such sustenance.

But somehow he could not make himself go back there into that yard at night.

Besides, from the looks of things, even in the dead of winter, the garden had not seemed to need him.

The garden not only continued to grow without Mudear's attentive presence and tender care. The garden seemed actually to outdo itself after Mudear's death, flourishing without her tender and daily attention and taking on a numinous beauty.

After she was no longer alive, the garden seemed to take on a life of its own: Georgia collard green plants that had grown to the size of a toddler under Mudear's hand now grew to the size of a full-grown child, while remaining tender and sweet. Rose bushes that had produced blossoms that Mudear could cup in one of her hands now bore roses that both hands of a grown man could not contain.

For years, folks in Mulberry had whispered that there must have been bodies buried in Esther Lovejoy's back yard for her to grow a garden of such prodigious proportions. With her dead, the gossip bubbling under the surface of small town life absolutely erupted.

"You know there was always something 'witchy-like' 'bout Esther Lovejoy," women, dissecting Mudear's life and death, would suggest to one another over their grocery carts at the Piggly Wiggly. "Hmmph, if I worked for the police department, I'd go back there with a warrant and a back hoe."

After Mudear died, the only upkeep performed on the garden was the nightly ritual of Poppa dragging his bony frame outside to the edge of the back yard at the corner of the driveway and turning on the rubber soaker hoses that wound their way through the foliage like fat, black, garden snakes. He didn't even bother to fertilize. The land Mudear had enriched for years with compost and cow and chicken manure didn't seem to need that nourishing anymore.

The vegetable and fruit plants—the Big Boy and Sweet 100 tomatoes, the shiny California Wonder green bell peppers and hot red cayenne, cowhorn and habanera peppers, the tall sturdy stalks of Silver Queen corn, the sweet watermelons and cantaloupe and honeydews—all flourished. The maze of tea olive bushes blossomed during the cold months of winter and the ferns and roses and ginger lilies came on back up as soon as the last frost of winter had passed as if Mudear were still out there giving them tender, loving care each and every night.

That's when she had done her gardening, at night. Many nights since her death, each one of her daughters—Betty, Emily or Annie Ruth—would have sworn that she had seen Mudear making her way through the dense greenery of the lush garden on some evening, when they had found themselves out at the house past dark. Emily had even run out into the yard one winter night, calling, "Mudear! Mudear? Is that you?"

Poppa had stood at the sliding glass doors in the family room leading to the patio watching his middle girl run from one sweet-smelling tea olive bush to another, then getting completely lost and confused in the labyrinth of bushes with shiny green leaves and tiny fragrant white flowers that had been her mother's favorite garden feature.

He hadn't wanted to go out there. He stayed out of that garden as much as possible and had never entered it at night on his own. But after nearly ten minutes of watching Emily stumble around by herself through the thick mulch that covered the ground, he finally slid the doors open and went out in his soft corduroy bedroom slippers to rescue her.

She was nearly babbling to herself by the time he reached her and slowed her down enough to turn her back toward the house.

"I know I saw Mudear out there," she kept telling her father. "I know it was her, but she was keeping just out of my reach. Didn't know she could move that fast, Poppa. But I know that was Mudear out there in her garden."

There was none like Mudear's garden in all of Sherwood Forest. Oh, folks had nice yards all up and down the streets that made up the subdivision. The sort of people who moved out there on the edge of town were the kind who prided themselves on keeping up good appearances.

"Strivers," Mudear had labeled them all with derision, easily classing herself off from them.

"All these strivers out here think they really something 'cause they living on 'Pork 'n' Bean Row' in one of these little cracker boxes made a' brick," she would say regularly whenever Poppa tried to make conversation after work about some home improvement he had noticed on a neighbor's lot. "Their little green painted shutters and add-on decks ain't nothing but pitiful to me. And ain't none of them got anything to match my back yard."

Esther could make little of just about anything, Ernest would think after she had silenced him with one of her disdainful remarks. He was proud of his house, nicest one anyone in his entire family had ever dreamed of living in.

But nice didn't seem to mean nothing to Mudear. She took nice for granted, then hocked and spat on it. That's how Poppa had felt around his wife for the last thirty years or so of his life. Spat upon.

Still, her passing had left such a gaping hole in his world that you could have driven a big Mack truck through it. His missing her, his mourning for her, his grieving for her didn't surprise him one little bit. But it sure left just about everyone else in Mulberry scratching and shaking their heads in wonderment.

Most town folks seemed to have expected Ernest to go running through the streets of Mulberry whooping and hollering in celebration at his wife's passing.

"Lord, if I found myself shed of that crazy woman who didn't never come out her house except after dark, I'd be so happy, you'd have to tie me down," one of Poppa's cronies from the kaolin mines told his barber as he got his hair trimmed at a corner shop in East Mulberry. Then, every man in the shop nodded his head in agreement as if each one of them had had to lay down their bodies for the past forty-five years next to Esther Lovejoy.

While Ernest was living with her, those years of marriage had seemed to just drag on. Looking back on them, however, he often wondered where the time had gone. Since Mudear had died, time didn't seem to mean too much of anything to Ernest. Even though Mudear had turned time upside-down and on its tail in their household decades before by sleeping all day, then rising late in the afternoon to eat something and watch prime-time television or flick aimlessly through the sixty or seventy premium cable channels, then fool around in her garden all night in her night clothes, there had still been some structure to his days.

For years, when Mudear was coming to bed at daybreak, he would be rising to get ready for work. When the girls were young and still living at home, they would prepare him his Sanka and breakfast and sit down with him and eat before doing their morning chores, getting ready for school, and heading off to the bus stop after he drove off to the kaolin mines where he had worked since he was almost still a boy.

His routine, seemingly tedious to outsiders, had given shape to his days, meaning to the passing of time.

Now that Mudear was no longer in the house, he found it hard even to keep up with time. Even when he thought he was paying attention to what was going on around him, he couldn't seem to tell the difference between a few minutes and a few hours. He would sit down on the edge of the sofa in the den for a few minutes and get lost in some memory of his wife when they had first married and she seemed genuinely proud of him, then look up at the clock on the wall in the kitchen to discover that hours had passed.

One evening earlier that spring while roaming the house from room to room with nothing to do, he had started to think about what he used to do, what his life had been like before Mudear had died. Sitting there in the gathering darkness holding his hands, he remembered The Place, his old hangout in downtown Mulberry on the corner of Broadway and Cherry Street. The last time he had been there was the night Mudear had died. That night he had left the hospital and driven straight there, walked in and ordered himself a cold Miller High Life. It was then, back in the fall, with his wife laying up dead at the hospital, that he had run into his old friend, Patrice.

Patrice had looked good, too, in her favorite, tight, black and white polka-dot dress, white round ear bobs clipped to her tiny seashell-shaped ears, her long narrow feet stuck down in cheap white leather flats, a white scarf tied around her dark neck. Weeks later, he still remembered how that dress looked on her tall, full frame, how her legs had been bare of stockings. Ernest knew from experience that she never wore hose. He remembered her as if he had dragged out his old Instamatic and snapped a picture that he could pull out of his worn leather wallet at any moment. He could still recall her scent as she leaned over his shoulder. She had smelled of liquor and perfume and Dentyne gum. The combination had smelled good to him, familiar. And she had sounded good, too, with her strong hoarse voice making him remember all the evenings he and she had sat talking over a cold beer before going to her shabby hotel room, then heading home to Mudear.

Folks liked to call Patrice a "Broadway Jessie," like she wasn't nothing but a whore looking for somebody to buy her a drink and a good time. Over the years, Ernest had bought her plenty of drinks and shared many good times, but he knew she was not merely a "Broadway Jessie." She had been kind when he had nearly forgotten what a kind woman sounded like. She had been accepting when Mudear had taught him that he was nothing she wanted.

"Shoot," he had muttered to himself in the quiet of the empty den, "I would'a bought Patrice a case 'a beers if she'da let me."

And right then, sitting alone in the dark on the edge of the sofa in his den, he had decided to drive downtown to The Place for a cold one.

With Mudear dead, he realized suddenly that he could do anything he wished. The thought of seeing some of his old cronies, men and one woman he had not seen since the night Mudear had died, of yelling across the bar, "Hey, man, how you got 'em?" and hearing the standard reply, "Aw, I ain't got 'em, man. You got 'em." Then, responding in kind, "Naw, man, I ain't got 'em. I had 'em, but they got away." The memory filled him with what he vaguely recalled as joy.

But by the time he took a shower and shaved, put some Vaseline on his face and hands, got dressed in a long-sleeved white dress shirt and starched creased khaki work pants that Betty had brought from the cleaners for him, and driven downtown in his old brown Ford Tempo, The Place was closed for the night. Standing by himself on the deserted corner of Broadway and Cherry, after peering into the plate glass windows of the darkened juke joint, he glanced at his watch to discover that it was three in the morning.

He had found himself turning around in circles like a confused dog chasing his tail. "Wha..what happened to the time?" he asked himself aloud, as he ran his hand over his greasy sweaty forehead and his closely cropped salt and pepper hair, becoming more bewildered and befuddled by the second.

Suddenly, he heard the memory of his dead wife's voice ring in his head, instructing his girls the way she used to, "Don't pay Ernest no attention. He a old man." And he simply turned back to his car and drove on back across the Ocawatchee to the house in Sherwood Forest. After that, he never even considered making the trip downtown again for a cold beer at his old haunt.

Instead, he spent night after night, sitting in the dark waiting for one of his daughters to stop by and remind him that he, unlike his wife, was still alive.

When he heard the back kitchen door open and the familiar footfalls of one of his girls on the tile floor, it took him by surprise. He knew it was Emily by the sound of her feet. All of them would have been shocked to know how well their father knew them: the pace of their steps, the smell of their perfume and shampoo and deodorant, the cadence of their voices, the calibration of the motors of their cars.

He knew he didn't have a good grasp on time, but he could have sworn that more than fifteen or twenty minutes had elapsed since he had heard his daughter's car pull up into the carport.

"Poppa? Poppa?" Emily called as soon as she entered the house through the kitchen door. Even before she had gotten inside, she had seen the shimmer of the colored light from the television screen through the frosted glass slats of the back door. "You still up?" she asked the figure sitting in the darkened den as if she fully expected to find her father stretched out in her parents' king-sized bed sleeping the slumber of the just.

She knew better than that. But as her sisters whispered when Emily wasn't present, "After all we been through, Emily still insist on living in some kinda' dream world."

The girls had hoped that things were going to be different after Mudear's death and burial. As they shed their stylish black outfits after their mother's funeral, they had continued to vow that their lives would be different, that they and circumstances indeed would change. But even Emily, usually the one to believe just about anything, hadn't been seriously waiting for any transformation. She, for one, still felt Mudear's spirit lingering too close to her shoulder for her to give any real thought to changing. She spent too many of her days merely try'na "hold the mule in the road," as Mudear had advised them over and over, to even consider change and "the mule going blind."

"Poppa," she said as she stood at her father's side, trying to decide whether or not to bend down and touch her smooth cool cheek to his stubbly one. She decided against the gesture and instead, reached over to turn on the floor lamp next to her father's chair. "It's so dark in here.

Can you see?"

She didn't wait for an answer. None of the girls really had conversations with their father, hardly ever bothering even to listen for his reply to their comments.

"I came to give you the good news about Annie Ruth," she continued in what she hoped was a light celebratory voice as she sort of waved her hand in Poppa's direction.

Ernest winced at the sound of his baby daughter's name.

He wasn't proud of it, but since the week of his wife's funeral the year before, he had not been able to bring himself to spend too much time with Annie Ruth or even to hear her name without shame. He knew he shouldn't have felt the way that he did. Annie Ruth certainly had never brought up the incident to his face. She didn't have to. It was seared in his brain. And he was ashamed.

The night before Mudear's funeral, Annie Ruth, fresh off the plane from her TV anchoring job in Los Angeles, had stayed at the house in Sherwood Forest rather than accompanying her sisters back to town and Betty's house for the night.

As always, big sister Betty had orchestrated the whole thing. She needed to. Things were beginning to fall apart. Ernest had heard it all unfold from his open bedroom window upstairs. As the girls had sat on the back porch drinking out of Mudear's good glasses, Annie Ruth had let it slip that she was pregnant and had no intention of getting rid of the baby and adhering to their girlhood vow never to have children.

Emily, bewildered and angry, had let Betty decide to end the discussion verging on a fight with, "Annie Ruth, maybe we better leave this for a little later. Why don't you go on up to bed and get some rest. Emily's going to stay with me."

Ernest heard Emily leaving with Betty and Annie Ruth taking her things into her old bedroom, but as far as the girls were concerned, he had no idea how it happened that Annie Ruth ended up spending the night. They hadn't let him in on their plans since before they were all in high school.

That night, unable to sleep in his empty bed, he had wandered downstairs alone. That was all he remembered clearly. The rest was merely vague images of him breaking down and crying, banging his head on the kitchen table in front of his baby girl Annie Ruth and having to be led and helped up to his bedroom by her like an old useless shell of a man.

The next morning when he awoke and every morning since, he had felt like an old juke joint character nicknamed "Cry Baby." Ernest hadn't seen "Cry Baby" in years but still remembered the roustabout from down at The Place who had the barroom talent for bursting into big believable tears on command.

Folks bored with the Bobby Blue Bland playing on the juke box or by the woman dancing by herself on the juke joint's tiny dance floor would look up and see "Cry Baby" sitting at the bar searching for someone to buy him a drink.

"Cry Baby!" one of them would yell over the din of the juke joint. "Cry Baby, cry for us."

Immediately, the short, squat, brown man's smooth face would crumble and big heavy tears would course down his cheeks as he moaned and sobbed as if somebody close to him had just died. If someone put an extra incentive of a couple of drinks on the counter near him, he would up the entertainment quotient by moaning and wailing, "Why they have to treat me like that?" or some other dialogue created right on the spot that told a little "cry baby" story.

For months, Ernest couldn't get the pathetic image of "Cry Baby" out of his head. He could hear the patrons at the Place whoop and holler and laugh at the weeping man. He could see Cry Baby thirstily guzzle down the beers that someone slid in front of him in payment for his antics. He would remember how some tender-hearted Broadway Jessie would look away in shame. And every time Ernest remembered that night after Mudear had died when Annie Ruth, his baby daughter, had caught him sitting and weeping into his cup of decaffeinated coffee at the kitchen table when she had had to put him to bed, he thought about "Cry Baby."

Many times since that night, his own "Cry Baby" night, Ernest would sit alone in the dark house and admonish himself out loud. "They ain't never had that much respect for me, my girls ain't. Not since their mother taught them to dismiss and disrespect me the way she did. But at least for all those years they ain't never seen me break down and cry, not in front of them. For all those years," he'd say and slap his thigh, hard, "they ain't never been able to say they seen their daddy a weak man, no matter what their mama said.

"But then I had to go and break down in front of my child, my baby daughter and prove everything Esther had said about me."

The memory of it all would make him want to break down and weep again.

Emily continued cutting on lights in the gloomy recreation room. "Why you sitting up here in the dark, Poppa? I got something to tell you. Guess what? Annie Ruth had her baby."

Emily was pleased the words didn't stick in her craw.

"It's a girl," she continued, attempting to sound all bright and cheery.

She thought she saw a shiver run through her father's wasted bony frame in the light from the TV. God, Poppa has gone to nothing, she thought.

"You cold, Poppa? It feels hot in here to me. Did you hear me, Poppa?" she asked as she stepped right in front of him and stood between him and the television screen he seemed to be having trouble focusing on.

"A girl, huh?" he asked after a little while of staring into space.

"Yeah, Poppa. A girl."

"Um, another Lovejoy girl, huh?" he muttered.

"Um-huh. A pretty little girl, Poppa. Looks just like Annie Ruth already."

"Lord," he said quietly as he considered the ramifications of Mudear's blood running through another female body on the earth, "help us all."

"Help you do what, Poppa, what can I do for you? What do you need from me? Some Sanka? I see an Entenmann's coffee cake in there on the kitchen counter. Did Betty leave that? Want some?"

Her thin, old father looked at his middle daughter for so long without saying anything that Emily started dancing from one foot to another like a nervous schoolgirl on recitation day. Then, he kind of chuckled to himself. And Emily realized that she had never heard her father chuckle before. She had seen him smile. Back when she was little before Mudear had changed and taken over the household, she remembered even hearing him truly laugh. She recalled his big old belly laughs ringing through the house when he ruled the roost and watched Jackie Gleason telling "Alice" he was going to send her to the moon or whatever other show he wanted to watch on the little black and white television set he had proudly brought home one Saturday evening.

But she had never seen or heard him truly chuckle, a dry wry chuckle, as he did before he looked her right in the eye and replied, "All I want or need is your love and understanding."

Emily actually hopped back a few inches in surprise at her Poppa's response, and bumped—bumped hard—into the edge of the rec room bar.

"What? What's that, Poppa?" she asked softly, sure that he wouldn't dare repeat his reply. She steadied herself with a hand on the Formica surface of the bar.

"All I want or need is my girls' love and understanding," he said again, with the same tone and inflection of sweet sincerity.

Poppa looked up into Emily's face as she edged away from him toward the back door. He could have kicked himself for opening up his big mouth again.

For a moment, she was stunned speechless. Then, all she said in reply was, "'Night, Poppa." And she turned and got out of there as quickly as she could. All she had said was, "'Night, Poppa," but as clear as day, he could hear his middle daughter thinking: "How can I give you that? Hell, I ain't got that to give myself!"

As he listened to the back kitchen door slam behind her, Poppa shook his head hopelessly and muttered. "Now, I done shamed myself in front of my second daughter, too."

And he could have sworn he heard his dead wife admonish him, *"Ernest, you are a old fool."*

CHAPTER 12

Lord, Ernest done gone from "sugar to shit!"

"Love and understanding," my ass.

Look at him sitting there in front of my wide screen television set tryn'a look all sad and pitiful.

Where was some of that love and understanding when I needed it? In the last few months since I been dead—Lord, ham mercy, has it only been a few months? Sometimes, it feel like a eternity up in here. Anyway, I ain't had nothing but time to look back over all those years I wasted tryn'a please that man. When everybody knows ain't no pleasing no man. _Ever!_ They don't give a damn 'bout you even after you turn your asshole inside out for 'em. They ain't _never_ satisfied.

If you skinny, they tell you to put some meat on your bones.

If you plump, they tell you you need to push back from the table a little more often.

If you yaller, they tell you you oughta' have a job out in the sun.

If you dark-skinned, they tell you don't wear no bright colors. "I ain't never seen no black house with no red shutters." They say things like that to break your little heart and your little spirit in two if they can.

Good thing I didn't never listen to none a' that talk. Well, not for long anyway.

Shortly after we got married is when he started that talk 'bout my looks and my bold ways and how it didn't seem like no real well-brought-up woman would want sex in all the ways I did.

I was right proud of myself even back then. And to tell the truth, it did sort of hurt my heart.

He even had the nerve one night to roll over in bed—little old narrow twin bed, too. He couldn't even afford no big double bed back then—to say Lil' Sis felt big and stretched out. He'd do that: come home for work, covered in that white kaoline chalk and make coarse comments and jokes about how it was a shame he didn't work in a alum factory 'cause I ought to think about sitting and soaking in a alum bath.

You know, back in those days they used to tell women—bad womens who had had lotsa' men—that their private parts were stretched out and the way to tighten it up again was to soak in a bathtub of water and alum. I guess the point was to tighten her up so men could continue getting some pleasure outa' her pussy and just stretch her out again.

"Can you feel that?" he'd ask while he was still up inside me. "Can you feel that? You don't feel none of that?"

I could tell just as good when Ernest had stopped off at that juke joint downtown—Lord, he loved to go downtown!—on his way home from work when he useta come in talking all that bawdy talk. Oh, for years he called himself having a girlfriend down there at The Place. Skinny, old rusty black woman named Patrice. And you know I ain't color struck. I woulda hated her just the same if she was a albino or white as Marilyn Monroe.

To tell the truth, I really didn't hate her for long. Only in the beginning. I was afraid he was gonna bring me home some nasty disease like the clap or some body lice or crabs or something. Then, after I decided to change my life and took what was mine, which was my life, I didn't care whether Ernest had a girlfriend or a boyfriend or both. It was all the same to me. _Me, I_ didn't want him.

I swear, it _still_ feel good to say that. "I didn't want him." Make me feel just as free as it did twenty or thirty years ago when I first said it and felt it. "I didn't want him."

Them girls don't know how lucky they are to have had a example of a free colored woman in their faces all their lives. Always complainin' 'bout me like I wa'n't no good mother.

Oh, well, I may not 'a done the job right to suit them girls, but I tell you one thing: that new little baby girl gon' know a thing or two 'bout life when I'm through with her.

I got plans for my grandchild. And them girls a' mine with their crazy ugly ways ain't gon' be able to do nothing 'bout it. HA!

CHAPTER **13**

As Emily backed out of the driveway, drove off, and left Poppa and the house out in Sherwood Forest, she knew there was something she had meant to do that she hadn't done. But for the life of her, she couldn't remember what.

She knew her thoughts could be scattered sometimes. Mudear used to say, "Lord, look at her in there running around digging kitty holes and cat holes and not knowing all the time that one would do." So, she had gotten in the habit of making lists in her head.

"I washed that river mud off of Betty's car before I went inside," she said aloud, ticking off the duties she had laid out for herself. "I checked on Poppa. I made sure he had Sanka in the cabinet. I told him about Annie Ruth's baby," Emily continued to herself as she came to the subdivision entrance.

Then, out of the corner of her eye, she caught sight of something next to her in the car. She let out a little "Lord!" and threw her hands up in the air in fright, thinking at first it might be one of Annie Ruth's "cats." But when the car began swerving crazily with no one at the helm, she grabbed the wheel, steadied the vehicle, steeled herself, and glanced to the right. There resting on the passenger's seat beside her was the white plastic hospital bag.

"Oh, shoot," she said, admonishing herself, and, without slowing down even one mile per hour, pulled the car around in a sharp u-turn under the black wrought-iron sign spanning the two mortar columns that spelled out SHERWOOD FOREST and sped back to her parent's driveway. She winced as she brought the Lexus to such a sudden stop at the entrance to the house that the tires squealed and the entire car rocked back and forth.

"Shit," she said under her breath. "If I get this damn car back to Betty in one piece, I swear to God I'm going to stick to my own little jalopy from now on."

Getting out of the car, she tried to be as quiet as she could, and hoped she would not disturb Poppa, whom she had left sitting up like a wooden Indian in the den, watching the flickering screen on her Mudear's wide-screen TV. She felt like a sneak thief slinking through the property at night past the tiny tool shed at the back of the house and hoped she wouldn't run up on a snake among the lush thicket back there.

All of a sudden, she heard Mudear's voice in her head, "'Sneak' and 'snake' have the same letters, and I'd rather be a snake than be a sneak." She bit her bottom lip at the thought of how many snakes there probably were slinking around Mudear's garden and remembered how often in her life she had felt like a sneak. Like the times—more than she cared to admit—she had sat outside an ex-boyfriend's house waiting in the shadows for him to return from a date with his new girlfriend. But she forged on.

Naturally, there were no lights on back there. Mudear had forbade artificial illumination in and around her garden.

"Don't need no lights," she reminded her family over and over. "I got night vision." She made the proclamation as if it she were saying "I got the gift of healing." or "I got my college degree in two years." She made it sound just that special. But then Mudear had the knack for that: making nothing seem like something. Unfortunately for her family, she also could do the converse: make something seem like nothing.

Even her girls had to admit that it was extraordinary the way the ordinary-looking mother could see so clearly in the dark. As a little girl, Emily would rise in the middle of the night to run to the bathroom with her eyes half shut, stepping lightly, trying not to wake herself in the process only to come fully and suddenly awake when she would run right into her mother walking around the darkened house as if it were high noon. Or later on as a teenager, fully awake on her nighttime trips to the toilet, she would sometimes look out the bathroom window and catch sight of a long pastel gown floating through the foliage of the garden and know that, even though the neighbors were likely up at their windows gawking and laughing at the strange woman roaming around outside in the night, all was right with the world because her Mudear was in her element.

Unlike her sisters, Emily was the least unnerved and embarrassed by her mother's nocturnal wanderings. Mudear made it seem so natural that a mother of three in a tiny Georgia town would sleep all day and garden all night and never even have a conversation, not even a telephone conversation, with anyone from the outside world, that Emily accepted her mother's routine without question.

Yet, how she longed to question it. All her life, she ached to get inside Mudear's head and discover the reason the woman took such solace in being alone, isolated, distanced from her family, from her community, from her girls, her own flesh and blood.

But Emily did not dare. More than anyone in that house in Sherwood Forest, Emily did not dare question how Mudear could build a hedge around her heart and still call herself a mother. As much as she yearned to know the answer, she just as much feared it. Could it be because of me, she wondered silently all her life. Could it be because I wasn't right, wasn't pretty enough, wasn't clever enough, wasn't right enough? Just wasn't enough?

Her struggle with that dichotomy of wanting to know while simultaneously fearing the knowledge, left Emily feeling unsettled her entire life. She and her sisters had few if any friends in school, and Emily didn't know about Betty and Annie Ruth, but she felt far too unsure about life—What does a mother do? How do you know someone loves you? Is everyone doomed to be the kind of adult their parents were? Does anyone love forever? What does forever mean?—to trust her friendship and secrets to anyone but her sisters. And even though from time to time, she had found herself strangely attracted to a woman she passed on the street or met in a club on Saturday night, she never pursued it. Emily could never trust herself, her life, her secrets, her heart to someone who might make her seem even more of an outsider to the world.

Even with her sisters, she was a bit uncertain, wobbly, forever a newborn colt, unable to stand firmly alone. Betty and Annie Ruth seemed to fit together so much better than she did with either one of them.

And that disconnect didn't end there for Emily. While she had lived in Mudear's house, Emily had always felt bewildered and disquieted by her surroundings, like an interloper who resided there. Yet, even after she was grown, though she knew Mudear would sometimes not even acknowledge her presence, let alone her visit, she had insisted on stopping at the house out in Sherwood Forest each week when she made the trip down from Atlanta to get her hair and nails done at Betty's shop. And still she always left feeling vaguely uneasy.

Now, with Mudear safely dead and buried for months, she continued the ritual and to feel the same way. And no matter how hard she tried to resist the temptation, whenever she was there, she would often find herself wandering through the lushness of Mudear's garden, still thriving on its own like a feral child.

As far as Emily could discern, that garden was all that her Mudear ever truly loved. And she longed to know why.

With the white plastic bag in one hand and her left breast clutched in the other, she tried to steel herself and perform the task she kept hearing described in her mind like a chant. Squaring her broad Lovejoy shoulders, she headed resolutely through the garden in the dark. But before she had made ten steps, she tripped suddenly over a large, flat, grey, river rock and fell headlong into the moist mulch and grass. More than ten years before, Mudear had made Poppa retrieve the rocks from the banks of the Ocawatchee and place them at the edge of her garden as natural focal points. Once in place, they seemed in exactly the right spot. Poppa had not had to drag them around the way he sometimes had to with the plants Mudear had ordered from catalogs or the county extension newsletter or the nursery out by Mulberry's farmer's market.

Lying there in the dew-damp grass with the wind knocked out of her from the fall, Emily could hear her Mudear cackle and say, *"Ha! Played so well, but tripped and fell!"* the way the woman had declared whenever she heard of some public disgrace suffered by one of her old friends in Mulberry.

Embarrassed and shaken, Emily lay on her side there in the moist grass for a few moments, rubbing her scuffed elbows and hoping the barking dog one street over was not going to bring her father to the window to investigate. She should have known better. If one of her sisters had been there with her, she would have told Emily that Poppa didn't have much curiosity or interest in much of anything anymore since Mudear had passed.

After a few seconds of getting her breath back, Emily raised herself up to her knees and felt around on the ground for the plastic bag she had dropped.

When she spotted the white sack against the wet dense grass, she felt a chill run down her spine that had nothing to do with the damp earth against her body. Catching sight of the white bag reminded her of Mudear's white garden—white roses, confederate jasmine, alyssum, tea olives—and how she had planted it to show her family what she, with her night vision, saw when she looked out on her yard at night.

"Get up, girl, and get on with what you got to do," Emily said out loud in a far harsher voice than she usually used with herself. She even sucked her own teeth at herself in the way she had heard Mudear do for so many years. Hearing her own voice strangely distorted in the night air startled her. However, it did get her moving.

She clambered to her feet, brushed off her fleshy bare thighs, snatched up the plastic bag and headed doggedly for Mudear's vegetable patch. Other than the collard and turnip greens—some of whose leaves were as big as the flagstones leading to the rose garden on the side of the house—every vegetable growing there was a "volunteer," coming up on its own from the garden Mudear had planted the previous spring. But none of the smaller hardy plants--California Wonder green peppers, Ichiban eggplant, Golden Globe summer squash—looked like volunteers. Year after year, they flourished like hybrids bred and grown to produce fruit one year with vigor and then, die. But they never died.

Grateful for the light from the mulberry moon and her memory of the yard, Emily passed all those plants and headed for the far corner patch of the huge garden where she remembered Mudear had planted Silver Queen corn the spring before. With each step, she felt her favorite red moccasins become more and more spoiled with the rich black loam that her mother had perfected over the years. But she couldn't seem to stop herself. She kept on walking until she reached the section where a few tiny green blades poked their tips up through the soil. Emily never grew a garden herself, but she knew that in a couple of months, that whole section would be crammed with tall thick corn stalks, loaded with fat ears, their greenish-golden silk undulating in the summer breeze.

Dropping to her knees in the soil, without hesitation, she began digging her freshly manicured scarlet nails into the dirt over and around the corn seedlings. When she felt a nail snap in the dirt, she still didn't stop or waver.

She felt as if she were standing far off in another corner of the yard watching herself as she went about her scratching and burrowing in Mudear's garden like a mole venturing out at night.

Mudear always said, When you dead you done. But Emily was beginning to doubt that. She almost expected to see her dead mother come walking down one of the cypress chip-covered paths between the raised garden beds, complaining, "Get out' the way, daughter. You don't know what you doing there."

In fact, Mudear's voice was beginning to come to her so strong in her head lately that Emily was starting to fear she was truly haunted. A couple of times, in the last weeks, Emily had considered calling her old therapist, Dr. Axelton, telling her about the voice and asking for advice on how to handle the latest aural manifestation of her dead mother. But she decided instead to ignore it until and if she heard her sisters complain about the same thing. She was the chameleon of the family and right now with Annie Ruth dealing with motherhood, Emily knew that her sisters wanted her to pretend to be sane even if it were all merely camouflage.

Gingerly, she took the thin wet membrane out of the bottom of the plastic bag where it lay as soft and pliable as when she had dropped it there at the hospital. Her fingers' contact with the moist piece of newly birthed skin, which hours before had been inside her sister's belly, sent shivers through Emily's being, but did not stop her. With just enough moonlight to see what she was doing, she gently laid her niece's birth caul in the freshly dug hole and spread it out with the palms of her dirty hands. Then, she pulled the pile of soil she had dug up back over the hole and patted it gently the way she had seen Mudear do hundreds of times.

Emily had planned to kneel there in her mother's garden a few minutes and catch her breath, but the neighbor's dog began raising such a ruckus again— howling and baying like some possessed thing—that as soon as she had finished burying the thin piece of skin, she jumped to her feet instead and ran back wildly to Betty's car, leaving the white plastic hospital bag lying on the ground among the corn seedlings like a ghostly garden marker.

CHAPTER 14

L ord! Would you look at that girl? Emily truly is out there in my garden digging kitty holes and cat holes.

Now, look at her. Good God! Emily don't hardly have the sense she was born with. Any fool know you got to tamp the soil down good and hard, not give it no baby pats, anytime you bury anything in the ground. Now if that corn don't grow up just right through that baby's, my grandbaby's birth caul, I'mo be mighty upset with that girl. That corn's gotta grow good and strong so that baby can gnaw on one a' those cobs a' corn when the stalks ripen and bear. That's the way it's gotta be!

I swear, I could just push that crazy daughter a' mine down in the dirt.

You know, I have raised a fool!

Shoot! Emily wearing me out! Humph, I tell you what,   now I'mo *have to concentrate on one of the other girls. Emily just too much work.*

I already done got Betty to just 'bout get that house of hers ready for me. Heh! She even out there planting a garden and don't even know why. Maybe that's who I'll concentrate on next. Or now that I think 'bout it, I might bypass all my girls and go straight for the gold. Yeah, now I think about it, I believe I will move on to my grandchild.

Now I got that baby's birth caul in the ground, all I got to do is get my hands on <u>her</u>.

And I'm already in that house of Betty's whether she knows it or not. Shoot, I'm having 'bout as good a time as I did out there in my garden at night. Now, this what I call <u>livin'</u>!

CHAPTER **15**

etty loved her house. *Loved* it.

It didn't surprise anyone in Mulberry when, in the late 1980s, Betty Lovejoy, a single woman, business owner, and eldest daughter of a kaolin miner and a reclusive housewife with only a high school education, purchased the spacious, grand house that had stood at the top of an historic African-American neighborhood for more than a century. Folks who didn't know that she had taken care of her parents, her family's household, and her sisters since the age of ten could still look at her and tell that Betty was a classic over-achiever by the set of her broad shoulders, the straight-forward common sense level of her gaze, and the success of her two hair care businesses.

But other than her sisters, there were few people on this earth who did know her, really know her past the sharp haircut, the beautifully tailored clothes, the late model cars, the Middle Georgia Businesswoman of the Year awards.

If they did, they would have known that although her beautifully appointed, orderly house looked like her prosperous, successful present, it was actually an exercise in banishing her chaotic, fear-filled past.

Each time she drove up the formal drive that curved from the street around her stately house to the edge of her lush back yard, she felt reassured that she had a home. She had a home, paid for and unencumbered, that no one could take away from her or ever banish her from. A place she could share with her sisters if need be. Where she could meet and tryst with whomever she wished. Where she could retire at the end of one of her marathon days or weeks or seasons and close the door behind her. Where she could even open those same doors to her father if he lived long enough to become too infirm to live on his own out at the house in Sherwood Forest.

Her father, in fact, was the reason she had bought the big house, the reason she still had to fight the demons of fear surrounding it

Some nights, when she was little, he'd come home from work with hell in him. If she allowed herself, she could still hear her father's voice from decades before.

"Get out!" Poppa had ordered Mudear and his children. First, it was only Betty and Emily, then, after Annie Ruth came, the three of them with their mother would have to hurriedly get their things together in the middle of the night and try to find shelter wherever they could. Sometimes, they found refuge at a distant relative's house. Neither of her parents seemed to have close family. Other times, they all ended up on the front room couch of one of Mudear's friends. Wherever it was, it never felt like safe haven to Betty. And it only lasted at most a few days or a week.

Then, Mudear would drag back home and beg Poppa to let them

return. Sometimes, she'd go alone, sometimes she'd take the girls and they would all have to beg and apologize – they never knew what for – just to get their father to let them back into their home.

"We sorry, Poppa," they would say as Mudear had instructed them. "We won' t do it no more."

Memory of those long ago forays into the night and back in shame was the reason she made such a sizable contribution four times a year to the battered women's homeless shelter in Mulberry County. It was the reason she strong-armed her stylists and shampoo girls to give generously, too.

But she didn't do it for the women in the present. Nor did she contribute to women's causes for the women who would come after her. She did it for the women in her past.

This forward-thinking modern woman was mired in the messy detritus of the past. Only those close to her—and only her sisters were truly close to her—knew she struggled not to take that glass or two of wine in the evening because she was afraid that she might have crossed over in the last few years from social drinker to problem drinker. That she ached for a cigarette most of the day and night. That even as she curled up under her twenty-year-old lover with a sigh of solace and release, she feared exposure and shame. That she was overwhelmed by the dark. That she feared growing old alone and unloved with no one but her sisters to care for her.

She didn't like to think it, but she knew that even picking Cinque, a man-child she could raise up to her own hand, was a reaction to the memories of Poppa ordering Mudear around in the old pre-change days. Whenever she and Cinque sat at her kitchen table to share a meal she had prepared, she relished how grateful he was for her efforts. He would never rap the tines of his fork on an empty spot on his plate to signal to her that he wanted more of what was missing the way that Poppa had done for years. Cinque would never have withheld money for her to get her hair fixed the way Poppa had when the girls were younger and he had the upper hand in his household. No, the fine young man who still sometimes slumped in Betty's high-backed Louis XIV dining room chairs and threw one of his long strong legs over the armrest when he forgot to try to be mature would never be like Poppa had been in the old days. Betty was queen of her castle, her domain, herself. And Cinque knew it.

"Put your dick right there in my hand," Betty had instructed Cinque when they began flirting with each other after hours as he performed odd jobs around her beauty shops.

"What, Miss Lovejoy?!" he had asked, incredulous and reverting to the appellation of respect he had dropped weeks before. "*What* did you say?" Even for the brazen woman who had stolen his heart and good sense, this was more than he could believe.

"You heard me," Betty had said with a chuckle at her own audacity as she ran one hand through her short dark hair and held the other one out. "You claim to be so hot for me, put your penis there and let me see how hot you really are."

Still a bit abashed, the lanky young man only took half a beat, then, stepped up. Moving languidly at first, then more resolutely with each step, he came to stand right in front of Betty next to the bank of state-of-the-art hair dryers and complied with her demand.

After that, there was no turning back or doubting by either one of them that Betty Lovejoy was a woman in charge of her life.

Even Stan, the old Casanova high school counselor whom everyone in town assumed was the only man in Betty's life, held no sway over her. When he wasn't trying to screw his former pupils and his teaching colleagues on the sly, he was merely in Betty's life to escort her to awards banquets and annual Christmas parties. For a while, before Cinque moved up in her hierarchy from the beauty shops' handyman to her "Handy Man," Stan had been Betty's boyfriend by default, filling the empty space in her bed from time to time if not in her heart. But shortly after she stopped fighting all sense of propriety and good morals and made the teen-ager her lover, she had ceased any semblance of a love affair with Stan.

"Stan," she finally told the former high school athlete who was on the cusp of portliness, "frankly, I don't know where your dick has been. And you probably don't know for sure either. So, from now on, it needs to stay outa' me."

And that was that for fucking Stan. He knew that Betty liked and enjoyed a healthy sexual life. It was one of the characteristics he most admired about her. He tried to put up a bit of a fight, attempting vaguely to argue his case. But he had known her long enough, since their own high school days, to recognize when she was serious and unmovable.

And anyway, even before she had ever actually slept with Cinque, Stan suspected that she was getting all the sex she wanted from the boy. The first time he had seen them together, standing casually and much too close together at the reception desk at her beauty shop, Lovejoy's 1 in East Mulberry, he recognized instantly the intimacy between his old girlfriend and the dark, lanky, errand boy who seemed to be able to do everything from fixing the dryers to buffing the floors to making his boss lady laugh. Only Stan's pride prevented him from rushing over and causing a scene right then.

Besides, he had always told Betty and anyone else who would listen, "I ain't no fighter, baby. I'm a lover." He was no Ernest Lovejoy from back in the day, no demon likely to turn ugly and abusive at the drop of a hat or the wrong word. Betty would not have stood for that. So, he accepted his new role as platonic friend and kept right on rolling.

In her house, Betty felt some sense of control over those demons that she kept hidden from most folks. Many days, even before her sisters returned to live with her, she said to herself over and over, if I can just get through this dinner for Mudear and Poppa, these tax records for the shop, this interminable staff meeting—and get back to my home and close that door and sit quietly in the library and have a drink, I'll be okay.

Oh, much of her work still awaited her in the home office she outfitted with every machine and piece of furniture and equipment she could think of. But that office was in her home, and her abode offered her asylum.

And it was an abode with which she was very familiar. Even with a housekeeper who came Monday through Friday, cleaning and washing and polishing and doing the household shopping, Betty knew her house as well as any housewife who spent the better part of her days and nights at home caring for it. Shoot, Betty knew her own home at the top of Pleasant Hill better than Mudear had known the house out in Sherwood Forest where she had spent nearly every waking and sleeping hour for more than two decades.

So, in late winter right after Annie Ruth had settled in, when items, little items at first—a candy dish, a hair brush, a mirror, the remote control for the small red TV in the kitchen—began showing up in strange and inappropriate places, Betty was a bit confused and irritated.

"Mrs. Andrews," she finally asked her conscientious housekeeper, "did you move my shampoo?" Betty prided herself on being a benevolent boss, and she tried to keep the vexation out of her voice even though she found the effort taxing. That's how she was in her two shops and that's what she strove for in her home.

"Shoot, Betty, you heap so much praise on your employees, they bound to disappoint you," Annie Ruth pointed out time and again.

"Annie Ruth," Betty finally told her sister, "you know as well as I do that we grew up without getting one sincere word of praise from the one we wanted to hear it from." Betty didn't even have to say she was talking about Mudear. "I be damned if I'm gonna be like that, too."

And she meant it. Praise just seemed to flow from Betty's heart.

It flowed as surely and strongly as her conviction not ever to be like her mother.

"Oh, the house smells so good, Mrs. Andrews," she would say on the few occasions when their paths crossed. The meticulous housekeeper, not more than fifteen years older than Betty even though a hardscrabble life left her looking decades older, was usually long gone when Betty finally dragged in at the end of her long workday. "And just how do you get these wood floors so shiny?"

It was no small thing that she was finally able to leave her home in some capable and caring hands. She had gone through what seemed like half of Mulberry looking for a housekeeper who didn't go through all her drawers and belongings as well as her well-stocked pantry and closets. When she finally found Mrs. Andrews, she recognized a treasure and strove to keep her with bonuses, respect, and understanding of her own home life that included a new second husband and three grown children at home with no jobs.

Yet despite her appreciation of her employees, she also demanded some sense of order in her life. The cans in her pantry all lined up evenly. The rolls of toilet tissue in all the bathroom cabinets had to be stacked just so. Her shoes in the big walk-in dressing room closet lined up by color and style.

She had to have some regularity in her days like she had to have some light in her nights. And the misplaced household items offended her sense of order.

"Now, what's that remote control doing out here on the ground?" she asked aloud on her way to work early one spring morning after she had stopped upstairs to check on Emily and Annie Ruth still asleep in their beds.

When she picked it up to return it to its proper place inside, the cold dew-damp plastic sent an unexpected chill through her body and she uttered a little cry, "Oh!" and nearly dropped it back on the steps on her way back into her house. She had to steel herself to dry it off with a couple of paper towels from the upright marble stand on the black granite kitchen counter before placing it firmly in its holder by the small red TV.

All day long, the memory of the sight of that wet channel changer kept messing with her head, popping up at the most unexpected times like spam on a computer screen. When she got home that night, she had to ask.

"Annie Ruth, Em-Em, did one of you by chance leave the remote for the kitchen television outside last night? I found it sitting right in the middle of the driveway out back."

They both looked at Betty as if she were crazy. Hearing the question out loud sounded a little nuts even to her.

"Uh, don't tell me things are getting up and walking around outside now, Betty?" Annie Ruth teased her and laughed. "This big old house of yours isn't haunted, is it?" Emily joined in the laughter a moment. Then, she turned serious.

"It's not, is it, Betty?" Emily asked with a nervous giggle.

Betty merely shook her head, laughed along with her sister and dropped the subject.

Then, a couple of days later, things weren't just misplaced; they started disappearing altogether.

The sisters had always loved wearing each other's clothes when they could fit into them. They had traded dresses and sweaters, earrings and shoes all their lives.

"Now, I know that pink cashmere sweater of mine didn't just get up and walk away by itself," Betty teased her sisters at the breakfast table after a morning of rummaging through her huge walk-in closet and dressing room.

"Betty, you know as well as I do, I can't wear pink," Emily said as she slathered pepper jelly on the biscuits Betty had just taken from the oven. "Red is my color, not pink. Not even the pretty rosy pink of that sweater."

"Don't look at me," Annie Ruth said as she sipped hot raspberry tea. "I couldn't fit these swollen titties and stomach in anything in your closet, including your shoes now. I will one day soon, but not right now."

"Well, what could have happened to it?" Betty wondered aloud.

For some reason that Betty could not put her finger on, the missing items not only vexed her. They frightened her and left her feeling oddly exposed. She couldn't shake the feeling that there was an intruder in her home, her sanctuary, who had no business there.

When her investigations kept coming up empty, leaving everyone who entered the house feeling defensive and on edge, Betty willed herself to ignore the missing and misplaced objects once and for all and put her energy and attention on getting the house ready for Annie Ruth's baby.

But every time one of her sisters asked innocently, "Hey, has anyone seen my bedroom slippers?" or "I can't for the life of me find the latest issue of InStyle I left in the bathroom. Did you take it?" it sent a chill right through Betty down to her bones.

Ignoring the strange occurrences, however, did not end them. As Mudear had told them all their lives, "When you don't pay attention to life, life will slam your head into a brick wall until you do."

Things got worse.

When Betty walked into her home office one evening after work and was sure that the hot spicy scent of red hots, the candy that Mudear had eaten incessantly as she lounged around her house in Sherwood Forest, was wafting on the air, she thought for a moment that she was losing her grip on reality.

"I know ain't none of us had no red hots up in this house," she said softly to herself. And just as suddenly, the aroma faded, leaving her more unsettled than the candy's scent had.

Then, another evening a few days later when she came in from work and found the pale wicker furniture rearranged in the solarium, her first thought was Oh-oh, Annie Ruth must be in the nesting stage of her pregnancy. But just as quickly, as she dropped her latest bags of purchases on the chaise lounge that was now situated over by the window, she remembered that Annie Ruth had told her that morning that lately she didn't have the energy to even put her clean laundry away.

When Emily and Annie Ruth came tumbling into the room to greet her like damp and motley five-year-olds from the side garden where they had been playing in the spray of the spinning sprinklers, Betty didn't get a chance to quiz either one of them about the changes.

"Oh, look, Em-Em," Annie Ruth had said as she flopped onto the chaise lounge and dug into Betty's packages. "Betty moved my favorite chair over to the windows so I could get more sunlight. Thanks, sis."

Betty didn't know what to respond. But that same coldness that she felt some mornings as she walked through her own new garden and wondered how all that flora could have sprung up on her land so quickly and profusely, flooded her being.

Oh, her home continued to offer her solace and joy. But with items missing and furniture moving and remote controls showing up in strange places, she was beginning to fear, really fear, that her home, her sanctuary of order and peace, was no longer a refuge. She suspected that her place of safety was beginning to turn on her.

Later, she would think ruefully to herself, Now, how in the world did I not see what all that meant? But that was later. And by then, it was too late.

CHAPTER 16

Betty ain't nearly as smart as everybody seem to think she is if she can't figure out who been moving her stuff and rearranging that furniture.

You know, before I died I hadn't even never been in Betty's house. Ain't been in nobody's house 'cept my own in what…twenty, thirty years. Betty was always tryn'a get me to come outa' my house and come see hers. When that didn't work—Now, what made her think it would?—she start leaving pictures of her place around my house for me to see and comment on. Heck, I didn't care nothing 'bout that little brick cracker box _I_ lived in. What in the world made her think I'd care about hers. Shoot, a house ain't nothing but something else to shackle you to the disappointments of this world. Just another link in the chain.

CHAPTER 17

As much thought and effort as Betty figured she had already put into preparing her house for the arrival of their new baby, one would have thought there was nothing else for her to do after the baby came.

In the midst of all her professional and personal duties—running two thriving salons; planning the Middle Georgia Spring Hair Care Fair; integrating Emily and Annie Ruth into her household; finding some secret moments to be with her Cinque—Betty had still found time to turn her home into the perfect refuge from the outside world for her sisters fleeing Atlanta and escaping from L.A., and the perfect nursery and first home for her new niece.

Neither Emily nor Annie Ruth had told the whole truth about the life each of them had left behind, but as the weeks wore on, the past seemed less and less important in the world they were creating right there in Mulberry. It was fresh life they were conceiving and making in their middle Georgia hometown and that existence was all tied up with the arrival of their new baby.

Even prior to her birth, the baby had become the very life breath of the house.

For weeks before Annie Ruth's due date, Betty had scoured the Internet and the countryside around Mulberry looking for the exactly right bassinet that would cradle her sister's baby. She found it at an antique store right in old downtown Mulberry, the last place she had expected to find anything worthwhile.

The old downtown business district of the tiny town was hardly a district at all anymore, let alone a thriving business center. As in most small towns and some large cities across the country at the end of the century, all the old downtown businesses had moved out to the enclosed malls located in burgeoning suburban areas decades before. In Mulberry, on the block where the cavernous Woolworth's had once stood, smelling like hard candy and tropical fish and coconut cake from the lunch counter and cheap paint on cheap trinkets "Made in Japan" when that label of provenance was a joke, there was only a parking lot with a cracking asphalt surface. Where the town's only true downtown department store had once reigned, there was now merely a deserted building with broken windows and squatters' ragged belongings cluttering the floors. Nearly all else was vacant lots and more deserted buildings. Once bustling banks and bakeries, shoe stores, dress shops, and theaters had disappeared like white rabbits in a magician's act.

But two businesses seemed to continue to thrive in the wasteland that was Mulberry's old downtown district: the antique shop owned by a meticulous older white woman named Jennette, and The Place, the signature juke joint and liquor store still owned, in part, by the richest black woman in town, Lena McPherson.

Poppa didn't think any of his girls thought much about his life outside the walls of the house in Sherwood Forest, so, he would have been surprised and chagrined to know that they knew The Place had been his favorite hangout for most of his life. It was true that they didn't think much about him at all—Mudear had taught them that. However, they knew a thing or two about his old habits. Betty even knew about Patrice, had even had a chance to study her once when she had sauntered into her beauty shop over in East Mulberry one Saturday morning for a wash and press on her short, dry, jet black hair. But Betty had never told her sisters about their father's juke joint girlfriend.

"God bless the child," is all that Betty could say about the relationship and the juke joint that she hoped had given her father some modicum of joy. For that reason alone, she had wanted to give The Place her liquor business.

But The Place didn't carry her favorite wine or the Rolling Rock beer that Cinque liked to drink every now and again, making him a bit tipsy like a schoolboy at his first basement party. So, Betty bypassed the downtown juke joint in favor of the chic new liquor store out by the mall.

In her frenzy of pre-baby shopping, The Place was about the only establishment in the region that didn't get some of her business. She had gone to the SAMs two towns over, in Macon, to purchase disposable diapers in bulk and had stacked them up in the walk-in linen closet at the top of the front staircase alongside mountains of cotton swabs and wet wipes and baby shampoo and baby oil.

She had commissioned Miss Evelyn, a seamstress in East Mulberry to produce piles of handmade baby wash cloths and soft stretch rompers and nighties in every pastel color they could find. With an eye to the future, she also ordered a one-of-a-kind ash wood crib from two black women artisans living alone in a pine cabin in the Georgia mountains, and crib blankets and padding in every color of the rainbow. She had even bought one light-weight baby-sized quilt that an old reclusive woman in the country outside the Mulberry city limits fashioned into the shape of a rainbow.

Whenever Emily or a steadily burgeoning Annie Ruth met their older sister coming in the back door with yet another load of baby products, Betty simply dismissed their "More, Betty?" with a familiar quote.

"Like Mudear used to say, 'It's better to have and not need than to need and not have,'" she'd say, brush past her sisters and add the new purchases to the bounty already secured in drawers and closets and spaces all over the house.

The pantry off the kitchen was full of jars of organic baby food and disposable bottles and formula that could be easily viewed through the glass panels of its old-fashioned doors.

The hall closet downstairs could not hold even another ball of cotton. And the bathroom cabinet was so full of more baby supplies and toiletries, Emily had to store extra towels, soap, and rolls of toilet tissue in one of her bedroom closets.

The state-of-the-art digital sound system that piped music all through the house at the touch of a finger was loaded with new cds of lullabies and Brazilian love songs and blues and soft jazz and anything else Betty could think of that might be soothing and stimulating to a newborn and her mother. She had already loaded up the library with her sisters' favorite classic children's book—Virginia Hamilton's *The People Could Fly, Just Us Women* by Jeannette Caines, Maurice Sendak's *Under the Juniper Tree*, Patricia McKissack's *Flossie and the Fox*, John Steptoe's Mufaro's *Beautiful Daughters*, and the entire line of Leap Frog learning books.

"We know she gon' be pretty, Lil' Sis," Betty assured Annie Ruth and Emily as she opened even more shopping bags filled with new literary purchases. "These are gonna make sure she knows she's smart, too. Like Mudear used to say, "Pretty ain't gon' get you where smarts will.'"

However, there were two assignments Betty and the girls had waited to do, and one was to purchase a doll.

That was a joy that all the girls were saving for an adventure they imagined having together with the baby. They all anticipated that shopping trip like children waiting for dessert.

Mudear had never bought any of her daughters a doll back in the days when she had actually gone out of the house to shop downtown in the Woolworth's or Dannenberg's department store. None of the Lovejoy girls had owned a doll in their entire lives. They hadn't even thought it odd until Emily and Annie Ruth were in college and their roommates had brought their favorite childhood doll or plush animal to school with them to prop up on their dormitory bed.

Later, the girls figured the lack of baby dolls in the house reflected Mudear's disdain for motherhood. Regardless, the very fact that Mudear had not done it for her daughters was the impetus for Betty to make sure she and her sisters would do it for their new baby girl. Mudear's life—including the time before the younger girls' recollection—was the blueprint for much of what the Lovejoy girls did and didn't do.

Only Betty remembered how it had been back then, before the change when they actually had a mother, a mother like all of their little friends, a mother who got dressed on Saturday afternoon in a clean pressed cotton dress and comfortable walking shoes and went out to shop for her family, a mother who rose early before everyone else on Sunday morning, put on a pot of coffee, roused her family and helped them get dressed for church. A mother who cooked dinner, then sat and ate it with them.

Those times were the stuff of fairy tales that Betty shared with her younger sisters after the change as she got them ready for bedtime or as they cleaned the house on Saturdays while Mudear slept until early evening.

"Mudear used to cook the best stew meat and potatoes you ever tasted," Betty had told them so many times as they were all growing up that the younger girls could almost taste the dish. "She used to buy the kind of stew meat that wasn't all lean, but the kind that had strips of fat in it so it tasted real rich and good and greasy. And she cut up onions and carrots...."

"With her own hands?" Annie Ruth would ask over and over right on cue.

"Yeah, Annie Ruth. With her own hands, and she didn't even complain about the onion odor clinging to her fingers. Not when Poppa was around anyway."

Although Emily and Annie Ruth couldn't clearly recall a time when Mudear didn't rule the roost and Poppa didn't kowtow to her every whim, Betty did. However, there weren't many happy stories. She remembered how Mudear had casually and venomously called Poppa "Mr. Bastard" behind his back and "Ernest" to his face. Mudear had called him that secretly when he was out of earshot, under her breath and to her friend Mamie on the phone for the first ten or so years of Betty's life. Betty knew Mudear had her reasons for that epithet.

She recalled seeing Poppa nonchalantly push Mudear to the rough wooden floor in the old house in East Mulberry on his way out the door one morning when she begged him for money to get her hair washed, straightened and curled. Betty could still close her eyes and see all three of the girls lined up in their tiny cot-like beds coughing and gasping for breath with whooping cough and Mudear running from bed to bed trying to stretch the little medicine they could afford three ways. And she remembered that first cold winter day when she and her sisters didn't eat until dark because Mudear decided to feed only herself then crawl back into bed for the day and Betty had to rustle up a meal of graham crackers and baloney for herself and her little sisters.

Betty tried not to remember. But she remembered. As she stocked her sub-zero refrigerator with Annie Ruth's favorite black olive tampenade, she remembered. As she checked the hundreds of diapers and boxes of wet wipes stashed away for the baby, she remembered. As she changed the 500-thread-count sheets on Annie Ruth's bed from persimmon to pristine white to turquoise and back, she remembered.

She didn't talk about it.

Sometimes, when she would find herself standing at her bedroom window facing the eastern side of her yard, watching the morning sunlight dance lightly through the fifty-year-old magnolia and oak trees on the lawn below, or on some winter day, when she suddenly caught sight of the peeling bark of a tall crepe myrtle at the edge of her neighbor's property, she longed to pick up the phone and call someone—one of her trusted employees at the beauty shops, her young lover, her old boyfriend Stan, her mother's old friend Miss Mamie—and ask, how did my sisters and I ever get out of all that alive and intact?

She never made the call. But she remembered.

She was Ishmael, the one chosen to remember, the repository of so much family history, forgotten, buried, or ignored, so weighed down that she felt some days as if she could barely lift one foot after another.

Her sisters had asked her about that history from time to time when they were growing up. "Betty, what was Poppa like before the change?" Annie Ruth would want to know as she swept up the kitchen after Betty had cooked and Emily had washed the dishes.

Betty would feel her spine become like steel as she feigned nonchalance and shrugged. "Oh, he was always Poppa," she'd reply.

Still, she couldn't make herself forget when he was "Mr. Bastard."

The second thing the Lovejoy sisters put off until the birth was the naming of their new baby girl. In fact, Annie Ruth had insisted that they postpone that discussion.

"Sisters," Annie Ruth had said firmly and sincerely each time one of her siblings tried to bring up the topic of baby names, "I have to keep something just for myself. I am the mama."

And that would stop the discussion—for a while.

"Hey, Em-Em, we got enough to be concerned about in getting ready for the baby without worrying about a name," Betty would say privately, trying to salve her sister's wounded feelings each time Annie Ruth pushed them away from naming her baby. "We got to get this house ready."

But with all that preparation, Betty and Emily still spent the entire morning after the birth bustling around the house getting ready for Annie Ruth to return the next day with their new baby. That's how all the girls thought of the newborn: "their baby."

Perhaps it was because Betty and Emily felt they would never have one of their own that from the time of discovering that Annie Ruth was pregnant and planned to keep it, that they began calling the child "our baby."

Emily had to acknowledge, if only to herself, that before Annie Ruth's pregnancy, she had not had much of a life.

For practically all her adult years, even for the brief time she was married, she kept returning home to the life she knew, making weekly trips down to Mulberry from her apartment in Atlanta to take care of much of her routine needs in her hometown.

She drove down to get her hair and nails done at Betty's shop in East Mulberry. She traveled down to go to her dental appointments and yearly medical checkups. She drove down to catch Joy dishwashing liquid and salmon fillets on sale at the local Piggly-Wiggly. And she returned weekly to visit Mudear, whether her mother seemed to notice her presence in her house and care or not.

The hour-and-a-half drive was no hardship to Emily. She felt it beat killing a weekend lying around with her left hand down the front of her panties, lazily watching the dust motes float in the sunbeams peeking through her bedroom window curtains. She got on the road home even when her car was not as road-worthy as she would have liked. Year after year, Betty insisted that Emily let her put her in a good new car.

"Em-Em, I worry about you on the road with that clunker of yours. Anything could happen. It's dangerous."

Emily would smile and shake her head, sweetly declining Betty's generous offer. But she always thought, Girl, you have no idea.

In fact, Emily's life was one big danger zone.

She still stopped to give strangers directions in the middle of Peachtree Street downtown. She continued to offer stranded folks the use of her cell phone for emergencies. Once or twice she had even stepped in to protect a woman she had seen getting her ass kicked by an irate boyfriend outside a Buckhead nightclub.

Shoot, Emily still picked up hitchhikers.

Yet she clung to the pretense of normalcy, the illusion of independence by continuing to drive the same red Datsun that she had made every payment on herself. Then, the week before Annie Ruth flew back to Georgia from California to wait out the final months of her pregnancy, Emily told her sisters that she had quit her job with the government, packed some stuff up in that ramshackle car and moved back to Mulberry and Betty's house "to help out" with Annie Ruth and the new baby. But that wasn't the truth.

She hadn't quit. She had been fired.

After more than fifteen years in the same job as an archivist with the same Georgia state employer in the same government complex near the gold-domed capitol, Emily had finally gone too far. She had, as her co-worker James Patrick told folks who asked about her, "shown her ass one time too many for these white folks."

Everyone there at the office figured that it was bound to happen sooner or later. Without the benefit of the safety net that her sisters provided, Emily walked a tightrope over a chasm called "Nutsville" every day of her life in Atlanta. Over the years, Emily had cussed out enough supervisors and clients to warrant her firing many times over. It had just never happened. But then Emily cursed out the wrong highly connected white woman the same morning she discovered that someone in the records office—she suspected the woman who had loud-talked her each time she came up for renewal of her benefits—had canceled her insurance benefits that paid the lion's share of Dr. Axelton's fees. Right there at her desk, she went totally off, calling folks "motherfuckers" and "sons-of-bitches" and "cock-suckers" and other names they had never even heard of, to say nothing of being called.

Then, Emily went throughout the massive government building starting in her own office and going down to the glass and steel lobby, cursing out everyone who came in her path, including the clerk from the benefits office who had the misfortune, on her way back from lunch, of running into Emily on the elevator.

The next day, she received her walking papers. That same afternoon, with only one small cardboard box under her arm, she walked out of the office she had occupied since college. Her co-workers stood at the bank of office windows overlooking the open parking lot next door and watched her depart.

"Emily Lovejoy has left the building," James Patrick said, half-joking, half-sad. And her former co-workers merely shook their heads and went back to work.

The following morning, she packed up her favorite clothes—most of them in varying shades of crimson and in different degrees of tightness—in her red Datsun and headed down the highway to Mulberry and Betty's house.

"I come to help out, Betty," Emily had announced obligingly as she dropped her luggage and tennis racket and cosmetics bag in one of the extra bedrooms as if she were checking into a luxury resort for a vacation.

Betty smiled appropriately, appreciatively, but underneath she was dreading the work she figured it would take to keep her younger sisters from ripping into each other in the coming weeks. For no one knew better than Betty the baggage that Emily brought with her, baggage that did not come in neat, identifiable suitcases and satchels.

As she stood folding and putting away Emily's clothes in the bedroom that Emily had chosen for her own, the one with the canopied bed and the mattress so high she needed a little square, wooden, antique footstool with a needlepoint pad on top to reach the mattress, Betty imagined conversations she knew would fill her house as soon as Annie Ruth arrived, and continue as a result of her two sisters being under one roof.

"Emily, sugar, you need to let those pants out on the side," Betty was sure Annie Ruth would say some morning soon. "You 'bout to bust out of them."

"Humph, you should talk, Annie Ruth, you getting big as this house."

"Well, at least I have an excuse..."

"Yeah, you pregnant!"

Betty was prepared for trouble bubbling up between her younger sisters at any moment. But it didn't happen. For the most part, the sisters kept their tongues and furies in check, spending most of their time loving and helping each other. And when that didn't seem possible, just staying out of each other's way.

In Betty's mind, Emily was going to be the biggest obstacle to peace. Instead, in between her bouts of quiet jealousy and inner rage, she ended up being a steppingstone, making light banter and looking for ways to distract and spoil her baby sister. And Betty discovered that she loved having her family, her sisters, all back together under one roof, her roof. It felt like old times without the stress and pain of Mudear mixed in. Being able to live together without the suffocating presence of their mother seemed like heaven, mother love without their mother.

Their life began to feel normal, or as normal as the girls could ever imagine.

"Emily, red birds playing in the sprinklers," Betty would say with a smile in her voice. Then, she would stand peacefully and watch her sister run to the nearest window to enjoy the sight of the flocks of cardinals dance and splash in the undulating water. Cardinals were Emily's favorite birds because she felt an affinity with their bright vermillion color. All her life she had been drawn to the color red: red dresses, red nail polish, red birds, red sunsets, red Christmas cards. And others, even animals, sensing the red in her, seemed to be attracted to her for that very reason. Even though hummingbirds made her sneeze, the creatures never failed to zip and buzz around her whenever she had played or strayed outside in the warm weather. And like so much in their family, Mudear's family, the Lovejoys had accepted as normal the vision of Emily standing sneezing as ruby-throated hummingbirds nuzzled her like a buddleia bush.

Despite the momentary unease Betty felt from the strange incidents of misplaced and moved objects, she began to look at the occurrences in her house in the same way she did Emily's hummingbirds. And over the late winter and early spring months, all three girls settled into an easy, unquestioning routine. After sleeping late in the morning until nearly eight o'clock, Betty left the house peaceful for Annie Ruth and Emily to sit and read, to plan the meals that Emily and Betty would cook later in the week, to try out new makeup, and model the flattering maternity clothes on Annie Ruth that her big sister ordered from Pea in the Pod.

Slipping into the house in the middle of the day for a quick lunch or rolling in at the end of a long evening, Betty would pause with true contentment in the downstairs hallway listening to the soft music playing, the familiar sound of her sisters' voices laughing, gossiping, and calling to each other from room to room.

"Oh, this is what family peace feels like," she'd say to herself and climb the stairs to join in.

From week to week, with Annie Ruth growing larger and more lush like the garden outside their house, with Emily seeming to settle into a less agitated routine, and Betty letting go of some of her professional duties and head-of-the-household, big-sister worries to enjoy her new-found family, they moved around the exquisitely appointed home like women in a modern Jane Austen novel of manners, drinking herbal and green tea poured from the antique silver service, reading elegantly bound books from Betty's wood-paneled library downstairs, writing well-crafted thank you notes on vellum paper to beauty shop customers and Los Angeles TV fans for the baby gifts that poured into the house.

Just writing the thank you notes became a daily job in itself. In the days before the birth, all three sisters were amazed at the stream of baby gifts that arrived at Betty's house, some from folks whom they had not heard from in decades, including friends of the family who had not even shown up at their mother's funeral. Folks who had not sent so much as a fifty-cent boxed condolence card, who had not even thought to bring pies or hams or cases of Cokes to be piled up in the kitchen and on the back porch for the hordes of mourners who never showed up after Mudear's funeral, suddenly acted as if they expected Annie Ruth's baby to call them "Auntie" and "Unc'."

It was as if the town had been waiting for an opportunity to welcome the Lovejoy girls into proper, sane society.

It was as if the town had taken out a full-page ad in *The Mulberry Times:* **"Your crazy ma Esther Lovejoy is good and dead. A new baby is on the way. Why don't you girls come on and join the regular world?"**

The people of Mulberry seemed to have no idea that the Lovejoy sisters—with Mudear out of the picture and a new baby girl about to take her place as the center of their universe—were as satisfied as they could be in their own little world, happily free of Mulberry and its gossip and judgment.

On Sundays in the weeks they waited for the baby to come, Betty's only day of relative rest, they would all gather in the kitchen and make a dinner fit for three queens and a princess in waiting.

Annie Ruth, still the baby, wasn't trusted with anything more advanced than chopping duties. She did the chopping by hand even though Betty seemed to have every appliance ever invented for the gourmet cook—a Cuisinart, a Poppeil chopper, an Ultimate Chopper, a wand blender, a Waring blender, an electric pepper mill, a spice grinder.

"Look at that girl chop those onions," Betty would say as she always had since her baby sister was old enough to hold a big butcher knife safely.

Then, Emily would look up from some more complicated culinary task and chime in, "Un-huh, can't nobody chop as good and fine as Annie Ruth."

And Annie Ruth would wiggle her shoulders, blush and just beam. Even after she got old enough to realize that they were merely humoring her to keep her from trying any of the other more complicated, satisfying tasks like making the gravy or mixing the potato salad or baking a pound cake, she pretended to fall for their false flattery. She knew her talents didn't lie there in the kitchen. Shoot, Mudear had told her where their skills rested over and over through her teen years and on into adulthood.

"Now, look at Betty over there," Mudear had intoned for years from her La-Z-Boy throne in the rec room in the house in Sherwood Forest. "She didn't never get no real college or higher schooling or anything like you other girls," Mudear would continue, ignoring Betty's continuing study of cosmetology. "But she know she can whip a meal together with a little bit a' nothing.

"Always could. That's why I always let her cook."

"Let her?" all the girls would mouth to each other but never voice.

"Now, Emily, she a fair cook," Mudear would continue. "But Annie Ruth, yeah, you just keep on studying your books 'cause your cooking ain't gon' never get you nowhere."

Without Mudear's dire pronouncements, kitchen detail for the Lovejoy girls had become a pure joy.

With chicken frying in the big, black, cast iron skillet or a juicy pork roast turning on the rotisserie or salmon sizzling on the indoor grill, Betty would wander happily from counter to counter in her own spacious sunny kitchen, looking over the shoulders of her sisters like a benevolent head chef.

"Not too fine, Annie Ruth. Now, watch that sharp knife. Don't you cut yourself. Em-Em, put those things in the dishwasher. You gon' ruin your pretty hands in all that harsh, hot, soapy water. And use an oven mitt, not a wet dish towel. I won't have either one of you burned or cut in my house. I won't have it."

Betty shuddered at the very idea. If anything ever happened to one of her sisters, she didn't know how she would survive it. They were all she had.

That is until their baby girl was born. Even before she was born, the little baby girl brought about a sea change in their household and routine. Despite the occasional bump or creak in the night, the sporadic missing item, the television in the study turning on by itself once or twice, peace seemed to settle on the house like a benediction. Emily would catch Betty standing at the kitchen window some mornings sipping a cup of coffee and gazing out at the early dappled sunlight playing on the luxuriant sweep of the back lawn and not even be able to articulate the new-found peace that nature and her surroundings seemed to give her.

No one even protested when Betty brought some early spring roses from her own new bushes into the house and placed them in a tall crystal vase on the kitchen counter the way Mudear sometimes had. Still, one or the other of the girls could not stop herself from saying, "Give me my roses while I'm still alive," whenever Betty brought the blossoms in the kitchen.

Mudear had always quoted some sweet person in her past—perhaps her mother or an old maiden aunt, the girls didn't know who—who had urged her loved ones to "gi' me my roses while I'm still 'live." But then, Mudear claimed she never was offered any roses at all during her whole life. And at her funeral, all three Lovejoy girls, as well as most of the town's gossips, noticed that she didn't get many roses in her death either.

Even though bits of their mother seemed to keep seeping in the house and into their lives, throughout the spring, they continued to feel a measure of safety, as if they were truly free of the dead woman who could not touch them any longer. None of them imagined life could get any better for them.

Then, Annie Ruth brought their new baby into the house.

CHAPTER 18

wow, now this is different! and cold, too. i'm used to it being warm and wet. but out here, it's dry and cold. is this what air is? i don't know if i'm gonna like this.

ummm, everything looks different, too. and so much room. now, a girl can really stretch. i am a girl, right? yep, i'm a girl! i really didn't even have to look. i just feel like a girl.

i seem to know so much and nothing at all at the same time. now, how do i know what air is if i never breathed it? and how do i know what cold is if i never felt it?

but sure as i'm born, i just know. heh, heh, just like i know that that's my mama there.

she looks a little wrung out, but she sure is pretty. i like her hair, i hope mine is like that. hey, do i have any hair?

too bad they don't have more mirrors around this place that i can reach. i can't see myself. man! and i think i'm cute, too.

shoot, this is definitely going to be a challenging world if they don't get some baby-sized mirrors up in here.

CHAPTER **19**

Humph, they think they so smart, them girls, quoting me whenever the mood suits them. Oh, yeah, they don't want to have nothing to do with me most days, but when it suit them to remember some golden nugget I let fall around them when they was growing up, they roll it out for their convenient.

Well, I'm glad they do it and it serve 'em right. 'Cause whether they know it or not, and I'll bet everything I got, which ain't much, that they don't have a clue that each and every time they mention my name I get a little bit stronger.

Keep talkin', daughters. Keep talkin'.

They can make fun if they want to, but I got all the roses I ever needed in my own garden. I ain't never needed nobody to give me *nothing. Especially not no flowers!*

Hell, if I did I sho' would'a been sadly disappointed.

Um, it's nice back here in Betty's yard by this fish pond that I had her get that man to dig for her in the garden behind her house. 'Course, she didn't know I got her to do it, but I did all the same.

When I was live, this is just the time of night when I'd be coming out into my garden out in back of the house in Sherwood Forest. Oh, Lord, how I loved it back there in my garden at night. That's the only time I gardened. At night. Couldn't stand all that sweating in the heat of the summer day. And didn't care much more about the sun in the cold a' winter.

But at night. That's when I really blossomed. Just like a moonflower.

You ever seen one of those big white moonflower blossoms unfurl? Ain't many people actually seen a moonflower open up. 'Cause most folks ain't privileged like me to have the time to pull up a wooden lawn chair and sit and watch for hours as the flowers on that pretty vine open up bit by bit.

Most regular ordinary everyday folks go to sleep when the flower is still a tight bud. And when they wake up the next morning, the best part of the whole thing is already over 'cause that big old, pretty, trumpet blossom is already wide open and nearly spent.

But now, I rarely even ever go out there to that garden in Sherwood Forest. Don't care to. Now, I like to stay here in Betty's yard. It's coming along right well, too. And Betty got the nerve to think she the one who planned and growed this garden. Ha!

She oughta' know better than that. Ha! She ain't never growed nothing in her life but hair.

But Annie Ruth, humph, now she 'un growed something right special.

Now, me, I don't care much for reading. Never did. My girls, they was always having their noses stuck in some book or other. But me,

I always just as soon look at something on the television as read. But somewhere in the last year or so—I think it was the last year. Time don't mean nothing to me no more—I read about a mother who carried a baby for her own daughter. Carried, gave birth to it and everything.

Lord, what science ain't come up with!

But right when I read that news story, I immediately thought about Annie Ruth and that baby she was carrying.

'Cause ever since I knew 'bout Annie Ruth messing up and getting pregnant, I've felt like that baby was more mine than it was hers. And she was only carrying it for me.

Um um um. You know, the Lord always provides a ram in the bush.

CHAPTER 20

nnie Ruth had no idea how long she had sat with her baby in her arms, rocking in the beautifully carved, antique oak chair Betty had bought for the mocha-colored nursery upstairs in the east wing of her house until she glanced up through the smoky cafe au lait sheers at the bay window and saw that darkness had nearly fallen over Pleasant Hill and Mulberry.

She was quietly giddy from the pleasure that silently and steadily rocking and nursing her child gave her. Betty had made sure that there was no phone connected in the nursery and except for the soft tones of lullabies playing all over the house, the room was as peaceful and quiet as a cathedral. Annie Ruth didn't even have the ring from her cell phone to interrupt her tranquility. Because she wanted to cut ties with all things California, all things having to do with her life before her pregnancy had begun to show, she had purposefully not brought her cell phone along with her when she had traveled from L.A. to Mulberry. She figured the tiny phone playing the chorus to the O'Jays' "Brick House" each time a call came in was still right where she had left it months before: on the lush, lavender down quilt on the bed in her beach house overlooking Highway One and the Pacific Ocean beyond.

No matter how many times she glanced down and kissed the top of her baby girl's tiny sweet-smelling head, she still could not wrap her mind around the concept of herself as a "mother." The word was not one that she and her sisters bandied about the way other women their age seemed to do.

"Uh, girl, I'm so sleepy. I stayed up talking to my mother on the phone 'til three o'clock this morning."

"Mama and I hit the malls this weekend and did some damage!"

"My mother is such a life-saver with my kids. I don't know what I'd do without her."

"You better not put off having children too long. Don't you want to be a mother?"

Other than "motherfucker," the word "mother" was hardly even in the Lovejoy girls' lexicon.

Annie Ruth had spent too much of her life making sure that the words that described her were: "sexy" "seductive," "stacked," "fine," "intriguing," "intelligent," "adventurous," "appetizing." Certainly not, "motherly," "maternal," "nurturing" or "protective." But amazingly, that's just the way she now felt. Even the realization that it would be quite some time before she could play her favorite all-pink gambit again without smelling like baby spit-up didn't faze her. She didn't think she would even miss the routine of slipping her favorite hot pink flannel sheets on her wide firm mattress, dusting herself with musky pomegranate body powder, putting on her tight, hot pink pjs, piling her hennaed curls on top of her head secured by a cherry-colored Scrunchie with a sequined fuchsia heart attached, rubbing her face lightly with a soft towel to smear her makeup slightly, then feigning surprise when her latest lover arrived at her door expecting to go out.

With only two days of motherhood under her belt—"Oh, I'll be able to wear belts again!" she muttered, a bit giddy at the thought—she knew for certain that she would gladly claw through barbed wire for this child—her baby. She also knew for a fact that her own mother never would have done the same for her. As far as Annie Ruth was concerned, Mudear was the barbed wire.

At the thought of Mudear, Annie Ruth could feel the muscles in her face tighten into an unattractive frown across her forehead, between her eyes and around her mouth, which she quickly tried to erase with a light brush of her fingertips.

"Ooo, don't be frowning like your mother, sweetheart," she said softly to her baby, then laughed at the word "mother."

"Frowny faces make frowny wrinkles, sugar. Your Mama'll be needing a couple shots of Botox if she keep that up."

Annie Ruth laughed again when the baby suddenly seemed to focus right on her and bob her little head as if in understanding.

She cut her laughter short, however, as a familiar scent wafted into the room from the yard. The bouquet floated up through the French doors leading out to a narrow balcony Betty had added to the house along with a new bathroom for Annie Ruth before she had arrived. Betty had envisioned her baby sister sitting out on that balcony rocking her own baby girl as mother and daughter looked out over Mulberry and the Ocawatchee River beyond the bottom of Pleasant Hill and envisioned a future of joy and unlimited possibilities. The mental picture had given Betty such pleasure that she stored it in her head along with other imaginary family snapshots from the past:

She and her sisters making mud pies in the side yard of the house in East Mulberry with a smiling, doting Mudear looking on. Shopping for a graduation dress downtown with Mudear. The entire family driving Annie Ruth off to college in Atlanta in the family car. They were all scenes that other families took for granted, but ones that had never happened in the Lovejoy household, only in Betty's dreams. In fact, all the girls had them, whether they admitted it or not.

It took Annie Ruth a moment to place the delightful fragrance. Then, it came to her.

"Mudear's tea olives!" she said and was startled to hear a tinge of fear mixed in with the amazement in her voice. "I can't believe Betty had the nerve to put Mudear's favorite plants in her own back yard." Although it had been a chore, in the two days since her own birthing pains began, Annie Ruth had labored not to think about her mother. She figured she and her sisters had gone through enough pain just living with the kind of mother who put her garden before her daughters, her creature comforts before her family, who remained in the house in body but left it completely in spirit, to let the selfish woman intrude on her first maternal moments. Annie Ruth had tried, but she had to admit she hadn't been totally successful in banishing Mudear from her mind for a mere forty-eight hours. But then, Mudear was never far from any of their thoughts.

The girls had spent their entire lives discussing and dissecting Mudear and found as women in their thirties and forties that lifetime habits are not easily broken.

As Annie Ruth swayed back and forth, she wondered if her Mudear had ever sat serenely rocking any of her three girls the way she was rocking her sweet baby. She knew Mudear had breast-fed Betty, her eldest, but had not shared that mother's milk with her or Emily. Whenever the three of them talked about that, Emily almost cried for herself and her sister, but Annie Ruth always said, "Good! She could keep her old sour milk. Probably would have turned my stomach, anyway."

I don't know why anybody was so surprised Mudear stopped cooking for us when we were little, Annie Ruth thought. Shoot, she didn't even want to feed us when her titties were supplying the milk for free, and she didn't even have to warm it up.

Annie Ruth had spent so much of her life thinking of Mudear as some kind of monster, "The Anti-Mother," that she couldn't for the life of her imagine Mudear being gentle and kind and maternal toward anyone, least of all her daughters, even as she had nursed one of them.

Sure, the strange selfish woman had granted her daughters some motherly endowments. But what maternal gifts they were. Where the girls imagined most mothers imparting words of wisdom to smooth their daughter's passage into womanhood—"Don't accept rides with strangers." "Don't kiss on the first date." "Don't drink anything at a party that you didn't mix." "Stay in school."—the Lovejoy girls knew their mother's insights were merely tools to control them whether they were up under her at home where she reigned, or out in the world where she sent them.

Mudear's "gifts" of wisdom still rang in her daughters' heads like the litany of the Eucharist in the minds of children who had attended parochial schools and been forced to attend daily Mass:

- Lovejoy women love pretty clothes.
- Lovejoy women don't wear no mammy-made clothes.
- Lovejoy women are strong as mules.
- But Lovejoy women go to nothing when they get a cold.
- Lovejoy women don't take no tea for the fever. (Mudear was kind enough to explain that one to her puzzled daughters. "It means you don't take no shit, is what it means. You so bad you won't even take a soothing tea to break your fever.")
- Lovejoy women can cook.
- Lovejoy women *keep* dirty noses.

- Lovejoy women can arrange *weeds.*
- Lovejoy women don't get no tapes.
- Lovejoy women don't wear no anklets.
- Lovejoy women have shoulders like men.
- Lovejoy women are terrible liars.
- Lovejoy women don't wear no cheap shoes.
- Lovejoy women don't wear no Hoyt's cologne.
- Lovejoy women don't wear no costume jewelry.

Mudear had made these pronouncements of "The Lovejoy Women" mythology for decades, from different residences, different beds, different kitchen chairs, different sofas and chaise lounges. She had repeated them so often that the girls took up the litany and completed each item without thinking as they cleaned her house and washed her clothes and prepared the meals and paid the bills: all the chores that kept the Lovejoy household running. All the chores that Mudear had unceremoniously dropped beginning one cold night in the family's first house over in East Mulberry when the girls were sick.

Yet on this warm spring evening with her sweet baby girl in her arms, Annie Ruth couldn't think of one single thing that Mudear had ever said about Lovejoy women that actually came in handy.

"I wish she had just left!" she said angrily and immediately regretted the venom she tasted in every word. "I will not let that old dead woman steal my joy today," she recanted, unwittingly mouthing Mudear's favorite dictum.

Mudear had always bragged to her girls that she enjoyed her life right in the moment, "'Cause when you dead you done..." But no matter how hard Annie Ruth and her sisters tried, their relationship with their mother was never done.

Still, Annie Ruth tried once more. She felt she owed her own child that much of an effort: to let the dead stay dead. Yet the scent of the tea olive plants continued somehow to haunt her. "And besides, aren't those tea olives supposed to be blooming in the wintertime?" she muttered to herself, angry at the plants for intruding on her mother-daughter time. "It's almost summer."

"Come on, sweet baby," she said to the child at her breast as she went back to rocking. "We're not gonna think about that old crazy woman, and we gon' 'Let the good times roll.'"

All through Annie Ruth's first full day back home, Betty and Emily and even Mrs. Andrews for a while had popped into the nursery every few minutes to make sure that Annie Ruth didn't need some immediate help with feeding and general care of the infant.

"Daughter," she had asked as she gently rocked the tiny sweet bundle in her arms, "will these folks ever leave us alone?"

At first, Annie Ruth had tried being pleasant, then a bit sterner and then, even firmer in her rejection of the unnecessary help. Finally, when none of those maneuvers worked, she had resorted to glaring nastily in the direction of the door as soon as she spied a crack and an eye there.

At last, it worked. The aperture in the door closed without her saying a word, and the prying eye disappeared and didn't reappear for hours.

She took advantage of the private time by sitting and staring into her baby girl's sweet face. Annie Ruth did that for a long time because she was so taken with the wonder of her own child's existence, but also because she didn't have the answer to the question the infant seemed to be asking her.

"What kind of mama are you gonna be?"

It was the query she had dreaded since she was a little girl. Long before she even got her period, she was afraid of that question.

What kind of mama are you gonna be?

For all of her adult years, she felt some measure of safety from that question. Each time she had popped her birth control pill—in her college dormitory room, in her first garden apartment, in a remote news truck as she covered a story as the first black reporter on a Texas television station, as the morning show host in D.C., on the set of the California station where she anchored the news—she would silently tell herself, if I have anything to do with it, Annie Ruth, you'll never be *any* kind'a mama.

But then, as her Mudear would say, she went and "broke a leg."

That year before, she couldn't believe it when she realized that she, who at thirty-four or thirty-five—even she wasn't completely sure of her exact age anymore—was as regular as Swiss clockwork, hadn't had a period in six weeks.

As a matter of course, the Lovejoy girls took their contraception duties very seriously. In more than two decades of sexual activity, which amounted to a whole lot of fucking, out of the three of them, only Emily had slipped up once and become pregnant in her twenties. So, barely two months before her mother died, Annie Ruth could hardly believe that her period was late. When she talked to her sisters on the phone, she didn't say a word to them about her worry, but she spent a couple of days running to the bathroom to check her panties. Then, when she finally accepted that there was not even the barest hint of a pink trail on the panty shields she insisted on wearing, she had to drive miles outside of the Los Angeles area, where the air waves from her station didn't reach, to purchase a home pregnancy test, all the while wishing she had cultivated at least one close friendship with one person she could have trusted with the errand. She didn't even know which pregnancy test to ask for. So, she bought all three brands on the shelf and used them all when she returned home to her small chic beach house in Malibu.

At first, Annie Ruth would not believe the positive results of any of them. She kept thinking, This blue strip is going to turn pink any moment now. Any moment now. Any moment now.

It didn't turn. And the other four tests that she went to another pharmacy in the next county to purchase didn't turn negative either. Even when she continued to make deals with God.

"Okay, now, Lord, I know I might fuck around a bit and lie about my age and just about everything else when it suits me, and that I almost hate my mother, but if You just get me out of this one scrape, I promise I won't..."

Unfortunately, she couldn't decide what she was willing to give up and really mean it. The only thing she ever gave up that she truly loved was marzipan candies one Lenten season when she was pretending to be Catholic for a cute Italian guy who led her to believe that his devout Neapolitan mother didn't care about her race, only her religion.

"My goodness, Annie Ruth," Emily had teased her when she told them about the Catholic ruse during one of their weekly sisters conference calls. "You will do anything for a good fuck."

Betty had been ready to jump into the conversation to douse water on the impending flare-up of a fight. Instead, Annie Ruth simply laughed at her sister's accusation and said, "Andddd, that's a bad thing? This from a woman who wears shorts primarily so she'll have an easier time just pulling the crotch to the side for a quick fuck."

Then, they both laughed.

Annie Ruth finally had to accept the results of the home pregnancy tests when she broke down and went to her own OB/GYN for a real test.

"Yes, Ms. Lovejoy, you are pregnant," her doctor informed her over the phone. "Is that a good thing?"

Annie Ruth was about to snap, "Hell, no, it's not a good thing, Martha Stewart." But then she thought about it and surprised her doctor and herself by responding, "Um, you know what? I think it is."

After that, there was never any doubt in her mind that she was going to have this baby. She just had no idea which one of her men friends was the daddy.

Yet even before she started to show good, she began looking for signs of strangeness that might pop up in genes from her side of the family: suicidal thoughts, obsessive behavior, pre-partum depression, manic selfishness, unusual sleeping habits.

Before she even told her sisters she was pregnant, she began obsessing about the white Mulberry mother murderer she had heard grown folks talk about when she was little, a mother who fed her children arsenic in their grits, then sat there and watched them slowly die.

Right up to the delivery, she had nightmares about the birth of her own child. And although her gynecologist in Los Angeles and Dr. Hamlin in Mulberry both assured her that the night terrors were normal occurrences, with some women dreaming that they had given birth to fish and kitchen appliances and strange mythical creatures, Annie Ruth's dreams left her fearful and expectant.

One night when she had fallen asleep downstairs where Emily had left one of her TBN preacher shows on the television, she had a nightmare straight out of the New Testament book of Revelation: the Four Horsemen of the Apocalypse and a fire-breathing dragon bearing down on her as she ran down a bloody road toward a desert with her newborn child clutched in her arms.

With daylight, she dismissed the dreams, but she could not shrug off the fear because the one huge question remained hovering over all that she thought: What if I'm a mother like Mudear?

Yet for a while, sitting and rocking in her big sister's house, nursing her perfect child and kissing her tiny fingers made Annie Ruth forget her fears as she clung to the newborn. She didn't think she would ever be able to leave her child's presence, but at the end of her first full day back home when she had successfully breast fed and had lain the baby down for the night, she missed her sisters' company and surprised them by making her way down the stairs to join them in the back sun room.

"Oh, look who's stirring," Betty said, delighted to see her sister standing at the entryway with a tired smile playing around her mouth.

"Ya'll talkin' 'bout me?" Annie Ruth asked gaily as both her sisters rose to help her to a comfortable chair.

"My ears were burning so I thought I'd come down here and investigate," she said playfully as she sank slowly onto the plump cushion in the other rocking chair Betty had brought for her and set up in the cheery glass enclosed room.

"What ya'll talking 'bout?" she asked when she got settled. Silence filled the comfortable room.

"Oh, I guess ya'll really were talking about me," Annie Ruth said with a raised arched eyebrow.

Emily and Betty exchanged sisterly glances, and Betty shrugged and went back to her knitting.

"Well, not really you," she said as she examined the tiny, lime green, nearly finished baby blanket. "We were talking about our new baby."

Emily jumped in with, "Yeah. We were talking about her name."

"Her name?" Annie Ruth asked innocently and smiled.

"Un-huh," Emily said, trying to sound as innocent as Annie Ruth. Then, she rushed on. "We noticed you haven't been that interested in talking 'bout names for our new baby girl, so, we left it alone. But now that she's home and all...."

Emily swallowed and paused again. She looked toward Betty, but Betty wouldn't look up and just kept knitting.

So, Emily took a deep breath and blustered on through. "And I was just saying why not name her after Mudear."

The suggestion landed in the room like a brick through the solarium's glass ceiling.

"Emily, have you finally lost your ever-loving mind for real?" Annie Ruth leaned forward and screamed. She was too through with her sister. And she was serious about doubting her sanity... again.

"Well, I know ya'll don't ever really listen to any of my ideas, but what is so wrong with naming our new baby girl after her grandmother?" Emily's voice was rising higher and higher the way it always did when she felt she had to defend herself.

"How about the fact that that selfish-assed crazy woman ruined our childhoods and tried to ruin our whole lives, for starters?" Annie Ruth shot back.

Betty continued concentrating on her knitting and tried not to be pulled into the fray.

"Knit five, purl three," she repeated again and again under her breath, trying not to drop a stitch. She really did want to have the baby blanket finished before the baby was walking and talking. But even more, she wanted to avoid a Lovejoy sisters' fight.

"How about the fact that Mudear was a crazy recluse who near about made us as crazy as she was?" Annie Ruth wanted to jump up from her seat and really get in Emily's face, but she was still too sore for any sudden movements. "How about the fact that ain't none of us ever had a good normal relationship with a man 'cause of her sick example? Or have we all forgotten about Poppa?"

"Knit three, slip one, purl four," Betty murmured to herself.

For weeks before the baby's birth, things had been going so smoothly in their household. The fights she had imagined had never fully materialized among the three women. But ever since the birth of the baby, Betty could see signs of wear and tear at the corners of their familial happiness.

Emily sniffed her sister's angry response away and that really made Annie Ruth furious.

"And for another thing, how about the fact that I wouldn't give a dog Mudear's name, let alone my baby girl! Shoot, I'd just as soon give my child a snake to play with as I would anything connected with that mean, evil woman."

"Well, she wasn't no snake, Annie Ruth," Emily said quietly. Then, she added with a voice a tad stronger, "After all, she was our mother."

"Emily, you been heading down that crazy road to Nutsville for a while now and I, for one," here Annie Ruth paused to cut her eyes at Betty who sat primly in her dotted swiss blouse and light blue pencil skirt that flared a bit at the hem and continued to focus on the soft green yarn on her knitting needles. "Knit one, purl three," she said softly to herself. She was still determined not to take part in what she knew was going to end in bitter tears and even harsher words. Betty could feel Annie Ruth, still weary from the long hard birth, was growing testier and testier with each comment Emily made.

"I, for one, refuse to let you do it," Annie Ruth continued. "For months now you been trying to resurrect Mudear as some kind of martyred saint who wasn't so bad. 'Mudear did teach us how to take care of our skin.' 'Mudear sure did have a way with flowers.' 'Mudear sure didn't care what folks thought about her.'

"Now, you tryna' hang that bitch's name on my child. It ain't gonna happen, you hear me, it ain't gonna happen."

"I'm not trying to hang anything anywhere," Emily retorted.

"Well, I tell you what, why don't you have your own child and name her after Mudear." As soon as she had spoken, Annie Ruth so regretted the comment that she could have bit her tongue right out of her mouth. But it was too late.

The cruel scornful words hung in the air a second like a nasty beer belch, then hit their mark and brought sharp quick tears to Emily's eyes and an incredulous little "o" to her lips. Annie Ruth didn't even have to look at Betty to see the horrified look she was shooting in her direction.

She could hear her sister's condemnation in the suddenly silent knitting needles.

When Annie Ruth looked over at Emily, all she could see on her fully made-up face was her sister's history with babies. She saw the decision the three of them had made two decades before when Annie Ruth started her period never to have children. She saw them all join their hands and take a solemn vow to be the only family they would ever need.

"I'll never be a mama." "Me neither." "Me neither."

She saw Betty driving her and Emily to her own gynecologist to get birth control pills when they were still in high school. She saw the clinic where she had accompanied Emily to get her abortion. She saw the look on the face of Ron, Emily's ex-husband, when he returned from work and found the two of them sitting there in the dark. She saw the words—"I can't stay with you. You flushed my baby down the toilet stool."—Ron had scrawled on a sheet of Emily's lavender stationery and left on their double bed when he walked out on her. She saw the string of failed relationships Emily had had since her divorce.

Instantly contrite, she leaned over in her rocking chair and reached for Emily's hand. But Emily snatched it out of her sister's reach, rose and hurried to the nearest panel of windows to look out on Betty's flourishing garden and weep.

In the lights from the garden and grounds, Betty and Annie Ruth could see the tremble in Emily's broad shoulders and both recalled how Mudear had casually intoned, "Lovejoy women got shoulders like men," as she had watched her teen-aged girls put on dainty strapless white pique dresses for some summer dance.

Caught between shame and defensiveness, Annie Ruth said, "Well, Emily, I thought you would have understood why I wouldn't name my child Esther."

Emily's back remained like quivering stone.

"I thought you would have been pleased that I wanted to name my little girl after you and Betty instead."

Annie Ruth saw her sister's shoulders become still and heard her weeping cease.

The room became quiet as a graveyard.

Emily couldn't seem to bring up a word in reply. Betty, still holding the knitting needles suspended at chest level, spoke first.

"After us?" she asked softly.

"Un-huh," Annie Ruth said shyly. She felt tears in her throat now.

Emily didn't turn from the window, but her tiny voice filled the room. "For real?"

"Un-huh," Annie Ruth said a little stronger, encouraged by Emily's voice. "I decided to name her 'MaeJean' for you and Betty. Your middle names. I know we all hate our names, but I thought you might like 'em better on our baby girl. Other than me, you two are all the family my baby's got."

None of the women in the room even thought about Poppa. They hadn't truly thought of him as family since they were girls.

Emily turned around and stood at the window with the outside lights forming a halo around her. "Mae...Mae Jean?" she asked with a tiny stutter.

Annie Ruth nodded. "One word: MaeJean," she explained.

Betty and Emily looked at each other, then, smiled tenuously.

"MaeJean?" they asked again, this time in unison.

Annie Ruth, feeling her earlier cold words warm and begin to melt in affection and gratitude, tilted her head back, smiled and nodded again.

"Her real given name?" Emily asked, almost afraid to believe it.

"It's what I put on the birth certificate, Em-Em, before I left the hospital," Annie Ruth said gently with a wide grin. "MaeJean Lovejoy. You gotta name 'em before they let you take 'em home."

Both women looked at each other for a moment. Betty let the knitting needles fall to the floor with a soft metallic clatter.

Emily brought her right hand up to her chest and clutched the plunging neckline of the red and white striped cotton sweater she was wearing with tight embossed jeans. Then, together, they swooped down on Annie Ruth with squeals and laughter and grabbed her up in a flurry of hugs, kisses, stripes, and swiss dots. Then, remembering their little namesake asleep upstairs in her wicker bassinet, they broke from their sisterly embrace so suddenly they nearly left Annie Ruth in mid-air and rushed for the stairs.

Laughing and calling, "MaeJean! MaeJean!" the two women fairly flew up the curved staircase in bare feet, trying to outrun each other to reach their niece first, and burst into the baby's room.

The commotion of love woke the child from a sound sleep and sent her into a crying squall.

Annie Ruth sat rocking contentedly downstairs and listened over the baby monitor on the glass-topped table at her elbow to the raucous coos and whispers of love her sisters were pouring all over her crying baby girl.

"MaeJean, MaeJean, why don't you be true? MaeJean."

"MaeJean, MaeJean, did you know that was your name? Baby girl, you named for us!"

"Oh, MaeJean! MaeJean! I could just call that name forever."

"Oh, Emily, wait 'til they hear 'bout this out at the shops."

Annie Ruth chuckled and shook her head at her sisters' joy. But her contentment instantly vanished as she caught sight of something out of the corner of her eye outside one of the sun room windows.

"Is that a cat climbing up that trellis?" she asked herself incredulously and realized suddenly that she was shivering and having trouble breathing.

omigod! these must be my aunties! aunt betty and aunt em-em. ooo-wee, they so loud!

they sure are some wild women! i think i like that!

oh, kisses, kisses, kisses. oh, i do believe i'm gonna like this world.

i know i like my name. maejean. oo, that sound like me. but i bet before it's over my mama's gon' be telling people, "you pronounce it 'may-jon' with the accent on 'jon.'" Heh-heh. she so funny! and she loves herself some me, huh?

hey, I know who my mama and my aunties are, but who is that old lady over there floating outside the window?

CHAPTER 22

"MaeJean?"

What kinda name is that for a child? Won't nobody never be able to spell it. "MaeJean." Ooo, it sound so country! And what? She ain't got no middle name? Shoot, "Esther" is such a better name. But of course, they don't want none a' that. Oh, them heifers got ugly ways! And now that Annie Ruth has gone and named that child after her two crazy sisters, I won't be able to tell none 'a them nothing no more.

Good thing I wasn't countin' on them to help carry out my plan.

Don't need 'em! Never did, really. For all the complaining and carping they did as girls around the house as they did their few little chores, it wasn't hardly worth it to me to have trained 'em to do 'em. Oh, well, that ain't the only time I wasted in the early part of my life, the part before I truly started living.

Oh, but I'm living now, dead as I am, I'm truly living. But then again, I been doing that for a number a' years since I decided to be a woman in my own shoes and take back my life. Lots a' women with a husband and children ain't as brave as I was in standing up and being free, insisting on being free, the way I did.

Oh, they can talk and yell 'bout their feminish and womanish selves now all they want, but they still ain't half as free as me! None of them, black or white. I seen them on television talking, on talk shows and moving pictures, real and play women, talking 'bout how they wish they had their lives back, how they wish they had made other choices, how they wish they hadn't gi' their whole lives over to some man or some house or some job or some ungrateful ugly-acting child.

Well, I say, wish in one hand, shit in the other and see which one fill up quicker.

But I gotta admit that it's right funny. I didn't even have to wish for things to start going my way with these girls a' mine. Ha! A cat, a cat of all things. Heh-heh, it's like a stroke 'a genius really. A cat! Ain't nothing in the world Annie Ruth more afraid of than cats. And rightfully so.

When she was just a baby, a stray cat sneaked into our old raggedy house over on Amber Street in East Mulberry and nearly slit her throat right there in that rickety baby crib that was already old and used when Betty first laid up in it.

You know what they say about cats, sneaky things, and how they'll suck the breath right out a' a newborn baby when they can smell milk in the baby's mouth. Well, that's just what that cat was doing to Annie Ruth, at least that's what I think. I walked into that room with her bottle in my hand – I couldn't breast feed Annie Ruth to save my life. She just wouldn't take the tit, and I got tired of her biting me and still not getting no milk and crying all night and day. She was the only one of my girls who I couldn't breast feed at all. I had a little trouble with Emily, too, but she finally took the tit a few times before my milk turned completely sour, and I had to resort to Carnation milk. I didn't never tell her nothing 'bout all that. But I give Annie Ruth a bottle almost right from the start. And when I saw that sneaky cat crawling over the white linens on that baby mattress — I could see the blood stain around the neck of Annie Ruth's little gown even from where I was standing at the door. You know, back then we bleached everything white to a farethewell — I screamed and dropped the bottle to the floor, and it broke and splattered all over the room. And the funniest thing, that cat didn't skedaddle out of there the way I thought he would. That bold creature just turned and looked me right in my eye with those old green cat eyes of his.

We both stood there for a while staring each other down. Oh, but that cat didn't know who he was dealin' with. He couldn't stare me down, not even back then. I might not 'a already claimed my life the way I did a few years later from old Ernest, but I sho' as hell wasn't gon' to give up my home to some filthy alley cat.

I stormed over to the baby bed, grabbed that cat and rung its neck like it was a chicken. And yet and still, them girls like to say I ain't never done nothing for 'em. Just goes to show you, people don't appreciate you no matter what you do for 'em. Shoot, Annie Ruth still got that little scar on her throat where that cat nicked her. That cat's nail only missed a artery by this much.

So, it was right funny when I looked up and I had turned into a cat. Who knew I'd be able to turn myself into anything else other than Esther Lovejoy? I was standing out in the garden listening to them girls talking inside and just thinking 'bout going up that trellis outside Betty's house to get up to the second floor to look in on my new grandbaby and all of a sudden, I was a cat!

A cat! Climbing up that trellis. Hah!

Them girls, with all their book learning and college degrees and business awards, don't know the half of it. They don't know nothing.

Shoot, even I don't know the half of it. I don't even know how it happened. But it seemed that after I died and as time went on on the earth, I just got stronger and stronger. Whether it was moving from one part of town to another with just a thought or passing back into time or, as it turned out, changing myself into a cat.

At first, after I passed up there in the Mulberry Hospital, why they call it the "Medical Center" like some television drama or something I will never understand, I was just happy to still be around. Then, when I was still laying up there in Parkinson Funeral Home with this ugly-assed navy blue dress on. I still can't forgive them girls for burying me in this navy blue dress when they know how pretty I look in pastels. Anyway, at first, it seemed I couldn't feel nothing, not the night chill on my skin, not the warmth of the afternoon sun, couldn't smell nothing, not that foul liquid they pumped into my body, not the cheap flowers they spread on other people's caskets. But as time went on, things changed.

Like I used to tell my girls, Keep living, daughters.

Well, anyway, you know what I mean. . . .

It seemed like I looked up one day before they even had the funeral – a small dignified affair. Surprised me! Anyhow, I looked up, and I was strolling down the paths of my garden out behind that little cracker box house in Sherwood Forest in the darkness of night. The one place I'd rather be at that moment than anywhere in the whole world – in my garden. Then, the next thing you know, I was inside the house listening to the girls sitting on the back porch drinking liquor from my good highball glasses and complaining about me, their own mother.

I never was much of a drinker. Didn't need it. Oh, folks in Mulberry used to say I was a drunk. Folks will talk, won't they? My old friend Mamie used to tell me, when I was still bothering to talk on the phone to people outside my house, she used to tell me what people were saying 'bout me. Said they said I was laying up in that house drunk out my head most days. Ha! Just shows you how little "folks" know. Most days,

I was just sleeping. It was the evenings and nights when I came alive. And I didn't need no liquor to make me do that. A good nine, ten, 'leven hours' sleep and the night air did that for me.

Uh, I love the night air. Heh, heh! Back ten or fifteen years, every time that song "I love the night life, I love to boogie" used to come on the MTV, I'd want to get up out my comfortable chair in the den, throw my head back and shout "Yeah!" 'Cause that's how I felt. Still do. After I made my big change back when the girls was little, I didn't never care much about change. I was pretty much satisfied with myself.

Oh, I know that them girls, and Ernest, too, used to talk about "Mudear's Change" like it was the change a' life or something. But they all knew better than that. It wasn't nothing to do with my body. It had to do with my soul and my decision, a woman's decision, that I wasn't gon' take no more a' Ernest's or anybody else's mess no more.

It sound easy. And to tell the truth, it wasn't that hard. Not after I had truly made up my mind to change my life. I just let things I didn't care about go, then sat back and watched somebody else taking care of 'em. Then, after they call themselves putting me in the cold cold ground, I wasn't in the ground at all. I was just about wherever I wanted to be. Sometimes, that was in my garden again and sometimes, I would be sitting on the edge of my bed back when I was a girl, and I could hear my mother singing to herself in the kitchen. I could her singing:

"When your meal barrel get empty
"The Lord will fill it up.
"When your meal barrel get empty
"The Lord will fill it up.
"Fill it up, fill it up with joy."

I think she made that song up herself. She was such a happy woman. I don't know why, but she was. Just naturally good-spirited, for all the good it got her. My daddy, he was a railroad man who was away a lot, he was more down to earth like me. I wasn't no daddy's girl or nothing, but I sorta' took after him. He was a man who did what he wanted to. I usta think I hated that about him 'cause I missed him lots a' times when he was on the rails working.

Guess I had to live long enough to see that that's the way it is. Some folks seem to always have to suffer a bit when one somebody else decide they gon' be free with their own life.

Oh, well, not a bad trade, if you ask me.

And then, it got even better after I died. It seemed like I didn't have to follow no rules of time or space. I could step into this swirling thing that looked to me like a stack of hundreds of golden loops like bangle bracelets on a woman's arm and I could step out again just about anywhere and any time I wanted to. So, some times—I don't know if it was days or weeks or what—but for some time I'd be able to just think about when I was a child and there I'd be. Just like it was when I was five or six years old. And my old neighborhood in East Mulberry would look the same as it did fifty years ago.

Don't ask me. I don't know how I did it.

Anyway, I stayed there in that place back in the past with my mother and all the folks I grew up with, in that place that wasn't here and wasn't there for what seemed like days and days, a good long time. But actually, when I looked up and I was back in my garden in Sherwood Forest, no more than a second had passed.

Other times, I'd move through time and space like something on "Star Trek: The Next Generation" and arrive back in Mulberry and discover that a few weeks had passed since my death. Didn't seem to be no rhyme or reason to it.

For a while, I'd move back and forth in time anytime it suited me. 'Course, couldn't nobody back there in the old times see me and I wasn't no child like I was then which as far as I'm concerned was a double good thing 'cause I always wanted to be grown and I have always liked to watch people and things when they couldn't watch me back. I guess that's one   reason I loved my cable television so much.

*I could walk through my mother's garden on the side of the little
shotgun house we lived in when I was a child. I swear I could almost
feel the damp soil under my feet, squeezing up between   my toes like I
didn't have on no shoes. Or I could sit in the classroom where I learned
to read or go to my first dance at the old church hall at the bottom of
Pleasant Hill.*

*And then, the next thing I know, the seasons had changed and it
was almost spring and I was moving through another garden at the top
of Pleasant Hill over in town. And lo and behold, it was Betty's.*

*Yeah, Betty who swore on her mother's grave that she wouldn't
never have no flower garden, not for anything in the world. Ha! Now
look a' her! Keep living, daughter! Keep living!*

*All I had to do was float through her big old front and back yards—
they was more like a park than a yard—and think about some beautiful
bush or plant that I loved, like a tea olive or something and I swear,
before I knew it, Betty's gardener, Mr. Something or Other, was driving
his brand-new Ford truck up her driveway with the back loaded with
shiny green healthy tea olive bushes. Shoot, I bet it was Betty's money
paid for most of the payments on that new truck of his.*

*Why, it was like when   I'd just think about a place and there I'd be.
I didn't even have to wish for it. I thought I'd get less and less as time
passed. But instead, I got more and more. More and more strong. More
and more powerful. More and more in charge.*

*And, heh heh, it's a funny thing. It seem like the more them girls
thought they was pushing me outa' their lives, the more I was in it. The
stronger they called <u>themselves</u> getting after putting me in my casket, the
stronger <u>I</u> was really becoming.*

*Every time they mentioned my name, I got stronger. Every time
they repeated some of my wise words, I could just feel the power and the
strength surging through my being, pumping into my blood or whatever*

it is now flowing through my veins. Whoo! I get stronger just thinkin' 'bout it.

Funny, ain't it? Ha! Yeah, keep living!

Back-fired on their asses! Ha! Serve 'em right for tryn'a get rid of their old dead grey-haired mother. Well, actually, I ain't got a grey hair on my head. Betty and her lotions and potions always took care 'a that! And that last dye job seems to be holding up right nicely.

I always told my girls to just "stand on the battlefield" and things would get better. But I had no idea how right I was. Shoot, I was just talking words I had heard my own Mudear say when I was a child and in trouble. Must'a been from a old hymn. My mama was a religious woman. Not like them fake Christian women who claimed to be my friend until I decided to live my own life. But a true Christian-hearted woman. Shoot, she'd give you the house dress off her back if you needed it.

Heh! I don't take after her no kinda way.

But that little one, that MaeJean a' Annie Ruth's - - humm, I still can't believe that that careless Annie Ruth went out and got pregnant and then had the nerve to name that child "MaeJean." Now that lil' one, that "MaeJean," she take after her Mudear. None of my own girls ever did. Oh, they learned a thing or two from me and my life.

They know 'bout how a man will lead you a dog's life if you let him get the upper hand. Emily found that out when she up and married that shell-shocked Negro from Vietcong. Marriage didn't last a good two years. And they know how to take care of themselves first. They know how to moisturize their skin every day and how to wash out their panties every night—I used to always do that, wash out my panties every night. That's 'bout the only thing I did after I made up my mind to be a free woman, a woman in my own shoes.

But them girls, no matter how independent they claim to be, they don't really take after me.

Wasn't none of them born with a veil over their faces like me. And now look at that baby come here with a caul and all.

Heck, they was my own flesh and blood and still they wasn't ever really my girls. Never could count on them to take my side. But that new little one. That MaeJean. Now she gon' be mine. She gon' take after her Mudear. I'm mo see to that. She gon' be mine for real, body and soul. And those girls ain't got nothing to say 'bout it.

CHAPTER 23

A ll through the night after seeing the cat on the trellis and into the next morning as she tossed and turned, throwing off the light soft cotton blanket one minute, reaching for it the next, Annie Ruth was torn between keeping secrets and baring her soul.

That was nothing new for her. That's how she had lived most of her life. Even as a child, she was tempted every month or so to tell a teacher or classmate how strange her mother and household truly were. But she always knew that within her household, that kind of honesty was treachery.

She had no idea what the cat climbing the trellis outside Betty's house meant, but she knew it did not augur well.

Ever since she discovered she was pregnant, she had thought, feared even, that the child she carried, the little girl sleeping soundly upstairs could possibly be the avatar, the incarnation of Mudear. But she had refused to speak it. Even the thought of it was too much to consider. So, she shared her fears with no one, as if keeping silent on the subject protected them all from the fate of a new Mudear.

Her second full day back in Betty's house from the hospital, Annie Ruth awoke bone-weary and bleary-eyed and moving deliberately and gingerly so as not to rip her stitches. She usually swung her legs out of bed when she awakened, but this morning she made do with slowly getting to her feet and stumbling to the bassinet with pink grosgrain ribbon woven through its rattan slats, to make sure she had not dreamed her tiny baby girl.

MaeJean lay there in the bassinet looking like a vision, pretty as she could be, but she was no dream. Annie Ruth could smell the fresh bowel movement from where she was standing. As she leaned over the bassinet, she heard herself crooning, "Well, ya'll, she ain't never said she was no rose." The voice, her voice, took her by surprise.

She stood straight up and wondered where that sweet baby talk had come from. Although the image of a rose immediately invoked Mudear and her love for flowers, Annie Ruth knew her mother was not the source of that or any other endearments. And she didn't think she had ever heard any doting mother or father tease a child with that rose joke.

Only a precious few of her friends back in California had children. Most of the women she knew were intent on keeping their pre-thirties figure, and the men she dated and worked with were too involved with their careers to give much attention to children. And the ones who did have children knew better than to impose any of their offspring on her by bringing them on dates or even talking about them incessantly.

Taking MaeJean in her arms, Annie Ruth cradled her gently, making sure she supported her small head in the crook of her arm. As she carried her to the changing table at the foot of the bed, she continued chuckling and cooing at her child. "Aw, they tryna say she smelling up the place. It ain't nothing but a little sugar water and cake, Mama," she said to the baby as she removed her diaper, wiped her little butt and leaned down to kiss it. "It's just a little boom-boom, huh, MaeJean?"

The infant lolled her head from side to side, stretched and kicked her legs happily.

"This a mama's angel," Annie Ruth sang. "This a mama's baby girl. This a mama's heart string. This a mama's heartbeat. This a mama's lil' shang-a-lang. This a mama's treasure here."

Annie Ruth sounded like a mother. It was an amazement. In all her thirty-four, or was it thirty-five, years, she had never talked sweet baby talk to anyone except some man she was trying to make hard. And she had certainly never heard those endearments whispered to her by Mudear.

She took her baby over to the mirror over the dresser and held her up next to her face. "Let's see how much you look like your mama," she suggested. She gave no thought to MaeJean's daddy and his possible resemblance. She hadn't heard from any of the likely fathers since she had been back in Mulberry. And although Emily had suggested a couple of times under her breath that they would eventually have to "round up the usual suspects," Annie Ruth had no intention of being in touch with any of the men she had left back in California. She didn't even know for certain if she would ever return to her life or her job there. She had taken a few months maternity leave, but Mulberry was feeling so good and comfortable...

"Oh, MaeJean, look! You do look like me. Ooo, but your mama don't look her best this morning." Annie Ruth examined her face in the mirror. "Oh, baby girl, let's see if mama can do something about those circles under her eyes," she said as she lay MaeJean back in her bassinet.

Annie Ruth had hardly gotten a wink of sleep the night before. She didn't know how she was going to survive without her normal nine or ten hours of solid sleep a night. Through every stage of her pregnancy, she had never failed to get a good night's sleep.

For weeks while she was back in California after her Mudear's death, she grew rounder, prettier and more at ease with her changing body and circumstances every day as she sat behind the anchor desk at her television station. Then after the 10 p.m. newscast, she'd get in her little vintage MG, head home, open all the windows to the beach house to the sound of the ocean, get in bed before midnight and sleep undisturbed until 9 or 10 the next morning.

In between glancing around for stray cats on the plane ride cross country to Atlanta and then for the short hop to Mulberry in what Annie Ruth, not the most intrepid flier, was happy to see was a small Brasilia jet, she fretted that being back in her hometown would stir up old memories—most of them surrounding her dead mother—she felt best left to rot, memories that would cause her stress and interrupt her peaceful nightly rest.

She laughed dryly as she recalled Raphael, her Dominican lover, asking in his sweet Caribbean accent when they were first getting to know each other a couple of years earlier, "And is mother still with us?"

She had snorted nastily before she caught herself and replied as sweetly and irony-free as she could, "Yes, 'mother' is indeed still with us."

Now, a mother herself, Annie Ruth hated to admit it, but she was beginning to see just how much 'mother', even in death, was still with all the Lovejoy girls.

Yet, surprisingly, the whole time she lived there in Betty's house waiting for the arrival of her baby daughter, she had slept like a baby herself every night. Rising rested and lovely each morning, she washed up, brushed her hair made suddenly thick and lustrous from her hormones and Betty's daily care, put on a new maternity outfit and descended the front stairs to the big country breakfast Betty had lovingly prepared and left warming for her sisters.

"You eating for two now, girl. You better enjoy it while you can," Betty would tell her on Sundays and the mornings she went into work late, as she dished up a heaping plate of buttery grits and scrambled eggs rich in cheese and sweet peppers, with biscuits she had made at dawn from scratch on the side.

But as soon as Annie Ruth arrived back at her big sister's house with her new baby girl from her two-night stay at the hospital, she sensed something had changed.

And it wasn't only the sight of that cat climbing up the trellis toward the second floor of Betty's house that had disturbed Annie Ruth's sleep. It was other things, too.

Annie Ruth's second night home from the hospital, as the girls prepared for bed, an unexpected rainstorm blew up and a strange and eerie noise began drifting through the house. Suddenly, all the windows in the house began to screech, squeal and sing at once, engulfing the girls and MaeJean in peals of what sounded like something from a banshee.

"Oh, that's just the wind up here in this old house on the top of Pleasant Hill," Betty explained breezily as she stuck her head in Annie Ruth's bedroom for one last look at MaeJean before heading downstairs. "It's been doing that for more than a century. The Realtor told me so."

Still, the eerie sound unnerved Annie Ruth. And Emily, too, who was more easily spooked.

"Well, why didn't the wind make that noise before now, Betty?" Emily asked from the top of the staircase.

Betty, busy checking the windows and doors for the night, simply shrugged and went over to the sound system controls and turned up the soft jazz playing throughout the house a notch.

And the "wind" wasn't the only sound that greeted the new mother and daughter on their return to the house.

"Betty, do you have squirrels in your attic?" Annie Ruth asked later, the second morning back at breakfast, as she tried and failed then tried again to get MaeJean to take her nipple and nurse. Her big nipples were swollen and tender. And her bottom was still a little sore from the stitches of the episiotomy. The discomfort of her body along with a sleepless night made her a bit irritable, though you wouldn't have known it by looking at her.

Despite her usual dark circles and a bit of puffiness, Annie Ruth, her rust curls tumbling to the shoulders of her pure white lace peignoir, looked like a slightly hung-over classic bronze Raphaelesque Madonna sitting at the table with her nursing baby in her arms and gentle morning sunlight streaming around them like a nimbus.

"Squirrels?" Betty replied as she brought her baby sister a plate full of softly scrambled eggs and cheese with fresh chopped tomatoes and a short stack of pancakes to the breakfast room table and poured all three of them tall glasses of freshly squeezed orange juice from a heavy crystal pitcher.

"Yeah, or some kind of little animal. Their scratching and scurrying around up there kept me up all night. Didn't you hear them?" Annie Ruth asked.

"Uh-uh, I didn't hear a thing," Betty answered with a confused little furrow forming between her eyebrows before she felt it there, immediately stretching her eyes, made her mouth into a circle the way she had read to do it in "Yoga for the Face" and smoothing out the creases.

You can't be dating no twenty-year-old boy and have wrinkles, she told herself as she pressed the skin on her forehead up toward her hairline leaving pancake batter spread across her brow.

"You sure you weren't dreaming, Annie Ruth?" Betty asked.

"Or just dozed off watching our MaeJean breathe?" she asked. Betty had to stop scrambling the bowl of eggs with no cheese for Emily and come over to her niece for a little sugar from the bottom of one of her tiny feet before returning to the stove.

"I told you I didn't sleep at all, let alone dream," Annie Ruth replied quickly. She wasn't used to functioning without her sleep and couldn't seem to keep the crankiness out of voice. "And don't tell me it was the wind."

Betty heard the edge to her sister's voice and made a mental note to take care of the scratching-in-the-attic situation that afternoon.

"Well, we can't have the little mama not getting her sleep, can we?" she said.

As soon as Betty got to Lovejoy 2, her beauty shop out at Mulberry Mall, before she checked the day's schedule of appointments for special customers or had her second cup of tea of the day, she called her regular exterminator, The Critter Gitter, and asked that he check out her attic immediately for varmints. Betty couldn't stand the idea of critters running around over her and her family's head all night while they slept.

The image of wild animals roaming so dangerously near her, her sisters and MaeJean reminded her too much of the time that stray cat had snuck into the house in East Mulberry and slashed Annie Ruth's throat when she was an infant lying in her crib.

"Not this baby," she promised herself. "Not this time."

However, after the exterminator made a thorough search of the huge space at the top of her house, he was left confused.

"Miss Lovejoy, I don't understand what you heard," he said when he called before lunch. "There's nothing in your attic now. I didn't find a thing up there. And what's more, I didn't find no nests or droppings or gnawed boxes or signs of a animal ever being up there at all. Not a squirrel or a possum or a rat or nothing."

"Really?" Betty said. She hadn't heard the noises herself, but she was sure Annie Ruth had. She could tell from the bags under her sister's eyes and the exhausted look on her face. All the Lovejoy girls had inherited the dark circles and slight puffiness under their eyes from Poppa's side of the family. But Annie Ruth's face that morning looked as if she had been out partying all night.

"And, Miss Lovejoy, you know your attic, this whole house, is as sound as a silver dollar, sound as any I ever seen. There're no cracks or holes or openings to the outside anywhere up there for a animal to get in."

"Well, okay," Betty had said reluctantly. She didn't know what else to say in the face of the man's adamancy.

Betty was at a loss for what to do next. She knew for a fact that, miraculously, the baby had slept almost all through the night. So, she couldn't understand what had kept Annie Ruth, a woman who treasured her full night's sleep, awake. As she went over the books that her accountant handed her at the end of the day, she wondered what to do for her baby sister.

She knew that Annie Ruth was known to hallucinate from time to time. The "cats" in the delivery room had been a good example of that. "Oh, God, is Annie Ruth *hearing things* now as well as seeing them?" She wondered aloud as she drove home that evening.

Later that very night, however, Annie Ruth was up again, kept awake by the scurrying and bumping sounds in Betty's attic. As she lay awake in her elegant bedroom suite, the sounds became louder, more insistent and somehow menacing. Annie Ruth rose from her bed, grabbed an embroidered quilted bed jacket from the foot of the bed and checked on little MaeJean lying in the bassinet next to her. The baby was sleeping soundly. Annie Ruth lowered her ear to the infant's tiny rosebud shaped mouth and smiled at the steady, breathy sound she heard and the sweet clean baby smell she inhaled.

"MaeJean," she said, "Mama loves you so much." Then, she giggled. She couldn't help herself. She chuckled every time she called herself "mother" or "mama" or "mom." Any maternal moniker connected to her sounded so strange and comical.

The baby stirred slightly at the sound of her mother's voice and slowly opened her eyes. Annie Ruth knew the baby could only see vague shapes at just a few days old, but it seemed to her that MaeJean looked right at her and sighed.

At the pure, dear sight of her baby looking up at her with infinite trust, Annie Ruth could not stop the tears. But just as suddenly, the sounds above her head brought her up short and stopped the tender moment. It sounded as if someone above her had knocked over a piece of furniture, a heavy piece of furniture.

Instinctively, Annie Ruth leaned over MaeJean in her delicate bassinet to cover her with her own body and looked up half-expecting something to crash through the ceiling.

Betty appeared at the bedroom door with a soft, peach, cashmere robe wrapped around her shoulders.

"Don't tell me you didn't hear *that*," Annie Ruth, still hovering over her baby girl, whispered sharply.

"Oh, yeah, I heard it that time," Betty answered, trying hard to keep her voice steady. "Is MaeJean okay?" she asked as she moved across to the baby's bed. Even in her half-frightened state, she had to keep herself from smiling at her little namesake.

She and Emily had so long ago resigned themselves to the fact that they would never be mothers, would never have a child to carry on their names, their blood, their DNA. Now, merely the thought of "MaeJean"—half of half of her name, half of half of her sister's name—gave her such solace she could almost feel it wrapped around her like her cashmere robe. Throughout her busy days, she found time to call home four or five times to check on the new mother and baby. Without the least bit of effort, she managed to bring her niece's name up in conversations with customers, employees, delivery men, Cinque, and even strangers.

Betty felt she had years of proud talk and joyous regalement and gloating glances stored up in her heart that MaeJean allowed her to release. It was a balm to her woman's heart to brag on her tiny niece.

After half a lifetime of loathing their names, they all found it funny that it took no time at all getting used to loving the sound of "MaeJean." Annie Ruth had successfully dropped the country-sounding "Annie" her first year in college and become just "Ruth" everywhere but at home in Mulberry. Emily, who loathed the "Mae" in her name, had relished the nickname of "Em-Em" that her baby sister had conferred upon her when as a toddler she couldn't pronounce "Emily." And Betty had resigned herself to explaining over and over that "Betty" wasn't short for anything every time she was introduced to someone new.

Now, Betty and Emily called the baby's name so often, Annie Ruth had chuckled and whispered to her daughter, "MaeJean, your aunties 'bout to make mama sorry she named you after them."

But even the sight of MaeJean couldn't settle the lump of fear Betty felt in the pit of her soul at the sounds coming from the floor above their bedrooms.

"MaeJean is okay?" she asked again nervously.

Annie Ruth tucked the covers closer around her baby and nodded.

Then, she said in a hoarse whisper, "I thought you said that the man came to check and didn't find any squirrels in the attic."

Betty shrugged her broad shoulders helplessly. "That's what he told me."

"Why you being so nonchalant about this, Betty? Didn't you hear those noises up there?" Annie Ruth didn't want to sound hysterical, but even she could hear the rising terror in her own voice.

"Well, yeah, I heard it," Betty said again as she came over to the crib and rearranged the delicate pastel linens around the baby.

"Well, what should we do?" Annie Ruth asked. "Should we investigate?"

"'Investigate?" Betty asked with a nervous giggle. "Who do you think we are? Miss Marple or Foxy Brown or somebody?"

"Well, we can't just sit here with all that going on over our heads," Annie Ruth countered as a loud banging sound started in the rafters above them.

Betty took a deep breath, glanced down at MaeJean again and squared her broad shoulders.

"Okay, I guess you're right. We do need to go see what that is. But first, make sure our baby girl is okay. Push her over into your bathroom where she's not directly under the attic just in case."

"Just in case what?" Annie Ruth asked as she carefully rolled the baby and bassinet into the new bathroom extension.

"I don't know," Betty said. "In case something breaks through the ceiling, I guess."

"Through the ceiling?" Annie Ruth repeated as she kissed MaeJean and pulled the bathroom door half-way closed.

"Look, I'm winging it here, Annie Ruth, I don't know what I'm saying, okay?"

Then, the two women tightened the sashes on their robes, gave each other a nodding high sign like black secret agents and headed for the hall.

"Hey, I never noticed that bedroom door creaking like that before," Annie Ruth said as they eased out into the dimly lit hall.

"Alright, Annie Ruth, don't you start bugging on me here," Betty chided her sister in a low serious tone. Then, she headed for the utility closet next to Annie Ruth's bedroom. "Here, I'll take the dust mop and you take this," she said as she extended a fluffy feather duster into Annie Ruth's hand.

"Oh, yeah, this should really protect us from some rabid wild animal or homeless person from down by the river," Annie Ruth sucked her teeth and said as she eyed her weapon.

"Well, it's the best I can do on short notice. Work with me, Baby Sis."

"Okay. But why are you whispering, Betty?"

"Annie Ruth! Stop it!" she hissed softly. "I'm wound tight enough as it...."

"What ya'll doing out here in the hall in the middle of the night?" Emily seemed to appear out of nowhere.

Betty's mop went flying one way and Annie Ruth's feather duster went the other, landing on the edge of the crystal chandelier hanging over the foyer and making the fixture give off an eerie tinkling tune that sounded like the cheap special effects of an Ed Woods horror film.

"For God's sake, Emily, don't be sneaking up on us like that!" Betty whispered as she clasped her robe at the throat and retrieved her mop from the top of the staircase. "Don't you see us on a mission?"

"A mission? What kinda mission? What are ya'll doing?"

"Well, maybe not a 'mission' exactly. But we trying to find out what that noise is in the attic. Didn't you hear it?"

"Yeah," Emily replied sheepishly as she tucked her hair under the red flowered silk scarf she had tied on Aunt Jemima-style. "But I was trying to ignore it. I thought it was just me. I, uh, hear things sometimes."

"Well, so do we, apparently," Annie Ruth interjected sardonically as she reached for her tossed duster and winced in pain at the effort. "Oh, fuck it. It wasn't much of a weapon anyway. Come on, Emily, you might as well join the hunt, too. Maybe, we'll outnumber them."

"Outnumber who?" Emily wanted to know. She sounded fearful, but she fell right in behind her sisters as they headed cautiously up the stairs to the third floor.

As they slowly climbed the stairs, they looked like little girls at a pajama party playing scary games to entertain themselves until someone's mother showed up to make them all quiet down and go to bed. When they reached the top landing, they instinctively reached for each other's hands and stood forming a link hoping that a three-string cord was indeed difficult to break.

They spent a few seconds arguing—"You open the door." "No, you open the door." "No, you're the oldest, you open the door." "No, you're the baddest, you open the door."—until Annie Ruth lost all patience and hissed, "Oh, hell, I'll open the damn door, but ya'll better have my back."

She reached for the door knob, then drew her hand back slowly.

"Betty, where's the light switch?" she asked.

"It's right inside the door on the wall to the left. You open the door, and I'll reach in and turn on the light, okay?"

"Okay."

"What'll I do?" Emily wanted to know, suddenly not wanting to be left out.

Before Annie Ruth could blurt out something rude, Betty hurriedly told Emily, "Em-Em, you just stand here at the door and be ready."

"Okay," she said, nodding seriously, placated, then, suddenly added, "Wait! Ready for what?"

Annie Ruth decided to act before Emily went to Nutsville on them. She turned the knob and flung the door to the attic open. Right on cue, Betty reached in and flipped on the overhead light, and Emily, true to form, slipped behind both of them and squeezed her eyes shut tightly.

They stood there for a moment, waiting and not knowing what they were waiting for. Then, all three of them leaned forward from the waists and peered into the cool crowded space.

"You see anything?" Emily asked from the back of the pack.

"No," Annie Ruth answered. "Betty?"

"Uh-uh," she said.

"Well, how can you tell? Betty, what is all this stuff up here?" Annie Ruth wanted to know. She eased a few inches inside the door and looked around at piles and piles of boxes and trunks and what looked like chairs and sofas and highboys and dressers covered with white sheets.

Neither Annie Ruth nor Emily remembered having ever explored Betty's attic. They had never thought about going up there or what might be there. Betty's house proper had been far too interesting and comfortable to think about venturing into what they assumed was a dark dusty attic. Now, everything their gaze landed on looked interesting.

"We're gonna have to come back up here in the daytime, Emily," Annie Ruth said as she peered around. "It looks like a high-priced flea market up here."

"Hey, is that a chaise lounge over there?" Emily asked. "Well, shoot, I been looking for...."

She didn't get a chance to finish. Just when they all thought they were safe and had been foolish for being fearful of what lurked in the attic, a small, dark figure seemed to appear out of nowhere and, running crouched down and on all fours, shoot past them from one side of the attic to the other.

"Oh my God! What in the world was that? What was that? Yewww! It brushed against my leg! It touched my leg! My God, was it a rat?" Annie Ruth wanted to know

"A rat? Oh, Lord, no. I know I don't have any rats in my attic," Betty said indignantly as she scanned the floor.

"Look! There it is again!" Emily screamed and pointed to a corner of the attic near an overstuffed wing-back chair. "Oh, Annie Ruth, look! It's not a rat. It's a cat! That is a cat, isn't it?"

"Oh, right, so I'm supposed to be the expert on cats now, huh?" Annie Ruth shot back angrily.

"For God's sake, Annie Ruth, this is no time to be sensitive. Did you or did you not see a cat in my attic?" Betty asked as she craned her neck around the open door edge and squinted to get a better look.

"A cat? A cat! Oh, of course. I forgot. A cat! Oh, God! Where's my head? I did see a cat. I don't mean now, but before," Annie Ruth said as she snapped her fingers. The popping sound seemed to echo in the cool dark space.

"Before where? In the delivery room?" Emily offered trying to be helpful.

"No! Right outside. Climbing up the side of the house. The first night I was back here. I didn't say anything about it because…you know, it was a cat and I didn't know if I had really seen it or you know.…"

"Just thought you saw it," Emily offered again eagerly , trying once more to be helpful in a stressful situation.

"Yes, Emily. Just thought I saw it. But it was going up the trellis outside the east side of the house, Betty. I saw it from out the solarium when ya'll ran up to see MaeJean. You think that's the same cat?"

"Um. Could be. Or it could just be our imagination playing tricks on us."

"Humph, that wasn't no 'trick' I felt running across my feet a minute ago," Annie Ruth said.

"Me neither," Emily put in.

At that exact moment, all three of them saw a sudden movement out the corners of their eyes, and they jumped in unison and looked at each other. Betty didn't say anything but she thought, Oh, great, now we're all seeing cats!

But when Betty ventured farther into the attic with her sisters to push the fluffy end of the dust mop she was carrying in the direction of the corner, they heard a sudden rustling from the opposite direction and turned just in time to see the dark creature scurry out the door and down the stairs behind them.

They screamed in unison again.

"Did you see that?" Annie Ruth whispered. She could hardly catch her breath.

"Oh, God, whatever it is is downstairs in the house now!" Emily exclaimed.

They stood there for a few seconds staring down the steps. Then, Annie Ruth grabbed Betty's arm.

"Betty! MaeJean! My baby! My child! MaeJean! She's downstairs by herself. Unprotected!" Annie Ruth yelled as she pushed past her sisters and flung herself down the stairs toward her bedroom.

As Annie Ruth ran, her right hand clasped between her legs, holding her aching vagina, and stumbled down the hall through her bedroom and toward the bathroom door, all she could think of was her baby girl lying exposed and vulnerable in her bassinet.

"Oh, God, what kind of mother am I leaving my baby all by herself," she admonished herself as she rushed to her child.

When she flung open the door to her bathroom where she had left the baby sleeping, it was all she could do to keep from passing out. She gasped, grasped the door jamb with one hand and clutched her breasts, still sore and tender from nursing MaeJean, with the other. What she saw was among her worst fears realized.

Standing over MaeJean's bassinet, with its wide, front white paws planted on either side of the baby was a huge black cat with a white breast. The sight of the cat standing there took Annie Ruth's breath away. And she nearly swooned at the vision. But just as she leaned on the bathroom door for support, the cat did something that quickly brought her back to her maternal strength and senses. As if in slow motion, the cat took its gaze off MaeJean and turned its big round head bit by bit, unhurriedly as if it had all the time in the world, and stared directly into Annie Ruth's face. Then, it slowly batted its eyelids in a few lazy blinks over its jet black marble eyes. One. Two. Three times. It was such a defiant, insolent, insulting gesture of power and one-upsmanship that Annie Ruth suddenly found herself not frightened but furious.

Just then, Betty and Emily came crashing into the bedroom behind her, saw the cat at the same time and both screamed, "A cat!" Annie Ruth took a deep breath that left her entire body shivering with rage, and leapt head-first, her arms stretched out in front of her toward her child and the cat.

"Muthafucka!" she exclaimed earnestly.

And then, just before Annie Ruth reached it—it looked to Betty and Emily as if their sister was poised for a few seconds in mid-air—the cat standing over MaeJean flexed its tiger-like muscles, turned languorously like a wisp of fog and leapt from the bassinet onto the bathroom window sill. It landed there with a light thud, and with its front paws, it pushed at the bottom of the antique, stained glass louvered window and sprung the latch holding it shut. With a quick final glance over its shoulder at MaeJean and then at Annie Ruth, the cat sprang out the window and disappeared into the night.

CHAPTER 24

uh, omigod, i know i don't have much of a neck yet, but it sure is stiff-feeling this morning. my mama had me sleeping all up under her all night and i couldn't stretch out even one time the way i like to.

and then again, it might be 'cause mama and auntie betty and em-em were all up on my neck last night poking and looking all around it—front, back and sides. i don't know what they were looking for. they kept asking, "blood? blood? you see any blood?" all loud and crazy-like, and mama was crying—i never seen her cry like that before. not like when she be looking at me and get all misty and everything, but real hard salty tears this time. but i don't know why they could have been looking for no blood. why?

anyway, after a while they must not have found anything, 'cause they all kind of settled down and we all went to bed except mama wouldn't let nobody hold me but her—which was nice— and instead of putting me in my own comfortable bed—i wonder where in the world they found 600-count baby sheets?—she tucked me in up under her arm and body in her bed. that's why i got this little crook in my neck this morning.

oh and i forgot. last night, i met my grandmama, too. she my grandmama, but she told me to call her "mudear." she came to see me in my bassinet. she don't look nothing, and i mean nothing, like my mama and aunties, and i don't think they get along all that much 'cause the moment they showed up running and screaming and hollering at her, my grandmama she skedaddled out the window. i don't know why she didn't just use the door.

oh oh oh, and i've already seen my granddaddy, too. it was right after i was born. i think it was my granddaddy. that's what he said anyway. i couldn't see so good. at first i could only make out big shapes and things and he was standing way across the room on the other side of a glass wall back at the place i remember being before coming home to aunt betty's house, but then he got the nurse to get me out my bed and bring me to him at the door. and when she did, he looked at me and said, "i'm your granddaddy." then, he shook his head and sucked his teeth and said, "lord, help us. she the spit a' her." whoever "her" is. then, he closed his eyes and bowed his head and said, "lord, please don't let her take after mudear."

then, he went away. well, now that i've met my big daddy, i wonder what my little daddy is like?

omigod, so much stuff and drama going on, and i only been here a few days.

this is exciting. i think i like drama.

CHAPTER 25

The first thing Betty did when she started stirring the next morning was call Mrs. Andrews and tell the puzzled woman not to come to work that day. The cleaning lady was used to Betty giving her an unexpected day off from time to time, especially when she knew her employer was expecting a sleepover visit from her young man. But that hadn't happened since Ms. Lovejoy's sisters had come to stay.

Mrs. Andrews had come to schedule her week's routine around her three-day-a-week visits to Betty Lovejoy's house. They were full days, leaving the heavy-set woman exhausted but satisfied with her day's work and her contribution to the smooth running of her employer's complicated household. Even with the addition of the two sisters, whom Mrs. Andrews knew from earlier visits, she was able to complete all her household tasks and errands in a reasonably long day. And the compensation she received for her work more than made up for any long days allowing her and her family to live comfortably on only that one job which still left her four days a week to enjoy her retired husband and grandchildren.

But she had to admit that Betty Lovejoy sounded right funny when she called that morning and Mrs. Andrews had a good mind to swing by the big house at the top of Pleasant Hill later that day to check on the Lovejoy girls anyway. Especially after Betty had sounded all defensive and worried when Mrs. Andrews had asked innocently, "Ya'll taking good care of that new baby girl?"

"MaeJean?" Betty had asked quickly, as if there were another new baby girl in that house. "Well, of course, we are. Why would you ask that? Why would you ever think we'd let anything ever happen to our baby girl?!"

Mrs. Andrews didn't quite know what to say, but before she could collect herself and explain that she was only kidding, Betty seemed to come back to herself. She laughed a little nervously, and said, "Oh, yeah, of course. Right. Don't worry, you know we're looking out for MaeJean, Mrs. Andrews." Then, she quickly hung up.

But still the older woman was a bit unsettled all day thinking about the sound of Betty's voice and the tension she felt over the line. Later, when folks in town talked about what transpired in the next couple of days around that house and the Lovejoys in general, she always had to keep from chiding herself for not investigating further.

"But then, even as a strong, Christian woman, what good would I have been other than to pray for them all? All of 'em!"

The second thing Betty did was grab a heavy ebony African ceremonial cane given to her as an award by a local businesswomen's group as an "elder in the Mulberry business community." She headed outside, determined not to be afraid and scoured every inch of her property in search of any signs of a feral cat. From her brief glimpse of the creature she and her sisters found hovering over their baby MaeJean the night before, she knew that the cat had to be wild. She could tell that from the untamed look in its eyes.

Betty was determined not to make it a cursory check. She looked around bushes and behind teak and white oak benches and side tables, under the cars and in the garage. She lifted flower pots and ran a rake through the sandy soil where the gardener had planted succulents and blooming cacti for signs that a cat had been using the area for a kitty box. But no matter how assiduously she searched, she found not one bit of evidence that a cat had been making itself familiar and comfortable anywhere on her property.

Still, she was not satisfied and returned to the house on edge and unsettled. Merely being outside in her yard had reminded her of Mudear and her garden. And suddenly, Betty was struck with the thought that the cat from the night before somehow put her in the mind of her mother.

What was it about the cat, she wondered as she walked into the bright sunny kitchen and poured herself a second cup of strong, black, Ethiopian coffee. Perhaps, she thought, as she sat for the first time that morning, it was the memory of the cat story from Annie Ruth's infancy that had stirred thoughts of Mudear. She shivered and couldn't stop herself for ten or fifteen seconds as she recalled how Mudear, more than thirty years earlier, had killed the cat she had found trying to slash Annie Ruth's little throat.

"Wrung that cat's neck like a chicken," Mudear always said when she told the story.

Betty knew it was true. She had seen her mother do just that and the image had never left her mind. Yet, that morning she did her best to erase the memory, especially since she spent the next couple of hours preparing a Sunday-style dinner of turkey with cornbread dressing, rice, gravy, and pole beans with yellow onions for the girls' evening meal. As she moved easily around her kitchen, a room she loved, she tried to keep her mind on the food and not on the image of a cat having its neck rung like poultry.

As soon as she had chopped the onions, celery, and bell pepper, softened the homemade pan of cornbread with steaming rich turkey stock, and slid the dressing into the lower oven, she wiped her hands on her Donna Reed apron, took it off and headed for the pantry.

There, she found a pair of rubber household gloves and a bucket and went to the pantry sink to run a pail of hot soapy Lysol water. She inhaled the fresh clean antiseptic smell as she climbed the back stairs to the second floor, then got down on her knees and cleaned all around the steps leading down from the attic, along the upstairs hall, and into Annie Ruth's bathroom. Anywhere she suspected that cat could have ventured the night before.

She hadn't cleaned like that since she had left Mudear's house in Sherwood Forest decades before. She didn't ask either of her sisters to join in and help her and when Emily tried to come in and pick up a brush to assist her, she merely shook her head furiously, tousling her short bouncy curls and shooed her away to the kitchen to make her special squash casserole for the evening meal.

Betty had to stop herself from admonishing her sister from ruining her pretty hands in the strong disinfecting solution. It would have sounded too much like something Mudear would have said. And, although the woman's presence seemed to cling to every surface in the house that morning, all the girls were diligently avoiding any mention of their dead mother.

But hard as they tried, not talking about her didn't seem to banish the dead woman's essence from the house.

CHAPTER 26

The first thing Annie Ruth did when she opened her eyes was look down to where her big belly had been. Even lying prone, her stomach wasn't exactly flat, but she thought, at least I can see my feet.

She wiggled her toes playfully for a few seconds, and then suddenly remembered MaeJean, the noises in the attic, the cat, and her child's safety. "What am I doing thinking about my shape? I need to be keeping watch," she chided herself and tried to rise from the bed.

"Owww," she screamed at the effort and ceased as she remembered how she had been running and leaping around the night before, to say nothing of the fact that she had indeed just given birth and was not yet healed.

"Oh my God, MaeJean," she exclaimed, then breathed a sigh of relief as she realized that she did not have to go in search of her child. After finding that cat breathing down on her in her bassinet, Annie Ruth had taken MaeJean into the bed with her for the rest of the night. MaeJean was tucked safely up under her right armpit.

Annie Ruth sighed again, but she couldn't afford to let out a true, fully relieved, breath. In fact, she felt unease all over her like a persistent body itch. And she didn't know if she would ever feel safe about MaeJean or if she would ever let the child out of her sight again.

Even as she cooed at and snuggled with her child, as she leaned down and sniffed MaeJean's little bottom to see if she needed changing, Annie Ruth could not get the image out of her head of that cat poised over the child's bassinet from the night before. After the cat had made its escape, she and her sisters had all made certain that MaeJean was fine, unharmed, no scratches, slashes, or welts on her throat or anywhere on her little body. Next, Betty and Emily had gone through the entire house together, closing, locking and double-checking all the windows and doors that led outside. Then, Betty had made them all a pot of chamomile tea, and Emily, never one to let a crisis ruin her appetite, ate some left-over broccoli and mushroom salad with ranch dressing and a salami sandwich. But they never really settled down.

They had sat up until nearly dawn, all clustered together in Betty's room, like in old times when they were little and huddled together for safety and solace waiting for a chance to whisper in the dark about their constantly evolving Mudear. With Annie Ruth rocking MaeJean long after she had fallen back to sleep following the vigorous examinations, the sisters had kept silent vigil. And although there seemed to be a presence, a spirit of some unknown provenance lurking around the edges of the room, like that black cat with white paws and a white vest that had menaced their baby girl earlier, none of the girls spoke of it.

Once, as the sound of crickets and tree frogs began droning on the other side of the luxurious draperies at the house's windows, Betty began to talk casually about her garden and how the grass and the herbs of her yard would certainly dry up and turn brown without the daily watering of the sprinkler and soaker hose system in the nearly drought conditions of that up-coming middle Georgia summer.

"That's kind of how life is, isn't it?" Betty offered. "The ones who put down deep roots, who aren't shallow and all on the surface of their lives are the ones who survive in hard times."

Annie Ruth, however, unable to bear hearing Betty speak of her garden as if she were some reincarnation of Mudear spouting her half-assed Bible quotes, shushed her big sister and went back to rocking like some old, weathered, weary, country woman keeping watch over a flickering home fire.

Later that morning, as Annie Ruth settled back into her bed, readjusted MaeJean snugly under her body, and looked down on her with a relieved sigh, she reminded herself: I have to keep a better watch over my child because the cats are trying to get her.

She shook her head in amazement at the way that idea sounded in her head. She repeated it aloud. "The cats are trying to get her. The cats are trying to get my child."

It sounded even crazier out loud.

A few hours ago, I wouldn't have dared let words like that even play around in my head, let alone say and consider them, she thought with a dry chuckle that came out sounding more like a tiny cry that made her gasp and shudder.

The events in the attic and at the bedside of her child the night before still left her shaken and afraid around the edges, frayed like the intentionally ragged edges of the tweed silk mohair Chanel suit that she wore on air. But the sight of MaeJean snuggling and gurgling and stretching her little body was calming her mother down bit by bit.

Betty and Emily, bleary-eyed from lack of sleep, had already stuck their heads into her bedroom four or five times that morning to check on them, offering breakfast in bed, a neck massage and even to take

MaeJean for a moment to give Annie Ruth a rest. However grateful for her sisters' vigilance and concern, she had turned down all offers. But merely knowing they were there for her and her baby gave her some measure of confidence.

Betty had even decided not to go into the shops to work that Saturday morning, instead declaring her intention of staying close until the entire household felt safer and steadier. Over coffee and biscuits that Betty had made before dawn, neither of the two older sisters came right out and mentioned the cat or the attic directly. When Emily started to ask Betty what she thought of the implications of all the Lovejoy girls seeing cats, she began shivering so violently that she shattered the bone china cup she was holding against its matching saucer, spilling hot coffee all over the kitchen table.

So, instead of exploring the cat in the attic, their fear for MaeJean's safety, and the implication of a house invasion, they kept getting up and checking on Annie Ruth and MaeJean as they slept.

"MaeJean, this is one of the few times I truly wish I had a man I could call on to help me protect you," Annie Ruth said softly, so her sisters wouldn't overhear when they stuck their heads in the bedroom.

For a second, Annie Ruth almost regretted not following the yearning that had struck her the day before to email a photo of her baby girl to her colleagues and acquaintances back in California. Annie Ruth couldn't help but smile with pride at the thought of them putting her baby's pretty image up on the screen with some cute story about MaeJean being the next star of the newsroom or something like that. But she had already just about separated herself from all those people back there. Besides, the last thing she wanted was to stir up a bunch of questions about how far her fucking range had actually extended and who her baby resembled within that radius.

As soon as she had gotten back to the West Coast from Mudear's funeral the previous autumn, she realized that she didn't want any of the possible daddies—and, truth be told, it was a fairly long list—to be the daddy. So, she didn't even try to lie to Delbert and tell him that he was the one the way she had planned. Raphael had already told her she had fucked too many men throughout the southern section of the state of California to pin him with the paternity. On introspection, she realized the rest of the men who had been in and out of her bed, some using condoms and some not, weren't good father material. And she knew that despite her high profile on television— usually a real plus in image-driven L.A.—she wasn't exactly what many men were looking for in a mother for their child.

"Good enough to fuck, not good enough to keep," she told herself again and then realized that she didn't know whether she was referring to the men or herself. Besides, the more she thought about it as she sat behind the news desk and stroked her growing belly, the more she warmed to the idea of raising her child alone with only her sisters' help and guidance.

"A man don't give a damn about you anyway," she heard herself say softly, then nearly jumped out of her skin. She glanced down quickly to see if MaeJean, sleeping in the crook of her body, had heard, then frowned at herself, sucking her teeth a little.

Mudear had drummed that into her daughters' heads so many times and Annie Ruth had rejected the philosophy as many times. I will not end up like Mudear, she would promise herself. I will not end up like Mudear. So, the sound of those words coming out of her mouth almost made her gag and throw up.

"But don't you be worrying about no men, baby girl," Annie Ruth whispered with a knowing little conspiratorial chuckle, the first true pleasant sound she had uttered in hours. "We got all the time in the world for me to tell you all I know 'bout men—the good and the ugly."

Annie Ruth gave MaeJean one last check and pulled the soft

down comforter on her high, four-poster bed up over both of them with a long deep sigh. But before she could close her eyes good, her rest was interrupted.

"Annie Ruth, you got a phone call," Emily said as she stuck her head in the door, easing all the way in to lean on the door jamb and hold out the portable phone.

"A phone call?" Annie Ruth grumbled. "Who could that be? Just take a message for me, Em-Em, okay?"

"Alright," she replied, turning slowly from the door with one hand still on the brass antique knob and the other holding the phone to her titties to muffle the sound. "But he say to tell you it's the 'daddy' calling."

Annie Ruth sat straight up, suddenly wide awake.

"Oh, shit!" Annie Ruth threw the covers back, picked up MaeJean and put her into her bassinet, reached for the silver brush on the night table next to her, and began fluffing up her hair. "That heifer Mudear was right," she muttered to MaeJean as she rearranged the small blanket to cover her baby's entire body, took a deep cleansing breath and reached for the phone. "Troubles don't never come single file. They always come in legions!"

CHAPTER 27

U h-uh. Don't nothing cross over the devil's back that don't buckle back up under his stomach. Here it come now!!
      I knew them mens out in California wasn't gon' just let Annie Ruth have that baby and not have some say-so 'bout it.

That's how men are. I know 'em. Know 'em just as good. Now, they didn't want to have a thing to do with her when she was all big and r'ared back. But now, soonst as she done dropped her load—and a pretty little load it is, too—here they come. Out the wood-work.

Heh!

Now, let's see how quick that lil' smart-ass Annie Ruth really is. I can't wait to see who she gon' try and lay that baby on. When I was a girl and a girl broke a leg and couldn't get no man to own up to it or if she like

Annie Ruth and got too many mens to pick from, she just try to lay that child on some stupid older man who was more than happy to take the credit and weight for siring a child in his old age. I wouldn't be surprised if that gal of mine won't end up doing something like that.

Lord, I wouldn'a gone on to my heavenly reward before now for nothing in the world. And miss this? Shoot!

First, I get a pretty little grandbaby—and it sho' was nice seeing her close up like that. I got so close, I could smell her mother's milk on her breath. And bless her lil' heart, she wasn't even scared of her Mudear even if I did look like an old black and white cat. She looked me right in the face and listened to me talking to her. Oh, she understood me alright.

Now, that was something special. And now this with Annie Ruth! Shoot, it's just now getting good. Huh! I ain't going nowhere!

CHAPTER 28

uh-oh!

CHAPTER 29

Annie Ruth hated to admit it. But she had no idea who would be on the other end of the phone when she picked it up.

She could hear Emily breathing heavily on the downstairs extension. So, before saying anything, she pressed the phone to her full, sore breasts, walked out slowly to the hallway outside her bedroom door and peered over the banister down the stairs. Emily was standing there in the foyer by the front table, a phone to her ear, her right palm cupped over the receiver.

"I got it, Em-Em," Annie Ruth yelled down the steps at the top of her sister's head. And Emily quickly clicked the phone to off and placed it softly on the hall table without looking up the stairs at her sister. When Annie Ruth saw her turn and walk in the direction of the dining room and kitchen, she took a deep breath, put the phone to her ear and said, "Hello."

"Hey, babes," the voice over the phone said casually. "What's new?"

Annie Ruth would have sworn on a stack of King James Bibles that she had gotten her hormones under control since MaeJean's birth, but she quickly discovered differently.

"'Hey, babes'? Motherfucker, who do you think you are calling here at my sister's house when I've just gone through hours and hours of labor to bring my baby girl into this...."

"A girl? It's a girl?" Raphael asked, his voice a bit breathless.

"Damn!" Annie Ruth uttered. She hadn't planned to divulge any pertinent information until she had had time to think her situation through a bit more. And her slip pissed her off even more.

"What the hell do you care if it's a girl or not, you trifling don't-want-to-talk-about-it motherfucker?" she started in again. "Why should you care since 'I have fucked half of Los Angeles County' and there's no way you're the father." She wished she could think of some other epithet than "motherfucker" since it seemed much too heavy with meaning. But nothing better or more satisfying came to mind. In fact, she didn't want to get emotional, let alone hysterical, with Raphael or any of the potential daddies at this point. She just couldn't seem to help herself.

And the more upset she became, the calmer Raphael seemed to become on the other end of the line.

"Well, now, babes," he broke in coolly, serenely, "that's not completely fair, is it?"

Had he always called her 'babes,' she wondered. If so, she had no idea before that she hated it so much. She was about to tell him precisely that when another voice broke in on the line.

"Excuse me for interrupting," Betty said, her voice floating on the line, as cool as Raphael's tone had been. "But I really need this line now for a business call, and Annie Ruth really should be resting. She'll call you back. Good-bye."

Then, Betty hit the receiver a few times until Annie Ruth heard a solid click on Raphael's end and then a dial tone.

"Hang up, Annie Ruth!" Betty called up the stairs. "And go on back to bed and your baby."

Annie Ruth looked at the phone in her hand a moment, put it down on the table outside her bedroom and walked back into her room as if in a trance.

As she quietly got back in bed, she felt that wrinkle-causing frown take over her face again.

"God, how did he know about MaeJean's birth?" she wondered aloud as she recalled against her will Raphael's broad, brown shoulders still muscular from years of swimming in the Caribbean as a boy and in some woman's pool since his move to California.

But as soon as she got settled back in her bed, Emily stuck her head in the door again.

"You got another phone call," she informed Annie Ruth. "It's 'Delbert' this time."

Annie Ruth closed her eyes and sucked her teeth in exasperation. Then, she extended her hand for the phone without even looking at Emily. She knew exactly how her sister was looking and what she was thinking.

Annie Ruth knew that despite her situation, Emily was fighting the good fight against a sea of jealousy that was roiling right below the surface.

"Hi, beautiful," Delbert greeted her as if they had just seen each other the night before. His deep rich voice reminded her of the Pacific when the waves rolled in after a storm.

Doesn't anybody on the West Coast call me by my real name, Annie Ruth wondered. She seemed to be having an out-of-body experience. She could hear Delbert's voice and his words, but they weren't making any sense to her.

She scrunched up her face in an effort to concentrate and look for an opening in his voice to interrupt and get him off the line, but she couldn't seem to find one in his seamless soliloquy.

"…. And so mama asked me what kind of man was I that I would let my own child be born back in some little backwater Southern town that nobody ever heard of and not step up to my responsibilities."

Did he just say "little backwater Southern town," she wondered. But still she could not seem to find her voice or clearly understand his words. He continued.

"She told me, 'Delly, you need to call that girl and do right by her.' That's what she said. So, I didn't even have to think twice, I picked up…"

Annie Ruth caught something out of the corner of her eye and her head cleared enough suddenly for her to shoot back, "Is this the same mama who told you ain't no telling where my coochie has been?"

"Well, now, sweetheart, we all make mistakes, don't we?" Delbert said soothingly. "We all say things we regret. Let's try to forgive and forget. For the sake of the baby."

His unexpected reference to MaeJean caught her off guard and left her feeling exposed and her baby girl unprotected. And she felt suddenly vulnerable and not quite as angry as she had been a moment earlier.

"Delbert, go on with your life and tell your, uh, mother…." Annie Ruth said weakly. Weak as she was feeling, however, she still had to stop herself from saying what she really meant: "your stuck-up mean ass mammy…" Now that she was a mother herself, she found it difficult to criticize any mother other than her own.

"Tell your mother, Delbert, that you did your duty, but this is not your responsibility. It's not your child. Go on with your life. All is forgiven. Just go on. Go the hell on."

Then, she hung up before she found herself saying something truly unpleasant and unforgivable. She threw the phone across the room into the cushions of the sofa, slid down in the soft, cozy bed and pulled the downy covers in over her head.

"Please, Lord," she prayed softly. "I don't ask for much. But please don't let that fool be my child's father."

She only stayed that way for a few minutes until she heard the door open and soft footsteps enter her room. Thinking only of MaeJean who was sleeping soundly in her bassinet next to the bed and her safety, Annie Ruth whipped the comforter off her head and, with her heart racing, sat up ready to fight.

But the only scary creatures she faced were her sisters who proceeded to circle her bed, find a comfy spot, and settle in.

Annie Ruth knew something was up.

Emily might have been jealous and even a little bit angry that Annie Ruth had so many men in her life that they were finally vying for the privilege of being her baby's daddy, but she was clear on one thing.

"Annie Ruth," Emily began, unusually focused and succinct. "We've been fielding calls from your men all morning, and we ain't gonna sit here and let this situation turn into a particularly bad episode of Jerry Springer with DNA testing and paternity suits."

Annie Ruth opened her mouth to refute that charge and set her sister straight, but at exactly that moment, the phone on the sofa rang. Betty and Emily looked at each other, then at Annie Ruth.

"It could be for one of you," she said.

Betty answered it, listened a moment and turned to Annie Ruth with an I-told-you-so look on her face.

"Annie Ruth," she said, not bothering to cover the receiver. "Delbert is on the phone again. He says he wants to talk to you about a new DNA procedure he was just reading about."

"Shit!" Annie Ruth said under her breath as if she could hide out if she kept her voice down.

"He sounded kinda nice, Annie Ruth, when he called before," Emily added with that "helpful" tone in her voice that drove her sisters crazy.

"Well, you fuck him, then," Annie Ruth shot back and grabbed the phone from Betty.

"Delbert," she said shortly. "Let me get your ass straight once and for all. There will be no DNA testing on my baby."

Then, she clicked the phone off without waiting for a reply and turned the ringer to off.

"Children sure know blood, don't they?" Betty said with a chuckle trying to lighten the atmosphere as she watched Emily pick up MaeJean with a nimble magic touch and confidently lay her down on the changing table and whip off her diaper. MaeJean didn't even wake up.

Emily was not the deftest woman around infants. Some people seemed instinctively to know how to handle a newborn child, how to hold the baby's back and cradle and support her head. Normally, Emily was not one of those people. But with MaeJean, it was a different matter.

MaeJean seemed to feel safe and content in Emily's hands as she finished changing her diaper and then gently laid the baby in the bassinet and pulled it closer to where she sat in the big bentwood rocking chair.

All three of the sisters let their gaze rest on MaeJean a moment longer simply because it pleased them to look at her. And as always, Annie Ruth took the opportunity to search her sweet face for any faint similarities to any of the men she had slept with nine months before. But each time she searched, she was relieved and overjoyed to see that her baby only favored her and her sisters.

Even though the scene of the three Lovejoy sisters smiling over their baby girl softened Betty's heart, she knew she still had a job to accomplish with her other sister.

"Annie Ruth, I do not know what made you think you were going to have this baby and all of those men in your life back in L.A. were just going to fade into the background knowing their child might be on the earth," Betty said gently from the foot of her baby sister's bed.

No matter how hard they tried not to do it now because it seemed to make them appear weak and needy, the girls kept finding themselves huddled together in one room like refugees. Either they congregated in the sunroom downstairs in the same configuration: the mother and aunts in a circle around the cynosure of the household, little MaeJean. Or they gathered in Annie Ruth's bedroom and sat on the bed or the pink silk overstuffed sofa and armchair and rocking chair with MaeJean safely in the middle of the bed or nestled in her bassinet at their side.

"Well, they didn't seem too crazy about the idea when I first mentioned it to them," Annie Ruth said defensively.

"How many did you tell, Lil' Sis?" Emily wanted to know. She was having trouble keeping the prurient interest out of her voice.

"Oh, now you and Betty teaming up on me. That's all ya'll seem able to talk about," Annie Ruth said with a true, self-protective tone creeping into her voice.

"How many, Annie Ruth?" Betty repeated Emily's question.

"Well, I told Raphael and Delbert...."

"Um-huh. And who else?"

"And there was the corporate insurance guy I called 'Executive Square."

"Um-huh. And....?"

Annie Ruth pursed her lips and widened her eyes prettily the way she had when she was little and trying to keep her big sister from asking if she had finished her homework and done her little baby chores.

"Annie Ruth, don't be tryna pull that cute shit on us," Betty said. "And besides, stop doing your eyes like that. You gonna' get crow's feet."

"Crow's feet?" Annie Ruth exclaimed as if that were her biggest concern and, holding the corners of her eyes lightly with the tips of her fingers, ran as best she could over to the nearest brightly lit mirror to inspect her face. "I don't have any crow's feet!" she said from the vanity.

"Keep living, daughter," Betty and Emily said in unison. And all three Lovejoy girls shivered a bit as if someone had walked over their graves or as if Mudear had suddenly entered the room.

"Keep living, daughter," had been the older woman's admonition for any situation. And as much as she had said it, the girls had tried not to let those words slip out of their mouths in months.

"Don't you use protection, Annie Ruth?" Emily asked as Betty cut her eye at her. Betty knew the question was more a chastisement than an inquiry.

"Well, of course, I always use protection, Emily," Annie Ruth answered in an exasperated tone as she returned to the bed. "You know how we Lovejoy girls are about our birth control. I guess I was that lucky one in a million."

Emily sighed heavily and sucked her teeth.

"She doesn't mean birth control protection, Annie Ruth," Betty explained softly, trying to keep the temper of the talk at a non-screaming pre-fight level. "She means STD protection, a condom."

"Oh, that. Sometimes," Annie Ruth said far too breezily for either of her sisters.

"Sometimes?" they both almost shouted in unison.

"'Sometimes', Baby Sis, don't get it," Betty explained as if she were talking to a wayward teenager.

"See, Betty, it's exactly like we were saying, she think she immune to everything 'cause everybody's always taken care of her."

"Oh, is that what 'ya'll' were saying?" Annie Ruth asked coldly. "So, you use a overcoat every time you and that boy of yours fuck, Betty?"

"Yes!" Betty answered emphatically. "He may be young, but I still have no idea where that twenty-year-old dick of his has been. Beside, you forget Cinque ain't never had a time in his life when there wasn't AIDS. In all our times together, I have never had to produce a condom.

He rolls with his stash and whips it out right away. Thank God!"

She was grateful for any number of things about Cinque, who had called a few hours earlier to check on her.

"Betty," he had said with real concern in his young voice. "You weren't at work and you don't sound that good. You okay? You want me to come over there? You want me to bring you something? Some barbeque? A Mudslide sundae from the DQ?"

Betty had to smile and almost bite back tears. Cinque sounded so sincere and ready to come to her aid. She realized that she had always considered herself the alpha dog in that relationship. It had never dawned on her that he might stand up for her. Oh, she had seen times when he had kind of mentally squared off with someone in the beauty shop or at a restaurant when they tried to play him cheap and hand the tab to her instead of to him, but she had never considered the possibility that he would actually think to come to her aid in times of distress.

She didn't know why not. Cinque was a tender-hearted boy not a tough. Betty had seen evidence of that time and time again. He hadn't actually come from the streets. He had two parents at home. His father was a surveyor with the county Department of Transportation. And his mother, Lizabeth, who Betty had been two years behind in school – "Thank God we weren't in the same class," she told her sisters. – was a fairly sophisticated small town woman. She only sounded country.

And their son, who inherited his father's smarts and his mother's unaffected charm, finally wore Betty down until she gave in to her true desires. She felt she indulged herself with so little. So a few days after they had put Mudear in the ground, she stopped pretending that she was interested in Stan, the high school coach who played around on her as much as his championship-winning students played on the football field, and put her attention where her heart really lay: into Cinque, the sweet-natured young man who had recently turned twenty.

If someone had told her six months before that she would be almost openly dating a man half her age, barely out of his teens, even though they only went out in public together in restaurants and theaters in surrounding counties, she would have thought them insane.

Betty started out slowly right after her mother's funeral. On their first true public date they went to Shoney's for a Big Boy burger and a hot fudge brownie dessert. Betty was fairly certain that Cinque could afford that on his entry level salary at her shop. She was careful not to put him in the embarrassing position of having to dig in his pants pockets for money that wasn't there to cover a hefty bill at one of her favorite restaurants in Atlanta. At the end of the meal, Cinque snatched up the bill with bravado, paid the waitress with a flourish and left a twenty percent tip. It made Betty smile and put them both in an even better mood for their time of quiet intimacy later that evening and into the next morning.

They had been spending so much time at her house and in her bed and the Jacuzzi tub in her master suite bathroom, that at first they were a little uncomfortable in public.

Once, Betty felt her face begin to burn with embarrassment when she looked around at the faces that were staring at them. But when Cinque noticed the patrons of the restaurant giving them the once-over, he stated proudly with a wide grin: "They can't believe I got somebody like you, Betty." Then, she couldn't stop smiling, either.

But, as Mudear also used to say, if it ain't one thing it's three. A few days before MaeJean was born, out of the blue, Cinque's mother called Betty up at the beauty shop in East Mulberry.

When Betty picked up the phone, she recognized Lizabeth's voice right away and her blood ran cold. She still sounded as if she had never moved out of the little backwater Southern town Delbert's mother was sure Annie Ruth hailed from.

"Hey, Girl, I bet you don't know who this is," Lizabeth drawled.

Betty chuckled uneasily. "I bet I do. How you doing, Lizabeth?"

"Girl, how you know it was me?"

"I would have known your voice anywhere," Betty said.

"Well, I guess you can take the girl outa' Mulberry..." she said and let it trail off with a laugh. "I didn't really want anything. You been on my mind lately. Just popped in my head. I'll let you go on back to work." And she hung up.

Later that week, Lizabeth snuck up on Betty as she was leaning on the front glass display case filled with artifacts from early black hairdressing—hot metal straightening combs and curling irons in all sizes, bright pink jars of Dixie Peach and a well-used burned wipe cloth—and stared out the side window off into the distance. Lizabeth grabbed Betty's shoulders in her big wide hands.

"Who you thinking 'bout? One a' those men a' yours?" Lizabeth asked with a sly laugh.

Betty had to work hard to keep her face straight and come up with a smile that wasn't sly at all. No, she wanted to say, I'm thinking 'bout that boy of yours.

Lord, this woman would cut me everywhere but on the bottom of my feet if she knew half of what Cinque and I have been up to, she thought as she struggled to carry on a casual conversation with Lizabeth. The last thing Betty wanted was for Cinque's mother to have a memory of some possibly under-handed comment Betty had made in conversation with her that in hind-sight implied she was making fun of her ignorance of her son's relationship with his mother's high school acquaintance. She continued to find it difficult to believe that no one in Mulberry had passed along the news of her and Cinque.

"I don't know what put it in my head to come out here to your shop, Betty," Lizabeth said as Betty trimmed her hair. "No offense, but even with Cinque working here, I've been going to my girlfriend's shop in my neighborhood for years."

"Um," Betty said. She thought that was a safe comment.

"But for some reason, I couldn't get it out of my head to come here and try you out."

"Oh," Betty replied. She didn't trust herself to say anything else. And blessedly, Lizabeth finally left.

Sometimes, over the last few months as their relationship naturally, casually solidified, Betty would sit at work and quietly spy Cinque go about some everyday task or movement—sweeping the snippets of hair from the floor, stand at the water dispenser studying the big bubbles that gurgled to the top of the tank—and get caught up in the veil of peace that settled on her from watching his mundane behavior. It made her feel almost like they were an old married couple: she, the wife, watching, him, the husband do something she had seen him do hundreds of times before and being calmed by the routine.

With the chaos caused by the intruding cat and the calls from potential daddies and the unacknowledged spirit of their dead mother suddenly raising its head, that's what she longed for: the routine in her life. Having her sisters back at home had spoiled her for the routine. Every day following the last in the same way, with the same peace, the same moments of laughter, of excitement, of boredom.

She wanted that with a partner, with Cinque. And before the upheaval of items going missing, doors suddenly standing open, and cats entering her house and stalking her baby girl niece, that seemed to be where she was headed. She wanted it back, that possibility of the routine, and as she sat at the foot of her baby sister's bed, glancing from time to time at her sleeping MaeJean, Betty realized that she was more than willing to fight for it.

"But wait. This isn't about me and my 'boy,' Annie Ruth." Betty interrupted her reverie. "It's about you and MaeJean's daddy. Okay?"

"Oh, he'll go away. They'll all go away," Annie Ruth said lightly. "They'll get bored with the idea of being somebody's daddy, especially if I'm not asking for any child support, which I'm not, and go on to the next new thing."

"Have you ever thought that that might not be the best thing?" Betty asked thoughtfully.

"What?"

"Annie Ruth, have you given any thought to us?" Betty continued.

"What do you mean?" Annie Ruth was truly baffled.

"Well, look at us and Poppa. We didn't really have a strong daddy in our lives. Not really."

"And we turned out just fine," Annie Ruth said lightly but defensively.

Neither Betty nor Emily could resist giving their baby sister the funny eye on that comment.

Betty decided to carry the ball.

"Well, we're okay, Lil' Sis. But I don't know if we turned out 'fine.' Especially as far as men are concerned."

Emily turned to the window with that far-away look she had when thinking about her ex, Ron, and their stormy past.

"And we have to admit Poppa's being ignored or dissed by…uh his… uh….wife," Betty continued, trying not to utter the word "Mudear." "Well, it had a lot to do with our messed-up history with men."

"Do you want the same thing for MaeJean?"

"Oh, Betty," Annie Ruth countered, fussing with the fluffy coverlet draped around her in bed. "You sound like you've been reading some of those psychology books down in your library. MaeJean doesn't need those half-stepping men of mine in her life. She's got us."

"Think about it, Lil' Sis," Betty insisted. "Let's not continue any generational curses, as the preachers say."

"Oh, great, now we're listening to preachers," Annie Ruth said with a dismissive laugh.

Emily suddenly seemed to emerge from her trance. "You might want to listen to Betty 'bout this," she offered. "When I went out to the house to tell Poppa 'bout you and MaeJean...."

"You been out to the house?" Betty asked, surprised. "You hadn't mentioned that."

"Oh, yeah, I, uh, went by to tell Poppa Annie Ruth had a girl."

"When?" Annie Ruth wanted to know.

Emily bit her bottom lip nervously and hesitated before answering, "Uh, the night MaeJean was born. Remember, I left the hospital before you, Betty."

"Oh, I gave him a call with the news, too," Betty said. "The next morning."

"Shoot," Annie Ruth said, a bit chagrined. "I haven't even given a thought to Poppa."

"Well, we can't be too fine if a daughter forgets to call her father to tell him she's had a child."

"Oh, Betty, we're fine and MaeJean will be fine with or without a so-called 'daddy,'" Annie Ruth assured her sister.

"Oh, you think so, huh?" Betty said.

"Yeah, I do. And besides, we got bigger fish to fry than Raphael and Delbert and 'Executive Square' and Poppa and them." Annie Ruth continued in a whisper, "I didn't want to say anything. Shoot, I wanted to pretend I didn't hear it. And you know, I was so mad with Delbert for having the nerve to even bring up some DNA test for my baby girl, I could only think about that."

"Okay, Annie Ruth, we understand you were distracted," Betty said impatiently, sensing something momentous was about to be shared and fearing what it could be. "Just tell us."

"Well," Annie Ruth said as she rose, went over to the bassinet and picked up MaeJean to nestle at her breast. "When I went out in the hall the last time to take that call, I could have sworn I felt something lurking around out there or maybe it was more of that scratching up in the attic again."

Then, all three girls tilted their family pointy chins toward the ceiling and silently looked in the direction of the stars.

CHAPTER 30

L ook at her laying up there in that bed sleeping like she ain't got a care in world. She better be getting up taking care a' that child a' mine.

Wake up, Annie Ruth, girl! You sleeping through your rights! I don't know what that means exactly. It's something my mudear used to say to me when I was in bed late on a pretty sunny day. I think it means I was missing out on something that was due me 'cause I was sleeping instead of doing.

Annie Ruth laying up there with those old big nursing titties a' hers. They don't even hardly look real. She look like this woman used to live over in East Mulberry that all the folks used to refer to as "Titty Mama." She'd come out to the corner grocery store every day to shop for her supper. That's how folks, women, used to have to do. Some didn't even have no real refrigerator, just a ice box, and they shopped for their groceries everyday. So, "Titty Mama" would come to the grocery store – this was back when I went out the house 'monst people – wearing these old flowered house dresses that all the women mostly wore, me included back then, and she'd be neat and clean as a pin except for her big old titties.

I swear, her dress where her titties stuck out would always be just as dirty and dusty as a motley-faced child's playsuit at the end of the day. Folks used to laugh and talk about it behind her back—right there is one reason I don't miss people right now—how her dress at the titties was always dirty. I tried to tell folks that if your titties as big as "Titty Mama's" you liable to brush up against just about anything you pass by: a wall, a door, a shelf, a bush. But it did look like her titties reached out and grabbed anything they came near and rubbed up against them.

Now, what in the world made me think about "Titty Mama?" I swear my mind is just coming and going lately.

I better look sharp 'cause I can't believe that after last night and me being in there with my grandbaby, even if I did look like a cat, that those girls a' mine ain't getting the idea that their Mudear is back and ain't never really left.

Not that they can do anything about it. But I better look sharp all the same.

CHAPTER 31

It came to Annie Ruth in a dream. She was wandering in a place that looked familiar yet foreign, the way many locations in dreams appear. At first, she thought it was the halls of Morehouse North dormitory from her freshman year at Spelman College. She dreamed about her alma mater all the time. Sometimes, it was during her college days and she had shown up for class and realized that she was naked. Other times, it was the present and she was back as an adult with her teen-aged dorm-mates.

This time, she realized that the dreamspace she wandered wasn't as large and anonymous as a college dormitory, yet it still seemed institutional somehow.

Suddenly, it came to her dream awareness: It was a hospital. She even said that in her dream: "It's a hospital." But not a large busy place like Mulberry Medical Center or Cedar-Sinai in L.A. where she had done special reports for sweeps week. It was a small and cozy place even though it did smell of antiseptic. And in a flash, she realized it was a hospital where she had never set foot but which she had seen in old black and white and sepia photographs in the research department of the Mulberry County Library.

In her dream, she was wandering the halls of the old private facility for colored folks in Mulberry that was called St. Luke's Hospital. It has been closed for decades. In her research for a college term paper one Christmas, she had studied the archival photographs day after day, fascinated with the dignity and professionalism of the medical staff, the equipment—state-of-the-art for the '40s and '50s—the quiet peace that seemed to emanate from the very images of the small brick building that was the prized jewel of the tiny town's black community for more than half a century. Comfortable and tranquil, she had experienced those same emotions in her dream.

However, her reverie was not without a sense of urgency. As she drifted through the narrow halls of St. Luke's in her dream, she realized that she was on a mission to find a precious and elusive item. She must have opened and closed twenty or thirty doors and explored as many wards and closets in her hunt for the treasure, all to no avail. And with each search, she found herself becoming more and more frantic, certain that she had to find her goal and find it soon or ...

She awoke with a start and instinctively reached for her baby. Just as she was about to jump up and run panicky through the house screaming , "Someone snatched my child! The cat snatched my child!!!" she realized she had placed MaeJean in her bassinet before dozing off, and the baby was still lying there unmolested and peaceful, her tiny mouth making sucking motions in her sleep.

Annie Ruth had to lie back down for a few minutes clutching her chest and waiting for her racing heart to slow down.

Half an hour later when Emily came in to hold MaeJean and reminded Annie Ruth she was supposed to walk a bit every day, she was still trying to quiet her throbbing pulse. But she still took that opportunity to go out in the hall and look for her older sister.

"Betty," she said when she found her big sister at the foot of the stairs leading to the attic.

"Good God, Annie Ruth, sugar, stop creeping up on me like that," Betty admonished, trying for the second time that morning to soften her tone with one of her sisters. "You took two years off my life. And you know I'm not getting any younger. 'Specially now with Cinque and everything, I need all the years I can get!" she added with a laugh. The first one that had passed her lips in the last twenty-four hours.

"Oh, I'm sorry, Big Sis. I guess we're all a little bit creeped out this morning, huh?"

"No. No, I'm okay. This my house, Annie Ruth. I promised a long time ago I wasn't never gonna feel uncomfortable in my own home. Ever again," she said.

Annie Ruth couldn't help herself. She looked down at the pail of hot sudsy water on the floor at their feet and made a little questioning face.

Before she could erase the expression, Betty saw it and responded.

"Oh, this? This is just a little cleaning I wanted to do"

"You been doing this all day, off and on. You gon' ever feel like we got the stench and germs of that filthy animal out of here?"

"Don't worry about it, Lil' Sis, hot water and Lysol kill everything. So, what's up? MaeJean's okay?"

"Oh, she's fine. Sleeping like a baby. Emily's in there with her. I don't think I'm ever gonna be able to leave her alone again."

"I know. I know. Really, I do, Lil' Sis. But we're gonna get through this little rough patch. That's all it is. Just a little rough patch. We've gotten through lots worse than this, haven't we," she stated rather than asked with a lilting tone of encouragement to her voice.

"Um-huh," Annie Ruth replied as she ran her hand along the upstairs balustrade that extended the length of the landing overlooking the entrance hall.

Betty knew her baby sister was having a hard time believing she'd ever feel safe again after the events of the night before, but she was determined to keep things as normal as possible.

"What's the matter? You hungry? I can make you a sandwich or a salad or some soup. We're gonna have dinner in a little while. We're waiting for the dressing. Gravy's made. The turkey's done. Emily made squash casserole for you and you know she can make some squash casserole."

"Um, sounds delicious. Smells good, too. No, I can wait 'til dinner time. I had a question for you, Betty."

Betty went back to her cleaning. "Hmm? What's that?"

"Was I hallucinating? Wait. Don't answer that. Or was MaeJean born with a caul over her face?" Annie Ruth asked.

Betty stopped her cleaning suddenly, leaving her big yellow sponge hanging loosely in her rubber-gloved hand, dripping soapy water on the rug runner.

"Hmm!" she said. "My goodness. You're right. I cannot believe I almost forgot to check on that."

"Me, too," Annie Ruth said. "I had forgotten all about it until a dream I just had reminded me. Isn't that funny?"

"Well, so much has been going on with us in the last few days. It's a wonder we remember how to tie our own shoes," Betty said.

"You're right about that."

"Don't worry," Betty said as she rose and collected her cleaning utensils. "We'll find out what happened to our baby's caul. I'll give Dr. Hamlin a call at home before we sit down to dinner. The old folks say you gotta keep up with something like that. If we ever lose the caul, they always called it a veil, then MaeJean is likely to be forgetful her whole life. We can't have that, can we?"

"I don't know, Betty," Annie Ruth answered as she followed her big sister down the hall to her bedroom. "Maybe there are things she'll want to forget."

"Stop, Annie Ruth. It'll be okay. After I talk with Dr. Hamlin and run that caul down, we'll have something to eat. Then, we'll all feel better."

When they sat down to dinner, even before they had taken a bite, Annie Ruth looked at MaeJean lying in her bassinet by the table between her and Betty's chairs, winked at Emily sitting across from her and joked, "Oooo, lil' girl, you must be mighty special. We're eating in Aunt Betty's dining room today. And look, we eating off the good china, too."

"Stop it, Annie Ruth," Betty said. "You know we eat in here just as much as we eat anywhere else in this house. Don't be telling my baby girl that. She'll be thinking her Auntie Betty is a phony baloney."

"Wouldn't think of it, Aunt Betty." Annie Ruth said. Then, she added quickly, "But we are gonna say grace today, aren't we?"

The sisters looked at each other. Unless they were dining with people who grabbed their hands and insisted on praying before a meal, the girls never said grace. They had early in their lives, back when they were little. Like most families back then in Mulberry, the girls and Mudear and Poppa had dropped their heads before each meal, closed their eyes and chanted, "God is great. God is good. And we thank Him for this food."

But they never really believed it—"God is good."—not after Mudear changed and cursed their lives. And after Mudear had changed, she either didn't dine with the family or when she did, she sat down and went right to eating without the preliminaries of blessing the food first. Sometimes, if the meal included some especially tasty item like collard greens fresh from her garden with juicy ripe tomatoes chopped on top, Mudear not only dispensed with the grace, she also eschewed the cutlery, holding her pinkie back against the palm of her hand and, presenting the very picture of hedonistic enjoyment, scooped up and ate the greens with the remaining four fingers.

"'Scuse my fingers," she'd say. But she didn't care whether her family excused her behavior or not. Mudear simply didn't care.

Mudear took not caring to new heights.

After her change, she didn't care about much of anything that didn't directly affect her peace and comfort. Mudear didn't care about the girls' grades or schooling. She wasn't concerned about their health, hygiene, or clothing. She ignored any talk of their fears, feelings, or fantasies. She didn't care about their souls either. The girls had attended church as children, more as a held-over habit from before Mudear's change when she got them all—everybody but Poppa—cleaned and dressed up early on Sunday mornings and accompanied them to the white brick church around the corner from their house in East Mulberry as a way to show off their new Sunday clothes. But with no one to insist they get out of bed on Sunday, their one day of relative rest, and the other Christians whispering about them behind their church fans, the girls discontinued that weekly Christian ritual before Betty turned thirteen.

After the change, the girls finally figured Mudear didn't care what they did. So, they did what they did—attended school plays, ironed clothes, kissed boo-boos, praised good report cards—for each other.

At the dinner table that Sunday afternoon, Betty, Emily, and Annie Ruth reached out, taking the hand of the sister next to her to form a circle around the table. At the last minute, Annie Ruth and Betty broke the circle and both reached over to touch the sides of the bassinet so MaeJean was included in the loop, too. Then, they bowed their heads, closed their eyes and prayed.

Betty, the eldest, the head of this little household, took the lead.

"Lord?" she said, unintentionally turning the opening into a query. She tried again, "Lord, bless our family here at this table. We are all we got."

The other girls nodded and MaeJean made a little gurgling sound that brought a smile to all their lips.

"But, Lord, especially bless and protect our little MaeJean. Oh, she is the most precious thing we have. The most precious. Don't ever let any harm come to her. Don't let us ever drop our guard around her. And don't you either. Keep this house and wherever she is safe from…"

Betty was at a loss. Annie Ruth picked up the prayer.

"Safe from anything that would do her harm, especially…"

Now, it was Annie Ruth's turn to be at a loss for words.

All was quiet for a moment until Emily spoke up.

"Especially from stray animals."

"Em-Em!" her sisters broke the circle and shouted.

"Well, ya'll wouldn't say it. And I'm hungry. Can we eat now?"

Annie Ruth rolled her big brown eyes at Emily. Betty sighed, shrugged, smiled, and said, "Amen."

Annie Ruth and Emily echoed the "amen." And all the sisters took and squeezed each others' hands before dropping them again and turning to the meal.

"Em-Em? Annie Ruth was asking about our baby girl's birth caul. And for the life of me, I can't remember what happened to it," Betty said as they began passing the steaming dishes around the table to each other with appreciative sighs and nods.

Emily's eyes widened a bit and she let out a nearly silent "Oh!" that was more of a breath than an exclamation. But no one at the table noticed even when she began nervously biting her bottom lip. Betty kept on talking and passing dishes.

"After Dr. Hamlin made such a big deal about it, I can't believe she'd let them throw it away. I called and left a message on her service and at her home asking her about it, but she hasn't called me back yet. And that's not like her. But I don't know. In all the confusion of the birth and all. Thank you, Annie Ruth for the drama…."

"Thank you, for all the stellar birthing advice and support. 'You got to do this yourself, Lil' Sis.'" Annie Ruth said with a giggle as she mimicked her big sister.

"Well, thank you for exploding shit all over everybody...."

"Oh, Betty, we're eating here!" Annie Ruth retorted with a laugh and a look at MaeJean in her bassinet.

"Oh, yeah, like I'm ever going to be able to get the memory of that moment from being seared in my brain," Betty retorted with a sly smile.

Suddenly, Annie Ruth and Betty realized that Emily, who was usually so good at this sisterly game of jonesing each other, hadn't said a word. They both stopped laughing and eyed Emily, then eyed each other, then Emily again.

"Em-Em," Annie Ruth said. "What you so quiet for?"

"Heh-heh," Emily chuckled.

"Heh-heh, my ass," Annie Ruth rejoined. "Is this about my baby's birth caul, Emily? What the hell is going on?" She knew her reaction to Emily's evasive laughter was over the top, but for the last twenty-four hours she had been feeling so on edge, she could not seem to control her emotions. And the thought that her crazy sister had some information about her child was making her temples throb.

"Going on? Nothing's going on," Emily retorted and reached for the squash casserole. "I mean, hee-hee, it's nothing really."

"What's nothing, really?" Annie Ruth asked as she slammed her fork down on the pale damask table cloth at the side of her plate.

"Okay, Annie Ruth, don't get upset, you'll pull out your stitches," Betty cautioned. "And don't be so loud, you'll scare the baby. She's got tender little ears, don't you, sweetheart?"

"Alright. Sorry, my hormones are still raging a little bit," Annie Ruth said, and began speaking in a light little sing-song pattern as she, too, looked over at MaeJean who was sleeping through the whole thing. "I'm not upset, and I'm lowering my voice, and I'm not making a bunch of noise.

"So, tell us what's going on, Em-Em," she continued.

"Okay, it was like this," Emily began. "I'd been kinda hearing this voice for a while…"

"Oh, shit!" Annie Ruth intoned as she pushed her high-backed teak chair from the table, leaned back, and crossed her arms over her big nursing titties.

"Come on, Annie Ruth," Betty said soothingly. "Let her talk.

"Okay, Emily, we know this sorta', kinda', sorta' can happen sometimes. I talk to myself all the time," Betty continued, nodding and looking back to Annie Ruth for some back-up.

Annie Ruth simply sat with her lips pursed, her arms folded, her face stone. She had no encouragement of Nutsville behavior to give.

Betty gave her a dirty look and went right on. "So, you were talking to yourself…."

"Naaahhhh, not exactly," Emily corrected her big sister as she reached for the delicate china gravy boat and ladled the rich, brown, buttery sauce over her rice, dressing, and squash casserole.

"You weren't exactly talking to yourself?" Betty asked.

"I wasn't talking to myself at all, Betty." Emily put the gravy boat down and, although she had not yet taken a bite of the scrumptious food on her plate, daubed at her mouth delicately with the linen napkin that had been draped across her lap. She dropped it back in her lap, leaned into the table so that her breasts nearly brushed the food off her plate, then, she continued softly. "A voice was talking *to me.*"

"And we're off!" Annie Ruth announced as she stood, threw her damask napkin to the embroidered seat of her dining chair and walked to the antique sideboard. There, she stood and speared an artichoke heart with a silver skewer lying next to the tray of antipasto.

"Annie Ruth, please!" Betty pleaded.

"God, Betty, she really is nuts!" Annie Ruth said.

"Oh, excuse me, 'Miss There's Something in This Hospital Room, Miss Cat Lady,'" Emily said to Annie Ruth before she could stop herself.

Annie Ruth dropped the artichoke back in the dish, spattering extra virgin olive oil all over the linen sideboard liner and spun around as best she could.

"Don't you dare say that three-letter word ever again in my or my child's presence," she ordered her sister. The force of her statement surprised even her.

None of them had uttered the c-word intentionally since they had discovered the cat perched over little MaeJean's bassinet.

"Look, let's calm down here," Betty commanded. "Everybody sit down. And let's get to the bottom of this without being mean and upset. Okay?"

Annie Ruth rolled her eyes again and reluctantly returned to the table. Emily leaned back and started playing with her food. Then, she began to eat again in earnest.

"Okay," Betty said. "Let's start again. Em-Em, no judgment, I swear, just tell us about the voice."

"Oh, yeah, the voice," Emily said absently as she continued eating her meal. "Well, I guess it started really a few weeks ago. Sort of vague talk, whispers and mutterings at first. Then, it got louder and more distinct and more and more and more specific."

" 'Specific?' What do you mean, Emily?" Betty asked.

"Oh, like it was talking directly to me. Just a little voice in my head telling me things. Sometimes, things to do. Sometimes, things to notice. You know, a pretty, blooming bottle brush plant by the side of the road, some purple and yellow verbena like I ain't never seen before in a deserted lot, an old song on the radio...."

"What you doing knowing about 'verbena'?" Annie Ruth wanted to know.

"Um, now that you mention it, I don't think I ever knew what a verbena looked like before," Emily said with a little interested lilt in her voice.

"Don't get her off track, Annie Ruth," Betty cautioned in a soft tempered tone.

"Yeah, you right. I don't care nothing 'bout no voice or no damn 'verbena,'" Annie Ruth shot back. "Emily Mae Lovejoy, tell me about what do you know about my baby's caul."

Emily and Betty both sat up straighter. Neither of them had ever heard Annie Ruth call either of her sisters by their entire hated names. It was sobering.

"Well, while everybody was looking at MaeJean and getting you settled, Annie Ruth, I whispered to one of the nurses to put the caul in one of those white hospital plastic bags for me," Emily explained.

"You did what?!" Annie Ruth was shouting again.

"I whispered to one of the nurses to put the caul in one of those white hospital plastic bags for me," Emily repeated.

"I heard you. I just do not believe you," Annie Ruth said. She truly was close to incredulous.

"What in the world would make you do that?" Betty wanted to know, too.

"Well, that's what the voice told me to do," Emily explained nearly indignant.

"Okay. Okay," Betty said calmly. "Then, what?"

"Well," Emily said, tilting her head to the side as she tried to remember. "I took the bag and laid it on the side table next to my purse so I wouldn't forget it. But you know me, I almost forgot it anyway."

"Why did you...?" Annie Ruth began, but Betty raised her hand and stopped her.

"Go on, Em-Em. Then, the voice told you to..." Betty prompted her.

"Yeah, that's one reason I left so quick. The voice said take that caul and get it in the earth. Whatever that meant."

"Emily, you took my child's birth caul out of the hospital?"

"Well, like I was trying to tell you, that's what I was told to do. It seemed like the only thing to do at the time."

Betty was trying her best to stay on point, but this was beginning to be too much even for her. She shook her head quickly to clear it, ran her fingers through her short hair and asked as calmly as she could, "Then, what did you do with it, Em-Em?"

"Well, I wasn't clear about what I was supposed to do, so you know me, I went down to the river. Oops!"

"You went down to the river by yourself again?" Now, Betty was getting off track.

"So, you were just riding all around town with my baby's caul in your raggedy-assed car?" Annie Ruth asked.

"I was in Betty's car," Emily corrected her sister primly.

When Betty saw Annie Ruth actually reach out for the silver carving knife laying next to the turkey platter, she knew it was time to step in again.

"Okay, Emily, let's try it again. You went down to the river..."

"Well, it was late and you know how exhausted and wrung out all of us were from the birth and all, and I had a joint in my purse. So, I went down there and smoked it."

"Of course," Annie Ruth muttered under her breath.

"Then, what?" Betty prompted.

"Well, let's go back. I'd been hearing this voice for a while, but right after MaeJean came, it was coming in like real loud and clear. And it said plainly for me to take the baby's veil—Now that I think about it, that's what the voice kept calling it: a 'veil' not a 'caul.' It, the voice, kept saying, 'Get that veil in the earth! Get that veil in the earth!' It kept saying that.

"So, at first, I thought I was supposed to throw it in the river 'cause that's where I ended up at first. But while I was there, it came to me that I should go home and take it to Mudear's garden."

Emily took a breath after the long explanation and quickly ate a few bites of the food on her plate as Betty and Annie Ruth exchanged glances verging on fear. Annie Ruth walked over to the bassinet, reached out and tucked the green baby blanket Betty had finally finished knitting tighter around MaeJean and balled her hands into fists when she realized that her fingers were trembling slightly. Then, she pulled the bassinet right close to her chair and sat down because suddenly her legs felt weak.

"Um, dinner's cold now," Emily said with a scowl as she dropped her fork back on her plate with disappointment. "I can pop everybody's plate in the microwave for a minute," she offered as she made as if to rise from the table.

"Don't you move a fucking muscle," Betty instructed her. "Finish your story."

"Oh," Emily said, surprised at Betty's harsh tone. "Well, just as I was about to throw the veil in the river, like I said, I saw or heard or felt something about Mudear's garden, and I just knew that was where I was supposed to 'put it in the earth.' In the dirt, not in the water. So, I finished off my joint and did just that."

Emily had the nerve to sound satisfied with herself. Betty and Annie Ruth could both feel their pulses throbbing at their temples.

"Exactly, what did you do?" Betty asked.

"I told you. I drove out to Sherwood Forest, walked right into Mudear's garden in back, well, I did trip and fall one time, it was dark. And I put the baby's caul in the ground over in the corn. Somehow, I knew it was supposed to be planted in the corn."

"And this 'voice' told you to do all that?" Betty asked.

"Well," Emily answered with her face kind of scrunched up as she thought, "yes and no. It wasn't so much that she told me as I felt it."

Annie Ruth spoke for the first time in a while. She asked quickly, "Why did you say 'she?'"

"What?' Emily asked.

"You said, 'It wasn't so much that *she* told me.' Why did you say 'she?' Was it a woman's voice speaking to you?"

"Um," Emily said as she pondered the idea. "I guess it was, now that you mention it. Gosh, you and Betty are so much better at this than I am.

"I wish Mudear had picked one of ya'll to talk to rather than me," Emily mumbled peevishly.

"What?" Betty and Annie Ruth both shot back at her.

"Uh, nothing," Emily muttered.

"Oh, don't give me that," Betty said before Annie Ruth could jump in. "Did you just say *Mudear* was the voice speaking to you, telling you what to do?"

Emily bit her bottom lip.

"Answer me, Emily."

Emily was silent. She wasn't being recalcitrant, she simply could not seem to find her voice. And her eyes were taking on that frantic, wild, wolfish look.

"Answer me, Emily," Betty repeated.

"I didn't want to say it before, Betty, but I think so," Emily said softly after taking a moment.

"Oh! My! God!" Annie Ruth whispered.

"Yeah," Betty nodded and agreed. "I knew there was something up. I just knew it. Ever since that cat showed up. Damn, Mudear's back," she said breathlessly. "She ain't dead. She's back."

"Heaven help us, ya'll," Annie Ruth said as revelation crept all over her face. "That's who that damn cat is. It's Mudear. That cat that's after my child is Mudear!"

And because it was Emily who uttered the next words, shivers shot down her sisters' spines.

"It's worse than that, sisters," Emily said and bit her bottom lip as she felt the idea truly dawn on her. "Mudear? She ain't just back. Mudear? I think she crazy!"

CHAPTER 32

Oh, so now I'm crazy, am I?

OOOooooo. They scared now!

Those girls, they need to quit. Now, they gon' try to play like they scared of their own mother.

I swear they get on my nerves more than just about anything in this world. Now the time when they need to be appreciating me instead of working against me. But instead of being glad that I'm still around – the way most daughters would who had lost their mothers – there they are being afraid of me like I'm some kind of scary ghost.

Well, maybe I am some kind of ghost or spirit or something. Tell the truth, I don't know exactly what I am. But I do know that I ain't nothing to be scared of. Not if I get what I want anyway.

And what I want is my grandbaby.

Naw, I ain't crazy, no matter what those girls say. I know I can't take care of the child myself. Not the way I am now. Besides, I didn't want to feed and burp and change my own children. So I ain't talking about taking the child like that. I just want to take her under my wings, so to speak, and teach her what I know. Make her mine.

And I plan to fight for her, too. The way my life is right now she's all I got to live for.

You know, you got t' fight in this life. It's true. Look in the newspaper any morning and see all those folks who didn't put up enough of a good fight. They right there in the obituaries. Me, I finally figured out why I'm still around here.

I know you got t' fight to live. And I for one ain't giving up without a good fight. My girls gon' find that thing out.

Yeah, they gon' find that thing out. Yeah, find that out....

You know, I was thinking 'bout Mamie. She was my friend at one time, back when I had friends.

I asked her one time, "What's beige?" and that was the last time we talked. I could just hear her get real quiet as she pondered my question and even more important, as I was concerned, she pondered my life. I couldn't stand that. Couldn't stand the idea that someone was actually thinking 'bout me and what kinda person I must be not to even know what "beige" was.

But you know it was back in the 1960s when all of a sudden, it seemed like to me, it was "beige this" and "beige that." Beige spring coats and pillbox hats. Beige furniture and beige leather pumps. I hadn't never heard of no "beige" before so I needed to know. You know, I like to know things, especially things that other run-of-the-mill folks seem to be aware of. That's why I looked at television so much, to know things. Well, and also, 'cause TV just downright entertained me.

But television was in black and white then. Ours was, anyway. And I was determined not to ask one of my girls what beige was 'cause everybody in the world seemed to know what it was but me.

OOoo, now how in the world did I get off on that? Oh, my mind must be drifting all of a sudden. I can't even remember what I was saying before I thought about Mamie and "beige."

Oh, yeah, my grandbaby. I think that's what I was thinking 'bout. Yeah, them girls can fight all they want. But they can't keep my grandchild from me.

CHAPTER 33

um, that little nap felt good. now i'm kinda hungry. and i think I smell food even
if it's not the kind I can eat just yet. but there's my mama and she got all the food I
need right now.

what they yelling about? i'm telling you, I 'bout to be sick of all this drama. it
was fun at first but this all they do. i want to do something else sometime other than
stress.

wonder what they stressing ´bout now.

if it's not about my daddy, whoever he is, it almost always seems to be about that
old lady who hangs around all the time that nobody seems to pay any attention to.

oh, yeah, she my grandmama. I don't know why I keep forgetting that.

i guess it's 'cause she don't seem to fit in this family at all. Don't none of us seem
to take after her at all.

CHAPTER 34

The girls knew, knew better than anyone else, that Esther Mudear Lovejoy was crazy. That's what nearly everyone in Mulberry over the age of thirty believed for a fact. It was what the townspeople had said and whispered and snickered throughout the girls' lives.

"That Esther Lovejoy crazy."

"She done stayed in that house so long, she done lost her mind."

"Stop doing that, child," they admonished their children. "You gon' end up being as crazy as Esther Lovejoy."

But the girls knew that if their mother was crazy, she wasn't just plain old ordinary crazy.

"Mudear," they had told each other for years as they cleaned the house, washed the clothes, did their homework, paid the bills, shopped for the household, and jumped up from taking a break to run and fetch for their reclining mother, "Mudear, she's crazy like a fox."

But the thought of a crazy mother living and breathing and moving about the family house and gardens, even in the dead of night, didn't hold a candle to the image of a dead mother, able to morph into any shape or creature she liked, invading their home and peace, skulking around the halls and rooms, getting into Emily's head, stalking their new baby girl MaeJean with the idea of doing God knows what to her. And they found themselves sitting silently around the dinner table contemplating their situation.

With tears in her eyes, Annie Ruth looked over at her baby sleeping soundly in the bassinet, then turned to her big sister. "Betty?" she asked. "What in the world are we going to do now?"

Betty surveyed her family silently for a moment. Then, she laid her hands palms down on the table like a mafia don and spoke.

"Okay, Annie Ruth, I know I'm the oldest and ya'll expect me to know everything. But with the situation we in now, I think it's about time that we listen to all comers.

"What you got, Em-Em?" Betty asked. "I can tell you got something on your mind."

"Well," Emily said slowly as she bit her bottom lip and bounced her breast in her hand. "I been thinking and noticing. All this stuff that's happening, it ain't all Mudear."

Annie Ruth was right on it. "What you mean, it ain't all Mudear? It's all her! It ain't nothing but her! It was Mudear telling you to take MaeJean's caul and bury it. It was Mudear who was that noise in the attic. It was Mudear who ran past us on the steps. And Jesus keep us near the cross, it was Mudear standing over my baby in the form of a cat last night trying to suck the breath out of her little body."

Betty closed her eyes and took a deep breath. Emily slid her hands under her bare thighs onto the upholstered seat of her chair to keep her entire body from shivering. Then, she took a couple of deep breaths the way Dr. Axelton had taught her and closed her eyes to think.

"I don't know how," Annie Ruth continued. "But I know it was Mudear. Dead or alive, it was all Mudear."

Emily sat nodding for a moment. Then, she spoke up.

"Yeah, I know she all up in it, and she started this, and she the one that wants our lil' MaeJean and all. But haven't you both noticed that everything we say seems to be coming true—good or bad?"

Her sisters stopped their minds from racing for a moment and tried to steady their thoughts.

Emily prompted them. "Remember, Betty, how we were talking earlier about who MaeJean's father was and you said those men weren't going to stay quiet about their possible child and the phone rang right then for Annie Ruth and it was Raphael?"

Betty nodded slowly.

"And then you said, 'We ain't seen the last of the daddies,' and Delbert's call came right after that?"

Betty nodded again.

"Oh, that's nothing, Emily," Annie Ruth said, trying to sound dismissive. "Of course, they were gonna call sooner or later."

"Yeah, but why now? And I bet you had been thinking yesterday about that old cat that Mudear killed that time when you were a baby and it was trying to cut your throat with its claw," Emily said, determined to make her point.

"Well, maybe," Annie Ruth conceded.

"Wait a minute, you two," Betty said, trying her best to insert some element of reason in this exchange. "Let's slow this runaway train down for a moment."

"Yeah, and why do you think you were asking about MaeJean's caul today? I was thinking about that caul all day. And what about when MaeJean was having that bad gas attack or something and crying her head off and we all said, 'I can't stand to see our baby girl in pain,' and just like magic, she gave a little burp and stopped crying without any of us touching her?"

"Oh, Emily, you just…" Annie Ruth began.

And Emily finished, "grasping at straws here like that silly woman named Annie Bea who used to come into Betty's first little raggedy shop when we were still teenagers."

Annie Ruth's eyes widened more and more as Emily finished her thought and her sentence.

"Oh my God, Em-Em," Annie Ruth said, even as she gasped at the words that were about to come out of her mouth. "You're right. You're dead right. You just said what I was gonna' say!"

"That's exactly what's been happening," Betty agreed. "We been reading each other's minds, influencing each other's thoughts and creating situations."

Emily bit her bottom lip smugly and nodded along with her sisters.

"Well, I been thinking some more," she said, basking in the glow of her sisters' newfound respect. "And I think we got more power than we think. Mudear ain't the only one who can make things happen. We can, too. That's what we been doing, right?"

Her sisters nodded slowly, uncertainly. The idea was still so new to them.

Together, they were as powerful as their self-centered, mad, dead mother.

"I've been thinking, too," Betty said suddenly as they all sat looking at their plates of cold food and contemplating their power and their situation.

"Yeah?" both her sisters answered cautiously.

"We've only got one choice,"

"What's that?" Emily asked.

"We've got to get that caul back!"

"Get it back?

"Yeah, it's the only way. As long as it's out there, Mudear can still get to MaeJean and to us. I don't know how or why, but I know she's using that caul."

"Wow, Betty, I was just thinking the exact same thing. Hmm," Annie Ruth said.

"Get it back?" Emily repeated.

"Yeah."

"But how are we gonna do it, Betty?" Annie Ruth wanted to know.

"We've got to go dig it up," Betty explained.

"What?" Emily exclaimed as she finished off a mouthful of cold squash casserole.

"We've got to go out to the house and dig it up," Betty explained.

"Dig it up?" Emily was truly on the verge of totally losing it. Just the thought of going back into that garden, getting down on her knees and ...

"Yes, Emily, and please stop repeating everything I'm saying. You're the one who put it there. You understand better than any of us what we got to do."

"Understand what?" Emily asked.

"Em-Em, stop playing like you some new little hip-hop teenager who doesn't know anything about old-time black folks and what they believe," Betty said indignantly as she nervously began taking platters of food off the dining room table. "You've spent almost as much time as I have out at Lovejoy's 1 listening to those old women talk while they're getting their hair washed, pressed, and curled not to have learned a thing or two about things. Like babies born with cauls and veils over their faces."

"Well, yeah, but..."

"Yeah, but nothing," Annie Ruth shot at Emily from her chair where she was suddenly nursing MaeJean without a bit of trouble. "You know a child born with a caul is special, able to see ghosts and spirits and tell the future and look in your eyes and read you and shit. That's why that old heifer Mudear who call herself our mother and ain't no more a mother that a stray cat had you bury that caul in her garden."

"See, Annie Ruth, you said 'Mudear' and 'cat' in one sentence, but when I say it, it's a big to-do," Emily chastised her sister.

"Don't start nitpicking with me, Em-Em," Annie Ruth cautioned. "And don't correct me. What you just better start doing is getting dressed to go on back out there to that garden and get my baby's caul back."

"I'm not going back into Mudear's garden," Emily said flatly.

"Oh, yes, you are," Annie Ruth said.

"Oh, no, I'm not!"

Betty broke in before it turned into a kindergarten bout of "Am"/ "Am not."

"Em-Em, you have to go. You know where it's buried. Without you, we could be out there digging kitty holes and cat holes all night."

"Digging in Mudear's garden again," Emily said softly with a far-away look in her eyes.

"Don't give us that dreamy, I'm not of this world bit, Emily Mae McPherson," Annie Ruth said fiercely. "I will whip your ass right here. I swear to God I will, stitches and all. I will take off these platinum hoop earrings and I will kick your natural born ass right here if you start flaking out on us now. I swear to God I will."

"God, Annie Ruth, ain't no need for that! Ain't no need for threatening violence up in here just 'cause I'm not up to everything you and Betty are."

"Emily. You took my child's birth caul, something that any fool knows has some kind of profound spiritual importance, even Dr. Hamlin, a woman of science, knew that. You took it out of the hospital, drove it all around Mulberry, took it down to the Ocawatchee River, dragged it out to Sherwood Forest, dug a hole and put it in the ground next to that woman's prized corn, and now, you want to act like this is something you can't do for your only—and I assure you she will be your only one from me—niece who is named after you."

"Annie Ruth, stop it. You know I'd do anything for MaeJean!"

"Well, then, let's get cracking and get the hell outa' Dodge," Annie Ruth commanded. "Besides, Em-Em, you're the one who said you think we're as powerful in our own way as she is. What you worried about?"

"Annie Ruth," Emily replied solemnly. "I got fired from my job. I got left by my husband. I drive a car that couldn't pass a safety inspection to save its life. I'm living with and off my big sister. And I just checked my stash and somebody or something has taken all my weed.

"I'll tell you what I'm worried about. What if I'm wrong about us?" Betty spoke up this time.

"You're not, Em-Em. This time, you're not wrong. I can feel it in my bones. As long as we stick together, we're more powerful than Mudear. We're more powerful together than she is alone, dead or alive."

Then, they all nodded, raised their crystal goblets of iced tea, clinked glasses, and headed upstairs to Annie Ruth's room.

"What about MaeJean?" Betty asked as she took Annie Ruth's arm and helped her carry the baby up the wide stairs. Betty was so relieved that things had quieted down a bit between her sisters before events had degenerated into a cat fight that she felt she could not possibly think more clearly.

"I mean what are we going to do with her while we're gone?" Betty wondered.

"We're not going to do anything with her. We're taking her with us. You don't think I'd leave MaeJean now, do you?" Annie Ruth asked incredulously.

"Well, we could get Mrs. Andrews to come over and stay a while, couldn't we, Betty?" Emily suggested.

"No!" was all Annie Ruth said as she entered her room and put MaeJean down in her cradle.

Even Betty was skeptical.

"Annie Ruth, she is just a little newborn baby. Do you think we should be taking her out in this night air already? Maybe, we should just wait until morning when it's warmer to do this."

"Oh, Betty, you know we need to take care of this right away. Mudear ain't sitting around waiting for morning. Anyway, don't be so old-fashioned," Annie Ruth admonished as she began throwing diapers and jumpsuits and baby blankets into a large pink baby bag. "You see young girls out with their babies at Wal-Mart the night after they give birth, and those children are just fine."

"Yeah," Emily retorted as Betty stepped out of the room to get her purse and a jacket, "but those are ghetto and trailer park babies."

Abruptly, Annie Ruth stopped changing MaeJean's diaper. "Emily. I cannot believe that we are standing here plotting how to save our baby girl from her crazy dead grandmother—a baby girl, I might add, whose daddy's identity we won't know unless we do a DNA test—and you got the nerve to be calling somebody 'ghetto.'"

"I didn't mean it like that," Emily explained as she pulled off one cherry red cotton sweater and picked up another just as crimson that she had grabbed from the deacon's bench in the upstairs hall. "I just meant those babies got more stamina and resilience 'cause they have to."

"Shoot," Annie Ruth retorted as she went back to powdering MaeJean's little bottom. She had awakened and seemed to be watching her mother and aunt with real glee. "I hope our baby got some of that ghetto 'stamina and resilience.' 'Cause she's gonna need it tonight."

"We are, too," Betty put in as she entered the room with her purse on one shoulder and the baby carrier on the other.

"Here," Emily said as she picked up the tiny mother-of-pearl-backed soft bristled baby brush and handed it to Annie Ruth. "You might want to run this over our baby's hair. You know Lovejoy women take care 'a their hair."

"My baby doesn't need her hair brushed," Annie Ruth replied indignantly. "Her hair is just beautiful the way it is."

"Um," Emily said as she bit her bottom lip. "Of course, MaeJean's hair is perfect. You know, we...."

Betty interrupted her.

"Emily, I swear if you say, 'We got Indian in our family,' I swear I'll lose it and have to hurt you," Betty said as she shifted the baby carrier on her hip.

Emily was offended. "I wasn't even thinking about saying that," she snapped at her sister and looked guilty because that was exactly what she was about to say.

She noticed again, especially in the last few hours, how often she and her sisters knew what the others were thinking. It's as if we can read each others' minds, she thought. And as close as they were, that was something new.

The other girls had noticed it, too. But because this time, as they prepared to confront Mudear's garden—the one thing that their mother loved more than her own comfort—the realization unsettled rather than strengthened them.

Annie Ruth merely decided to ignore the new phenomenon. And instead of leaping into the fray, she picked up MaeJean, headed for the bedroom door and announced, "Let's ride. Mudear ain't getting' no deader."

CHAPTER 35

woooo, road trip! i call shotgun!

now this what i'm talkin' 'bout. some real fun, not just some old drama for my mama.

my mama, she something else, huh?

Hmmph, she may look all cute and everything, but, wooo, don't get my mama mad, okay? She don't play.

i wonder would she really kick aunt em-em's ass over me. i bet she would. tee-hee tee-hee.

yeah, my mama just might do that.

man, how much fun are my mama and aunties gon' be? they always got something going on. and it ain't just drama.

but i still don't know what all the fuss is about my grandmama. she don't seem that bad to me, just a little sad even when she laughing or looking at me. she just a old lady.

and now it looks like i'm gonna get to see her garden and what all the talk is about. i don't think i ever even seen a garden other than aunt betty's.

and for some reason, all this talk about taking me out at night makes me think the nighttime is the right time.

CHAPTER 36

U h-uh. Look out! Here come the posse. Look at 'em. They think they bad asses now.

Those girls think they can just round up all their little strength and pack that baby's clothes and bring her out into this night air to stop me from getting my hands on her. Then, they bigger fools than I give 'em credit for.

Can't nothing in heaven or on earth stop me from getting that child.

Well, at least them girls a' mine doing something. I guess I should gi' 'em credit for that, at least.

It's like I used to tell them girls when I heard 'em complain among themselves as teenagers about to having to go to school but still wanted to get jobs so they could get out my house, "Root, hog, or die po'."

It ain't gon' do 'em no good, but I like to see my girls putting up a fight. Even if it's against me.

"Bright lights, big city, gone to my baby's head."

Now I don't know where that came from. It just seem that little bits and pieces of songs and poems and conversations will just float through my head and out' my mouth from time to time, 'specially in the last couple a' days. I don't know why. I hope I ain't getting crazy like my daughters in my old age. Well, my old death.

I got the shock of my life today. I was walking down Betty's hall, well, I was moving really, 'cause when I ain't taking on the shape of some living thing like a cat or something, I can't really walk and touch and feel and smell. But I was still going to visit my grandchild in her room just to look at her 'cause that's all I could do, when I passed a big gold-framed mirror. Lord, Betty got more mirrors in that house than a little. Just go to show you how vain she is. I ain't raised her to be that conceited, but that's how she turned out. Anyway, I got a glimpse of myself in that mirror. Ain't seen myself in a mirror in I don't know how long. Didn't think I had no reflection no more. But all of a certain, there I was looking back at myself in Betty's upstairs hall.

And you know what, I ain't nearly as cute as I always thought I was. Of course, I still have on this ugly-assed navy blue dress they buried me in. Out of all the things I seem able to change, my wardrobe ain't one of them. So my attire may 'a had something to do with it, but, like I said, I didn't look anywhere as good as I thought.

It took me by surprise so much I just stopped and stared at myself for a good long while. Annie Ruth came out the baby's room with the telephone in her hand and looked up and down the hall and up toward the attic. I guess she could feel me nearby.

She finally went on back in her room, but a little bit later when Betty and Emily come up there, that's when it hit me. With all the girls sitting there together it hit me that I was seeing myself in their faces, in their walks and stance and bodies.

And I ain't nowhere as good-looking as them! I wouldn't   tell them that even if I could for nothing in the world.

Like I say, they all conceited as hell already. Besides, everybody know pretty women a dime a dozen on this earth.

CHAPTER 37

When the girls pulled up to the Lovejoy house in Sherwood Forest, Emily half expected to hear creepy organ music playing like that from an old Bela Lagosi horror movie. From Betty's car, the women could see the outline of the brick ranch-style house and the edge of the backyard garden in the ghostly light that streamed from the carport through the fog.

"I wonder what made Poppa turn on that outside light tonight," Betty wondered aloud.

"Shoot, he's probably scared of the dark," Emily offered. "And besides, look at this fog. Where did it come from?" she asked as she squinted toward the house.

They had all noticed the gathering mist that seemed to enshroud the car on the silent ride across town to their destination. And although Betty, who usually had a lead foot, had driven slowly to compensate for the limited visibility, none of them dared mention the fog until Emily spoke up.

"It's foggy down by the river lots of nights," she continued. "But I don't think I've ever seen it foggy out here at night."

"Sure, it has been," Betty offered bravely. "You just don't remember. I've seen it foggy out here at Mud...."

She stopped in mid-word, wishing she had not even uttered the beginning of their mother's name. As soon as it was said, they could all feel her presence in the interior of the car and simultaneously reached for the door handles to exit the vehicle.

None of them had stated their resolve not to utter Mudear's name, but they had all made that decision around the same time when they noticed that each time they said it aloud—"Mudear"—they felt a chill run up their spines as if a cat had walked over their graves.

"For God's sake, Emily, stop thinking the worst!" Betty commanded. "Remember, we're not only thinking the same thoughts, but for whatever reason, everything we think and say is coming true."

"Oh, yeah, right, Betty," Emily said. "I just forgot there for a minute."

Then, she closed her eyes tightly and repeated, "Think good thoughts! Think good thoughts!"

Betty turned in the driver's seat to make sure Emily could handle unhooking the baby seat and lifting it and MaeJean out of the back seat while Annie Ruth tried to negotiate the steps involved in going from a sitting to a standing position by the side of the car.

"Don't bother taking the seat out, Em-Em," Annie Ruth said as she struggled to stand. "I got my Bjorn baby carrier, and it'll be easier and safer for me to have MaeJean right here at my breast."

She stopped her struggle for a moment and pulled the green blanket Betty had knitted for her niece out of the baby bag and to tuck around

MaeJean to protect her from the damp air and whatever else might be waiting for them in the night. Betty's blanket was not as heavy as two others she had packed, but Annie Ruth felt it carried more spiritual protection.

Betty was about to run around and help Annie Ruth when she remembered something and, with a snap of her fingers, reached across the front seat, opened the glove compartment and removed the big heavy shiny blue Magnalite flashlight. Then, as she was about to close the glove compartment she reached back in, felt around for a moment and took out a miniature version of the bigger flashlight and passed it to her middle sister as Emily handed the baby to Annie Ruth who had finally lifted herself out of the passenger's seat.

Betty didn't bother to test either one of the lights. She knew they worked. It was part of her m.o. to be prepared. And on this strange foggy night, she knew she needed all the grounding and foresight she could muster.

"Okay," she said, as the three Lovejoy women stood clustered around MaeJean snuggled in her soft baby carrier on her mother's breast. "This is the plan."

"Good," Emily said with a sigh. "We got a plan."

"Well, such as it is," Betty said. "The plan is to get in there, find the spot where you buried MaeJean's caul, dig it up, then get back in the car with it and get the hell outa' here."

Emily looked toward the garden.

"Ya'll know this is creepy, don't you?" she asked.

Her sisters didn't answer. They didn't have to. They could feel the goose bumps and the tiny hairs raised on their arms and the backs of their necks as well as Emily could.

"Are we gon' tell Poppa we here?" Emily asked softly.

"Please!" Annie Ruth said softly but intensely. "Poppa can't help us. Besides, the quicker we get in that garden, find that caul you planted in the ground, Emily, the sooner we can get the hell outa' here and back to Betty's nice, safe house."

Her sisters nodded their agreement. All of them, however, silently questioned whether they would ever feel completely safe anywhere again. Since the episode with the cat at Betty's house the night before, even the house at the top of Pleasant Hill didn't feel like the haven it always had. Still, they moved closer to one another and headed for the garden in the backyard like a division of soldiers on a life-or-death mission.

From time to time, Annie Ruth remembered to bounce MaeJean in her carrier, but for the most part she was concentrating so hard on holding the baby close to her chest that she forgot to comfort her in the strange surroundings in the night air. If she had had sufficient light and the presence of mind to notice, however, Annie Ruth would have seen that MaeJean was just as comfortable and content as she could be snuggled against her mother under her Aunt Betty's blanket. Her eyes, still barely able to distinguish shapes and colors, had a life to them, sparkling in the dark like glowing coals as never before in her short life.

"Okay, Em-Em," Betty said as they came to the perimeter of Mudear's garden and stopped. "Just where in the corn field did you plant MaeJean's caul?"

Emily stopped, put her hands on her hips and stood surveying the entire dark yard as she slowly bit her bottom lip.

"Well," she said deliberately as she recalled the night of MaeJean's birth. "Over there is where I tripped over that river stone and nearly broke a nail."

"Um-hmmm," Betty said softly, trying to encourage her sister's memory.

"And over there is where I dropped the plastic hospital bag with the caul after I got up and brushed myself off," Emily continued.

"Okay," Betty said.

"Oh, oh, and over there – Remember, Betty?" Emily said as she trained the flashlight on another section of the thickly planted yard. "There is where I hid for a whole afternoon when I was sixteen and my face had broken out so bad."

"Okay, that's it, Em-Em!" Annie Ruth shouted. "Where the fuck did you bury the damn caul?"

"Shhh!" Emily and Betty cautioned their baby sister.

"Shit! Don't 'shush' me," Annie Ruth said in a harsh whisper. "I got my child out here in the damp night air surrounded by fog as thick as London pea soup looking for my baby's precious birth caul that this one buried in the dirt, and she's taking us on a stroll down memory fucking lane. What the fuck?!"

"Okay, shhh. I'm sorry. You're right, Lil' Sis," Betty said. "Just keep it down so we don't disturb Poppa and half of the neighborhood. They think we strange enough without half of Mulberry finding us out here in the middle of the night digging in our dead mother's garden."

Annie Ruth merely pulled the soft blanket around the baby and sucked her teeth at her sisters. Emily, hardly mollified by her big sister's apology on her behalf, rolled her eyes at Annie Ruth, but then softened when MaeJean made a little mewling noise that sounded almost like a sneeze.

"Oh, my goodness!" she exclaimed softly. "Is this baby catching a little cold? Okay, Aunt Em-Em is going to hurry up."

And she did. Marching resolutely right into the heart of the garden, Emily headed for the corner where the blades of corn had begun to peek through the rich dark soil.

The other women followed her cautiously through the fog with the flashlights illuminating their paths.

Emily looked around on the ground for a moment, then pointed to a mound of fresh dirt.

"Right there," she declared. "Right there. I'm sure of it. Right there is where I dug that hole and put the caul."

Betty and Emily shone their lights on the spot she designated, and

Betty and Annie Ruth looked at each other. Both of them were afraid to take the next step, but they didn't have to. Emily handed her flashlight to Annie Ruth, dropped to her knees without any encouragement and began to dig in the dirt. But before she had excavated more than two or three handfuls of soil, she suddenly stopped.

"What's the matter?" Betty asked cautiously, half-afraid of the answer.

"Something's not right here," Emily said slowly and she looked around her, then back to the original spot. "Something's not right."

Annie Ruth took a step closer, sticking the small flashlight in the infant holder and cradling the baby with both hands. "What do you mean, 'not right'?" she asked.

"Well, I know this is where I buried the caul," Emily stated flatly. "I can tell that much," she added emphatically. "But the caul's not here. I didn't bury it that deep, and it's not here. Besides, something's been digging around the spot other than me."

"What?" Betty asked as she swung the light from her big blue flashlight around the spot in the garden. She tried to control her voice so it didn't reveal the sudden shot of fear she was feeling, but it didn't work. And the sound of their normally calm big sister's fear upset Annie Ruth and Emily even more.

"You heard me," Emily said sharply as she began frantically digging in the soil. "Something's been digging out here. I can see the claw prints in the dirt. Look!"

And the other two women bent over Emily's broad shoulders for a closer inspection.

"Oh, my God, she's right," Annie Ruth whispered not making any effort to disguise her rising terror. "It looks just like...."

"Who's that out there in the yard?" Poppa shouted from the end of the carport.

All three women jumped at the sound of their father's voice and turned their flashlights in the direction of the house where he stood. The women could see that he had something in his hand but couldn't make out exactly what it was.

"It's just us, Poppa," Betty replied quickly. "Don't shoot!" Then, she giggled nervously at her silly comment.

"Betty? Emily? Annie Ruth? Good God, is that you all out there? Don't tell me you got that newborn child out there in the yard in the middle of the night? All of ya'll, get in this house. Good God!"

The women couldn't remember when they had heard their father order them around like that. Annie Ruth had never experienced that. But they all automatically obeyed and headed for the house.

"What in the world has gotten into you girls tonight?" Poppa asked as the three women filed past him into the back kitchen door, Annie Ruth bringing up the rear with MaeJean wrapped in her arms. He rested the baseball bat he was holding against the wall.

"Annie Ruth, you a mother now. You oughta know better," he chastised his youngest daughter as he guided her and MaeJean to his own chair in the den.

Annie Ruth was just about to get some lie together to give her father when he moved on to a more important subject.

"And take all those things off my new grandbaby and let me get a good look at her," he said with a smile none of his daughters had ever seen on his face. His dark, clear skin that had taken on an ashen aspect in the last few years, seemed to light up and his eyes crinkled up in the corners with what looked like delight.

"Well, she a pretty girl, ain't she?" Poppa cooed. "Why, she look just like her Mu.... Just like her mother. She look just like you, Annie Ruth."

All the girls forgot their task for a moment in the glow of their father's unfamiliar smile and began preening over the baby, too. But just as they were about to enjoy showing MaeJean off to her grandfather, the sound of trash cans being knocked over outside drew their attention.

First, they looked out the back sliding glass doors leading to the screened back porch, then over to their father for an explanation.

"Oh, that's probably some old cat that's been hanging out here lately," Poppa said lightly and went back to smiling at his new granddaughter.

"Cat?" Annie Ruth asked, her voice managing to break over the one-syllable word.

"Oh, it's a real cat alright, Annie Ruth," her father answered without thinking. Even though neither Mudear nor any of his daughters had ever discussed it with him, he knew all about Annie Ruth's predilection for seeing cats out of the corner of her eyes. He even knew that the condition began the year she turned thirteen, something that her mother and sisters would probably be hard-pressed to remember.

In fact, he knew more about his girls than any of them would ever surmise. He knew that Betty could not abide the cold and the dark. He blamed himself for that. He knew that Emily was allergic to hummingbirds whose presence made her sneeze uncontrollably. And that still, the tiny creatures seemed to seek her out and hum and zip around her as if she were a butterfly bush in full bloom.

And he knew there were few things other than aging that Annie Ruth feared more than cats, real and imagined, but especially imagined.

CHAPTER 38

"Some old cat?" "Some old cat?"
Is that what that old burned-out light bulb of a husband a' mine had the nerve to refer to me as? I got a good mind to march right into that cracker box of a house of his and...
What am I talking about? I can do anything I want to do. Shoot, I did that before I was dead. I sho' can do it now.

CHAPTER 39

uh-uh. here come my grandmama. i know she want me to call her "mudear," but i don't like the sound of that for some reason.

with her here, i know there gon' be some drama up in here now.

but at least, my whole family'll finally be together. well, except for my daddy, and i got a feeling it's gon' be a while before he's allowed to show his face.

CHAPTER 40

As the girls watched their Poppa play with his granddaughter, they were tempted to allow themselves to relax a tiny bit. They all wanted to heave a little sigh and lean back in their seats in the den.

However, when they began to relax a bit, they realized how tense they had become, planning their foray into the night, stalking around in their dead mother's garden, digging in the dirt for a piece of buried membrane, looking over their shoulders for God knows what.

So each time they came close to real relaxation, trying to enjoy the family scene in front of them, the sound of what Poppa had called "some stray cat" knocking over what sounded like tin garbage cans and metal garden tools outside made them sit up straight and tense again.

The three girls kept glancing at the sliding glass door that led to the screened porch at the back of the house expecting their father to rise from his seat at any moment, hand MaeJean back to Annie Ruth and walk out to chase the bothersome creature away from his property. But he didn't. The noise didn't seem to faze him at all.

And though no one said it, Betty, Emily, and Annie Ruth all thought the frightening racket was getting closer and closer to the house.

All three girls had come out of their wraps soon after entering the house. In fact, they had all made the move to remove their coats and jackets at the same time, which creeped them out a bit when they realized that even their movements, like their thoughts, were becoming synchronized.

Lord, old folks keep their houses so hot, Betty thought. Even to me, it's hot up in here.

Betty had been responsible for purchasing Poppa's medicine most of her adult life and knew that after a little heart scare a few years earlier, he had been taking blood thinners that left him cold most of the time, no matter the weather. But even with thin blood, Betty had never remembered her father turning the heat up so high on a spring night. Even a damp foggy one.

Poppa's getting old, she thought. And she found herself surprised at the realization that her father's life was continuing to dwindle out whether his daughters gave him much thought or not. It continued to amaze her the way the sun still rose in the east and the birds kept on singing in the trees, life continuing unabated, after Mudear had died.

Other than feeling like the tropics, the den looked the same as it had when Mudear was alive. The early American furniture Betty had bought for them years before was arranged in the same spots as before. The heavy rugs in the same places on the clean tile floor. Even the lights were turned on low the way Mudear, with her night vision, liked them set after dark. It seemed her father hadn't changed a thing other than the temperature since Mudear had died.

Poppa looked around the room at Annie Ruth holding MaeJean, then at his other daughters and seemed about to speak when he caught sight of Emily's dirty hands.

"Emily!" he said suddenly, confusion and surprise in his voice. "Your hands are filthy. What you been doin', girl?"

Annie Ruth and Betty looked over at their sister. And Emily slipped her hands behind her back like a child caught being naughty.

"Go on in there to the kitchen sink and wash 'em with some of that Octagon soap there in the drain," Poppa instructed. "There's a brush there, too. Use that."

Emily rose and quietly obeyed.

"Is that what ya'll were doing out there in the garden?" he asked Betty. "Digging in the dirt?"

Poppa couldn't remember a time when he had chastised his daughters so much at one time. Not when they were children. Not when they were teenagers. And certainly not after they became women.

When none of the girls responded, he felt suddenly strange and uncomfortable doing it, playing the stern father role so late in the game. The girls simply didn't know what to say in explanation.

"Mudear's back from the dead, and she's trying to get her hands on MaeJean."

"Your dead wife can turn herself into a cat and has been prowling around Betty's house trying to snatch our baby girl."

"A voice in Emily's head that we think belongs to Mudear told her to take MaeJean's birth caul and bury it in the corn field out back. And now we need to dig it up and keep it safe so Mudear can't get it and have some kind of power over our baby girl."

Now, all of those statements were true. And the sisters believed every one of them. But not one of the girls could force herself to say any of them aloud to their father.

Poppa took their silence as admonishment of him as a father and bit his bottom lip to hold back the hurt.

Emily returned from the kitchen holding up her clean hands for her father to see, but he was no longer looking at her or any of the others girls. He was staring at the floor, deep in thought. Emily took her seat again and tried to look relaxed.

After a few moments of tense silence, Poppa cleared his throat as if he were a boy about to give a Sunday school speech, handed MaeJean back to her mother, looked around the room at his daughters and grandbaby, then cleared his throat again. But instead of saying anything, he dropped his head with his chin nearly resting on his chest and remained silent.

He stayed that way for so long that the girls grew even more uncomfortable in the silence and looked at each other with raised eyebrows and shrugs.

Poppa knew what he wanted to say, but he was so full of snapshots from the past of missed opportunities with his daughters and images from the future of little MaeJean going on errands with her Granddaddy, of running in a ruffled swimsuit through the sprinklers in the front yard in the summer, of him taking her to school in a freshly pressed plaid dress and leather Mary Janes on a crisp fall day. The swirl of images nearly crowded out his other thoughts.

Just as Betty was about to break the tense silence and attempt to explain what they were doing out in the night with the baby poking around in his yard, Poppa spoke up.

"I know I ain't always been there for you girls," he said without looking up at them. His voice started out softly but seemed to grow stronger with each word he spoke. Then, finally, he raised his head and tried to look them all, one by one, in their eyes.

Emily and Betty exchanged glances, but Annie Ruth merely continued playing and fussing with MaeJean, evading her father's gaze. Annie Ruth realized that Poppa had been avoiding her presence ever since the night before Mudear's funeral when he had broken down in tears at the kitchen table and had to be led by her, his baby daughter, weeping to his bed. And she was just fine with that. She had no idea what to do with the memory of that night, so she had pushed it way back in her mind and tried not to think about it.

"Ya'll ain't got to say nothing," he continued. "You know it's true, and I know it's true, and I know you know it. I been thinking 'bout this for some time. Ain't had nothing but time in the last few months to do nothing else but think, the house being so quiet and empty and all."

Though his comments kept drifting off with no real end, the girls could tell somehow that he was nowhere near finished even as they sat there in the gaps of silence.

Then, he spoke up again.

"You know, a daughter is a special thing to a man. Oh, I know men always talking 'bout their sons and somebody to carry on their names and such. But any man who's truly honest with himself will admit that it's his daughters who have his heart."

Poppa's unusual personal talk was making all his daughters uneasy. They felt surprised and off-kilter, the way they had the night the previous fall when Annie Ruth had arrived for Mudear's funeral, and he had delivered a little unexpected speech about putting Mudear in the ground right away. That, along with the odd and steady noises outside, made Betty, Annie Ruth, and especially Emily about ready to jump out of their skin.

"Poppa," she piped up suddenly, "you had your Sanka this evening? Want me to make you a cup?"

But Poppa merely ignored Emily's offer and continued what the girls felt was becoming another speech. They didn't really know what to make of it. It was beginning to sound like an apology, but they just didn't know.

"Yeah, it's his girls that really mean something to a man. I know I always felt that way about you girls. 'Course, you wouldn'a known it by the way I conducted myself or…" Here he paused as if he were deciding whether to say the next words or not.

"Or for that matter, the way I allowed your mother to conduct herself."

At the mention of Mudear, one of the huge terra cotta flower boxes fell from the ledge that lined the perimeter of the screened porch and crashed onto the brick terrace below. The house, the sisters, and Poppa shook from the reverberation.

Poppa and his daughters all leapt to their feet.

Betty gasped.

Annie Ruth cried softly, "Oh."

Emily yelled, "Lord have mercy!"

And MaeJean let out a little short baby cry at the abrupt movement of her mother's sudden jerking stance.

Looking annoyed, Poppa reached down and patted MaeJean's head tenderly.

"Look at 'em," he said "Scaring that baby with all that noise and jumping up all of a sudden. What's the matter wi' these folks? Huh, MaeJean?" It was as near as any of his daughters had ever heard him speaking in baby talk.

Then, he turned to Annie Ruth as if he would never get to tell her all that he had to share. "Love that name, Annie Ruth. I love that name 'MaeJean.' Bet Betty and Emily love it, too," he added with a smile.

Though tense and frightened, Annie Ruth found herself smiling back fondly at her father for the first time that she could remember.

However, another crash from out back broke the gentle moment and brought them all back to the present.

"Damn that cat!" Poppa exclaimed as he turned from his girls and strode resolutely toward the back kitchen door and the Louisville Slugger he had leaned against the wall.

Before she could stop herself, Annie Ruth cried, "Don't leave us alone in here, Poppa."

And both Emily and Betty swung around and stared unbelievingly at their baby sister, who stood shakily holding MaeJean in her arms. Annie Ruth's voice was so fragile, her plea to their father so plaintive, that her sisters felt a stab of empathy in their guts and began moving closer to her as she sank to the sofa with the baby snuggled at her breast.

But it was too late. Poppa had already opened the back kitchen door and stepped out leaving it ajar.

"Get on 'way from here," Poppa yelled as he brandished the baseball bat in the night air, slicing through the fog that still draped everything outside the house.

"Poppa," Betty called even more loudly over her shoulder as she sat next to her sisters and MaeJean on the plaid Early American style sofa. But she knew he couldn't hear her. She could see that he had moved off beyond the carport into the back yard by the trash cans and disappeared into the fog.

They sat there in silence with nervous perspiration beading up on their top lips and beginning to soak through their clothes even without their shawls and jackets on. The sudden quiet after all the racket outdoors didn't relieve the tension. It added to it.

"Maybe, we should close that door," Emily suggested as they all sat staring at the gaping kitchen door. It was the first time they had spoken to each other since they had entered the house.

None of them made a move. Nothing was said, but they were all thinking about those claw marks they had seen in the dirt around the corn where Emily said she had buried MaeJean's birth caul. It seemed they hardly needed to speak at all to communicate with each other.

"Yeah," Betty agreed. "Maybe, we should."

Still, no one moved.

Suddenly, Annie Ruth began to shiver, and she clutched MaeJean, sleeping in her arms, closer to her chest for warmth and protection.

The three girls sat so closely on the sofa that they all had felt it when their baby sister began to shake.

"What's the matter, Annie Ruth?" Betty asked. "You chilly?"

Betty didn't have to wait for a response. As soon as she asked the question, she felt a blast of frigid air wash over her like an arctic wave. And she, too, began to shiver.

"My God," Emily exclaimed as she wrapped her arms around herself and began rocking back and forth. "It just got freezing cold in here."

Suddenly, a small but unmistakable sound at the open kitchen door drew their attention. They certainly had not spent any time around animals, cats especially—not real ones anyway. But they immediately recognized the meooowwww that they heard there.

They turned back to the open door just in time to see a cat—the same black cat with white paws and a white vest that they had last spied leaping through Annie Ruth's bathroom window the night before, the same cat that had stood astride their little MaeJean's bassinet, the same cat that had disturbed their sleep and the peace of their household making scratching noises in the attic—come strolling languidly into the house.

At the sight, they all drew in a quick frightened breath and for a good long time, forgot to exhale.

The cat continued walking arrogantly into the kitchen, then, through the doorway leading into the den, and stopped right in the middle of the room on a thick, grey, oval-shaped rug.

Emily suddenly remembered the time when she had been going through the divorce with Ron and simply could not seem to get it together enough to rise, dress, and go back to Atlanta and her job, and how Mudear had proclaimed from her own cozy bed, "Craziness is hanging 'round this damn house like a hungry cat smelling fish!"

And as she watched this new arrival, what looked like a wild cat sitting in the center of Mudear's house licking itself, she thought, that's exactly what this thing looks like, a hungry cat smelling fish.

Finally, before they became dizzy and passed out, Betty, Emily, and Annie Ruth remembered to exhale and breathe, but they still did not move. It was not that they chose to remain motionless. It was that they could not make their bodies respond to the command of "Run!" that their brains were sending out.

And with all their hearts they wished they had been able to obey their first mind to flee when the intruding cat stopped licking herself, turned her marble-eyed gaze upon the three of them and Maejean, opened her small furry mouth and spoke.

"Now, ya'll on my territory," the cat said.

They didn't bother to consult one another. All the girls recognized their mother's voice.

And together, they let out a blood-curdling scream, "AAAAaaaaa-iiiiiiiiiiiiiii!"

"God Lee Moses!" Poppa exclaimed as he ran back into the house at the sound of his daughters screaming, his long rangy arms hanging by his side with the baseball bat held loosely in his right hand. He strode into the den.

"What the hell is going on up in here?"

CHAPTER 41

omigod! now what?

there is always something going on with this family. i ain't been around but a couple of days, and i'm already almost stressed out. this is too much drama for a little baby girl.

well, i tell you what, i'm just gon' do some deep breaths, check out for a while, and try to get some sleep. yeah, beauty sleep. can't get too much a' that. that's what i heard my mama say.

yeah, i'm like my mama i need my beauty sleep. well, children don't take after strangers.

CHAPTER 42

It was difficult for the girls to believe or comprehend. However, they couldn't deny it. Mudear was standing right there in front of them, talking like herself, but looking like a cat.

Betty and Emily, still screaming, reached out their hands for each other and moved in even closer to Annie Ruth to sit in the gap between MaeJean and Mudear, making a semi-circle around the baby.

"Girls! Girls!" Poppa yelled. He had to in order to be heard over their screams. "Settle down! What's the matter? What's the matter? You gon' scare the baby. What's wrong?" he asked as he leaned the bat against the entranceway to the den and entered.

Betty, Emily and Annie Ruth couldn't stop crying, but they managed to lower their pitch and eased into a muted whimper as they each pointed to the cat in the middle of the room. The shrieks had, of course, awakened MaeJean, but she simply looked at her mama and aunties and didn't join in their cries.

"My God, it's just that old cat," Poppa said in a puzzled, exasperated tone of voice as he turned and headed toward the animal to capture it and take it back outside. "Betty, Emily, I'm surprised at you. You'd think it was a ..."

But just as he came within a few feet of the cat, he stopped in his tracks. He stood completely still for a moment, blinking a few times, then rubbing his eyes with the backs of his calloused hands.

"What the..." he said incredulously and took a couple of steps backward. It was a good thing that he did. Right before his eyes, the cat was transforming, wavering and bending, becoming fuzzy and indistinct around its edges. Then, it began to enlarge, growing quickly to two, four, six, eight, ten times its original size, losing its body hair and standing upright in the process.

It was an incredible metamorphosis that left Mudear looking like her old pre-death self standing before her family in her burial navy blue dress. The girls all gasped, their eyes big as teacups, their legs became like cooked spaghetti. None of them could understand how they could still be standing until they looked down and realized they weren't. But Betty and Emily managed to move in even closer around Annie Ruth and the baby.

Poppa, his dark face nearly blanched, began feeling sick to his stomach.

Before he could regain his composure and doubt what he was seeing, Mudear shook herself all over as if to settle into her new body shape and spoke.

"*Having trouble believing your own old eyes, huh, Ernest?*" Mudear said, sounding like her usual feisty self.

Poppa tried to speak, but all he could do was sway in the spot he was standing and sputter.

"What's the matter, Mr. Bastard? Cat got your tongue?" she asked and laughed a high dry cackle.

The laugh was new, but the taunting tone of her voice was vintage Mudear.

Mudear looked at her girls cowering on the sofa and taunted them, too, like in the old days.

"I thought ya'll were such bad asses," she said. *"Come riding out here in the dead a' night with my granddaughter in tow to dig around in my garden. Ya'll don't seem so bad now."*

Mudear's mocking tone was like a cold hand slapping them in their faces and clearing their heads. They looked at each other cringing and trembling on the sofa like scared little girls and, without speaking a word to each other, determined to stand up to this frightening spirit.

"I ain't scared of you, Mudear," Emily said bravely, speaking first and surprising everyone in the room.

"Yes, you are," Mudear said evenly. *"I can smell it on you."*

Emily paused and stood. She was a bit shaky on her feet, but still she stood, moving slightly away from her sisters to face Mudear "Maybe, I am," she replied. "But that ain't gon' stop me from doing what's right."

"Hmmph. So ya'll all think ya'll grown now. Can stand up to Mudear, huh?"

No one said a word in reply, but Betty and Annie Ruth stood without even consulting each other and stepped up close behind Emily and that seemed to make the old lady angry.

"Well, you ain't never gon' be grown enough to combat me," she said, her voice turning into more mewing than speaking, her visage becoming more feline than human. *"And look at you, old man, weak as water, frail as a old dying bush. You couldn't withstand me when I was alive. Now that I'm dead, you ain't got no idea how strong I am."*

Everyone in the room could feel the intensity with which Mudear was directing her energy toward Poppa. Even MaeJean felt the heat that seemed to emanate from the cat lady across the dim cold room and shoot into the lanky frail man's body.

He stood at the edge of the room, a few feet away from the back kitchen door, first studying the specter of his dead wife standing in the center of the room. Then, he shifted his gaze to his daughters standing on the opposite side of the room by the sofa, Annie Ruth holding her baby tightly in her arms.

They had always seemed like strong inscrutable creatures to him, the flesh of Mudear, but more loveable. Now, standing together as they did, facing this incredible, frightening presence, they appeared almost invincible. And he was humbled by the sight.

For her part, Emily didn't think she had ever been called upon to gird up her loins and truly fight for any good cause.

Oh, she had fought the good fight to stay out of some state institution for the slightly insane. She had battled all her life not to tip the scale at a number that was too high for an acceptable image of herself. And she certainly had wrestled with all kinds of mental demons for the privilege of working a steady job, paying the rent on her apartment, and keeping pretty crimson-colored clothes on her big butt.

But fought the good fight for a genuine good cause, one larger and more momentous and important than the size of her ass or even the freedom to walk the streets of Atlanta without wearing a straitjacket? Never.

Now, along with her sisters, she was all up in the fight of her life.

When not one of her daughters or her husband buckled under the weight of her gaze or her mere presence, Mudear eased back toward human form and sound and decided to try reasoning.

"For God's sake, just look at the child. She take after me," Mudear said. "She was born with a veil just like her grandmama. She more like me than any of ya'll. Shoot, ya'll don't even hardly know nothing about no veil."

"We know enough to know you got scared and went out in that

godforsaken garden of yours and dug that caul up, trying to get back some of the power you felt slipping away when you knew we were coming to get it," Betty said, as she leaned around Emily and rested her hand protectively on Annie Ruth's shoulder.

"We know enough to know this baby is Annie Ruth's and not yours," she continued when Mudear looked surprised at her insight. "And God willing, never will be anything like you."

At first, Mudear looked genuinely wounded by the comment. Then, she smirked and rallied. She looked into the faces of each of her daughters, trying to size them up the way she had done effortlessly in the past. This time, it wasn't quite so easy.

She didn't bother to look at Poppa, who was still standing a bit behind her and off to her right.

He noted her disregard of him and recalled how often he had overheard her telling the girls, "Don't pay Ernest no attention. He a old man."

"Well, if you read your Bible," Mudear said finally, trying a new strategy, *"you'll see that when Moses came down..."*

"Don't you dare quote the Bible to us, old lady. Don't you dare do that," Annie Ruth said, low and serious. "Besides, what do you know about the Bible or being a good Christian or anything good at all?"

"Well, I'll tell you this much," Mudear replied. *"I'm the only one in this room 'cept MaeJean who been to the other side recently and that's closer to God than any a' ya'll been with your divorces and your abortions and your sleeping with young boys."*

"Just 'cause you dead don't mean you close to God, Esther," Poppa spoke up for the first time.

As Mudear spun around on him, Emily stood there rubbing her head trying to wrap her mind around what was taking place right in front of her. She was used to seeing and hearing strange things, things other folks didn't see or hear. But all this: her entire family standing in the family house talking with their dead mother who sometimes looked like a woman and sometimes still seemed like a cat, mewing her comments as well as speaking them. This was all much too much for someone teetering on the edge of reason as she was.

"*So now you think you can talk back to me, old man,*" Mudear said menacingly.

Poppa stood his ground. In fact, he squared his bony shoulders and even took a step toward his dead wife.

"*Watch what you say to me, old man,*" Mudear continued. "*Words once spoken are like eggs once broken.*"

Poppa merely snorted a kind of sad derisive laugh and that seemed to really incense his dead wife.

"*Now, you laughin' at me?*" Mudear couldn't believe it. "*You got some nerve. Where you get some of that nerve from? You ain't had none of that in years, you dried up ole fool!*"

"Lots a' things changed since you been gone, Esther," Poppa said boldly, more boldly, in fact, than he felt.

Still, his bravado unsettled her. For the first time since her arrival, Mudear looked a bit unsure of herself, but she quickly recovered. Yet not before Annie Ruth spoke up.

"What are you really after, old woman?" she asked.

"*I just come back to see my grandchild,*" Mudear lied, trying to make her voice quake and quiver with sincerity and age. It sounded like a lie to every adult in the room.

"Don't none of us believe that, Mudear," Annie Ruth replied. "We know you. Know you better than anybody in the world. You trying to get your hands on MaeJean and take her from us."

"*Shoot, I don't want to take her nowhere. I just want to have a hand in raising her. The way I didn't get the chance to raise ya'll.*"

"And whose fault was that?" Betty asked, surprising herself with her boldness in the face of her dead mother.

"*You tryn'a get smart with me, Betty?*" Mudear turned and asked quietly, menacingly.

Betty didn't answer. Not because she was afraid. Betty suddenly realized that she did not fear her mother's specter as much as she was repulsed by it. Simply speaking with Mudear now seemed to take all her breath away and leave her a bit nauseated.

"All I'm looking for is a second chance," Mudear meowed, changing her tactics and trying hard to make herself sound all pathetic and weak.

Annie Ruth wasn't falling for it.

"Well, you ain't gon' get no 'second chance,' with my child," she said so low and softly that Mudear had to perk up her ears to hear her.

Um, I thought I saw somewhere that cats supposed to have extra good hearing. No, maybe it was they could smell real good, Mudear thought. Whatever it was, her hearing was good enough to detect the steely resolve in Annie Ruth's voice. Mudear looked her youngest daughter up and down, taking in this new woman who stood steadfast between her own mother – who now favored a cat – and her own child.

"Mudear, you're not going to get our baby. Not this one," Annie Ruth said quietly as she clutched MaeJean to her breast. The child was also strangely quiet, so quiet that Annie Ruth paused to put her ear to the baby's bud-shaped mouth to hear her breathe. "You had your chance to be a mother. Three chances, in fact. You don't get another chance with my child.

"No, ma'am, I will fight you to the death, to my own death, on this one," Annie Ruth continued, still speaking calmly. "This is my child. *My child!* And I will kick your dead ass over this one. Betty and Emily will, too. Even Poppa will fight you on this one."

"'Poppa?!'" Mudear said derisively and almost spat in the middle of the floor. " 'Poppa'? *The hell with your Poppa. I don't give a damn 'bout that man. And if you had any sense you wouldn't either.*

"You may be too young to remember how he was, but you...." Mudear

continued as she spun around and turned on her eldest. *"You, Betty, you remember. You tell her. Go on, tell her!"*

Betty squared her shoulders again, moved closer to Annie Ruth and the baby and said evenly, "I ain't got nothing to tell her."

Mudear sucked her teeth at her eldest daughter, but the sound came out more like a hiss, and it struck Betty as so sinister that she had to close her eyes for a moment and gather her strength all over again.

Poppa saw Betty's effort and inched a little closer to his daughters. It was a tiny paternal movement, but the girls all saw it.

"Even dead, even after all this, you still don't know nothing about life , do you, Mudear?" Emily asked.

"Oh, so, now you, you lil' crazy heifer, you gon' try ta get smart with me, too?" Mudear asked nastily.

"Naw, Mudear, I ain't trying to get smart. I ain't really trying to do anything but tell you that what I know is this: forgiveness got to come sometimes. I know I may be crazy, but I forgave you a long time ago, Mudear. Betty and Annie Ruth, they thought I was crazy for doing that. But I wasn't crazy, I was just too weary to spend all that time and energy hating you the way they seemed to. And besides, I never could truly hate you.

"Even now, even after I see what you tryn'a do with our lil' baby girl MaeJean, I still don't really hate you. I feel sorry for you, but..."

"Well, lil' fanatical fool, you can keep your lil' feel sorry for yourself. You couldn't even follow simple instructions about getting them to name that child 'Esther' because I..."

"You didn't let me finish, Mudear. You didn't let me finish. You never let me finish. But I'mo finish this."

Mudear stood there on the grey rug looking like a cat, then looking like herself, then looking like a cat again, strobing from one image to another like a hologram.

"What was I saying?" Emily asked, confused and fascinated by the sight of her changing mother. Then, she remembered. "Oh, yeah, I feel sorry for you 'cause you my mama. You carried me nine months, and you brought me into this world. But that's not gonna stop me from standing with my sisters, standing with my family, against you.

"And you can't win, Mudear. It's over for you. But like always, you just won't admit it. Mudear, you said it yourself. When you dead you done."

Emily's comments seemed to outrage Mudear more than all the others' combined. Emily, her crazy daughter, the "fanatical fool" who she felt she could manipulate more than her other girls had the nerve to be trying to stand up to her Mudear. And it sent the woman into a true rage.

With a high-pitched whine, she began spinning around like some chimerical animal–part cat, part woman, part spirit–chasing its own tail until she was practically a blur in the middle of the floor. It was such an extraordinarily frightening and disturbing sight that Annie Ruth reached down and pulled Betty's baby blanket farther up over MaeJean's face to make sure she didn't witness any of the apparition's gyration.

my mama may not really mean that she would have hurt auntie em-em 'bout me the way she said when everybody was sitting around the dinner table, but somehow i know for a fact she really would kick my grandmama's ass 'bout bothering me.

i realize i haven't been here for long and i don't know that much, but that can't be right, can it? kicking an old lady's ass like that. that don't seem quite right.

while i been lying here letting everybody make over me, and hold me tight, i been thinking 'bout a lot a' stuff that may not be right. from the way everybody's carrying on over my grandmama looking like a cat sometimes and like a old lady other times, maybe that's not right either.

since i come here, it seems like I been seeing lots of stuff that i just know and lots a' stuff that just confuses my lil' mind.

for instance, what about those twinkly little white lights that dance all over my head 'til i go to sleep every night. i know i don't see all that well, but they don't seem to dance over my mama when she's sleeping in her own bed without me.

and that little song one of the twinkly lights sings to me every night:

"*When your meal barrel get empty*
"*The Lord will fill it up.*
"*When your meal barrel get empty*
"*The Lord will fill it up.*
"*Fill it up, fill it up with joy.*"

i love that song! i just *love* it!

now, i'm beginning to wonder if everybody hears it or just me.

CHAPTER 44

Neither Betty nor Emily nor Annie Ruth could hardly bear to watch as Mudear spun around crazily in the middle of the den. But Poppa didn't have that problem. He watched in what looked like a fascinated trance and remembered how he had once compared his young bride to Fourth of July sparklers. That's what she looked like again as she twirled around like a whirling dervish on the thick rug.

He watched her until she began growing fainter and fainter in the gradually warming den.

Somehow, Poppa knew this moment was his only, his last chance. His last chance to set things right. His last chance to do right by his girls. His last chance to protect his little granddaughter, MaeJean. His last chance to be a man.

Poppa moved in the direction of the baseball bat he had left leaning against the den wall by the kitchen door. But Mudear stopped spinning and slipped her still-glowing body, stealthily as a cat, between him and the Louisville Slugger.

"What you think you gon' do with that, Ernest?" Mudear asked with a small cackle.

"I'm gonna protect my family," he answered.

Mudear chuckled and asked, *"And I ain't your family?"*

"Esther," he said, inching closer and closer to her and the bat. "You ain't been nobody's nothing in a long time."

"Hmmmph, maybe so," Mudear said, as she began to spin and twirl again, her voice noticeably more assured than when she had spoken before. It was as if she drew strength from Poppa's resolve to take action. *"But I know one thing. You ain't man enough to get that bat if I don't want you to have it,"* she stated flatly.

Poppa thought for a moment and smiled ruefully. He recalled the things he was proud of in his life and the things that brought him shame. Then, he looked over his shoulder at his girls, all four of them, and smiled again.

Without hesitating a moment more, he turned back to the apparition of his dead wife and, like a man years younger, he plunged head-first into the glowing spinning swirl, extinguishing the shimmering light of Mudear's final moments and disappearing with her.

CHAPTER 45

As the sun began to rise through the trees in the yard of Betty's house, the three sisters marched slowly in through the back door with MaeJean and collapsed in the solarium. They simply could not go any farther.

The Lovejoy women felt as if they had been dragged down thirty miles of hard road. Betty's joints and muscles actually ached as if she had been in a wrestling match. And Annie Ruth couldn't tell where the soreness from MaeJean's birth ended and the aches from the night's encounter with their dead mother began.

They barely remembered the ride home. For the life of her, Emily could not recall if she had driven or if Betty had slid behind the wheel after they walked out of Mudear and Poppa's house before dawn without bothering to cut the lights off or to lock the doors. Anything done to safeguard that house seemed pointless to all of them.

They knew they had a great deal to confront and deal with from that night. The first task being how they were going to explain their father's disappearance to the authorities. No body, no evidence of foul play, no suicide note, no record of a bus ticket out of town, no missing automobile, no money withdrawn from the bank, no nothing.

The Lovejoy women's collective memory was the only evidence that Poppa had finally, staunchly stood up for his girls and had made sure that they would be safe, as safe as he could make them.

That his granddaughter could grow up and move on with her life without the fear that her mad peculiar grandmother would be haunting her for her entire existence.

That his own baby girl could raise her own daughter without the interference of ghosts of the past.

That his two oldest daughters might actually have a shot at happiness and peace.

Annie Ruth silently wished that she had been able to retrieve MaeJean's caul from Mudear's possession before she and Poppa had disappeared into what she figured was the Great Beyond. She had briefly considered searching the yard and house for the caul, but knew that Mudear was far too clever to have left it in such an obvious place. Besides, she and her sisters were simply too weary to begin such a scavenger hunt after the night they had had.

So, she comforted herself with the image of Mudear being kept in check by Poppa's presence and decided to find some peace about its loss.

No telling where Mudear put that caul, Annie Ruth thought as she sat and gazed down at MaeJean and gave the baby her nipple. It was the first time MaeJean had seemed to want to nurse since they had left for Mudear and Poppa's house the night before.

The women also knew they would have to decide how to dispose of the house and gardens in Sherwood Forest. The idea of keeping it in the family was unthinkable, but the prospect of selling it to some poor unsuspecting family felt down-right criminal.

And they, especially Emily, had no idea how many years of therapy it was going to take to get the image of their dead mother walking and talking and stalking as a cat out of their heads and psyches.

However, Betty, Emily and Annie Ruth, stronger and surer of themselves than they had ever been, were certain that they could somehow face whatever they had to deal with when the time came.

Betty even said it after she found the last little bit of strength to get up and drag MaeJean's bassinet in from the dining room into the solarium, then, flopped down on her favorite seat.

"I don't think anybody on this earth will ever be able to fuck with my head ever again." Then, she exhaled a good long breath and felt her heart begin to beat in a regular rhythm for the first time in hours.

But for the moment, they decided that what they all needed to do was get some rest. Even Emily didn't suggest that they warm up some of last night's dinner before getting some sleep all together in the solarium.

But as Annie Ruth settled a slumbering MaeJean into the bassinet, she whispered to the baby the first line of a silly rhyme she suddenly recalled Poppa reciting over her as a child.

" 'To bed. To bed,' said Sleepy Head."

" 'Wait a while,' said Slow," Betty added.

" 'Put on the pot,' said Greedy Gut," Emily put in.

" 'And we'll eat before we go,' " the three Lovejoy sisters chimed in together.

CHAPTER 46

that's so funny. " 'put on the pot,' said greedy gut." hee-hee.

ooo. it feels so good to be back in my own bed in my own house. i mean i love being up in my mama's arms and everything, but i was ready to stretch out.

" 'put on the pot,' said greedy gut." hee-hee. they so funny.

i love my mama. i love my aunties. i love my life.

i sure hope i take after them.